# A Noble Place

*By the same author*

The Gentle Wind's Caress

# A Noble Place

Anne Whitfield

ROBERT HALE · LONDON

First published in Great Britain 2007

ISBN 978-0-7090-8365-8

Robert Hale Limited
Clerkenwell House
Clerkenwell Green
London EC1R 0HT



2 4 6 8 10 9 7 5 3 1



Typeset in 10/13pt Palatino
by Derek Doyle & Associates, Shaw Heath
Printed and bound in Great Britain
by Biddles Limited, King's Lynn

To those wonderful Victorian women who kept diaries and journals of their experiences as they started new lives in a foreign and challenging land. Your spirits live on in *A Noble Place.*

It is with sincere gratitude that I thank my husband and children for their patience when Mum is always at the computer, and I know *A Noble Place* is a better book due to the members of Historical Fiction Critique, especially Ginger, Anita, Diane and Rosemary.

It lies not in our power to love or hate,
For will in us is over-ruled by fate.

Marlowe, *Hero and Leander*

# CHAPTER ONE

Sydney, Australia – October 1850

Phillippa Noble lifted her face to the sun and listened to the soft murmur of the waves slapping the rocks below. A delicate breeze ruffled the six inches of fine lace at the hem of her blue linen dress. She breathed in deeply, filling her lungs with air so pure it was intoxicating.

'Pippa, if you keep on allowing the sun to touch your face you'll tan, or worse, develop freckles,' Hilary tutted and, hitching up her skirts, climbed back up to the bush path. 'I'm not going down any further. Your madness to explore will most likely cause me a twisted ankle.'

'Oh, do shush, Hil. The day you start moaning like Mother is the day I'll renounce you as my twin.' Pippa grinned, but seeing Hilary frown as she dusted down her pale-pink skirts, she gave up the idea of investigating the little bay below and turned back for the bush track that led from town. 'I need to find a new advantage point to paint from, but I guess I can do it another day. Shall we walk on around the headland then?'

'I think not. It is miles.' Hilary softened her words by smiling and linking her arm through Pippa's. 'Perhaps we can return now and look at some shop window displays instead?'

Pippa sighed. 'Why that gives you pleasure I have no idea. We spent this month's allowance last month.'

'You might have spent *yours*, but *I* saved some shillings.'

'Well, I was out of paint and charcoal.' She shrugged one shoulder. 'I know, let us stop by the stables and check on the horses?'

Hilary groaned. 'We checked them yesterday. They are perfectly fine. They survived the journey in the ship's hold so I'm certain they'll survive living in comfortable stables.'

In silent, mutual consent they returned the way they came. Large gangly trees, that they now knew to be called eucalyptus or gum trees, loomed above them in colours of grey and blue-green. The sandy track, one of many, snaked through the bushland bordering the outskirts of Sydney Town. To their right the wide expanse of the harbour shimmered in dazzling splendour, a host to watervessels of all shapes and sizes.

'I'll never be tired of looking at all this,' Pippa whispered. 'How could anyone ever say this was the land of the forgotten?'

'It was though, in its infancy.' Hilary squeezed Pippa's hand where it rested on her arm. 'Not everyone here arrived of their own will. Many do not appreciate it as you do.'

'I understand that you and Mother prefer England, but to me this country affords me the opportunities I'd never have back home. Here I can breathe.' She closed her eyes in excitement. 'I have so many plans . . .'

'I know you do, dearest, but I do worry you'll be disappointed. Standards and society still hold sway here as they do back home. You're a woman and not as free as you'd wish.'

'True, but I've heard of other women here who have done well for themselves, like Elizabeth MacArthur.'

'Yes, but she and her husband have money, something we lack. Women can only do great things if they have money or sponsors who have money. We have little of both.'

'Thanks to Father,' Pippa murmured. She gazed through the trees and over the water to the dense blue-green forest on the other side. No, not forest. It's called 'The Bush' here, she had to remind herself. She and Hilary had read numerous books before and during the voyage from England, but despite knowing that Australia was built as a convict country, she had become enthralled with sketches and paintings of the dry, untamed land. Its diversity fascinated her.

'Oh, look, Hil.' To the side of the track a large deep hole went at right angles under exposed tree roots. 'I believe it is a tunnel for those fat furry beasts.'

Hilary kept strolling. 'Come away, Pippa, for heaven's sake the thing could come and attack us.'

Pippa hesitated, studying the hole's entrance. 'No, I don't think they do attack, not like lions or anything. If I remember rightly I think they sleep all day . . .' After another long look, she hurried to catch up. 'I want to know everything there is to know about this country. I want to know all the animals' names, the birds, the flowers.'

Stooping, Hilary picked a small yellow wild flower from the sparse undergrowth. 'How can you admire it so much? Nothing is lush here. Everything is hot, dry and dusty. You must miss England some?'

'Not likely!' She snorted. 'Moving from house to house around the country, never settling down in one place, dodging creditors? Why on earth would I miss England?'

'Because it's home.'

'Not any more. This country is our home now. Here we have a chance of bettering our lives. When the house is built and we are selling the best horseflesh in the country, we'll never have to worry again. We must believe it.'

Hilary slowed, her gaze earnest. 'Don't place all your hopes on Father, dearest. You know he has a ... tendency to ... let us down despite his good intentions.'

Pippa glanced away to the right and feasted on the harbour view, trying to ignore Hil's warning. 'Father promised us this time would be different. We could build a home here, a future of wealth and social acceptance.'

'I hope we do ...'

'But you aren't confident?'

Hilary shrugged one slender shoulder. 'I'd also like to think Father will keep his promises this time too, but we know better, don't we?'

'Here he doesn't have his friends to help him lose money either at the card tables or the races, or to spur him on to invest unwisely.'

'His friends may not be here but the gambling is.'

'I will not let him ruin everything again.' Frustration, her old enemy, grew. She strode on. 'I'm tired of living well one minute with servants, good food, riding hunters and then living like paupers the next after selling everything we cherish to pay Father's debts!'

'Slow down.'

She eased her stride to suit Hil's and gave her a wry smile. 'Sorry, my temper gets the better of me.'

'Don't I know it?' Hilary frowned. 'Father tries hard to give us a good life, he always has. I suppose we mustn't be too harsh on him and this new start of ours has inspired him to believe in himself. We must try to do the same, it's...it's our duty. Poor Papa.'

Sighing, Pippa swooped down to pick up a stick and walked on in silence. The family's move to the other side of the world had surprised everyone. Immediate friends and family knew of her father's debts but even so, this venture seemed extreme. However, from its first conception she had championed the idea, imploring her sister and mother to take this chance of adventure. It was as though she'd been waiting her whole twenty-one years to flee their unstable life. Her father promised a new start in a country that offered everything to those who had the courage to grab it with both hands.

Well, *she* was going to grab whatever came their way. Her father couldn't always be relied upon to keep them safe and secure, so it was up to her. She held no false illusions. Out of the family she was the strongest, it was commonly said. Oh, it had caused talk amongst her mother's acquaintances back home, but in this country no one knew her. Well, the Henderson family they'd travelled on the ship with now knew her a little, but they weren't important regardless of Hilary and Mother's attempt to include them in every outing they took.

No. The family's future lay with her, not Father, he was only the figurehead, so to speak, which reminded her that she must talk with him about the money they brought with them. Investiture money. Money lent to them by her father's cousin Lindfield, who had inherited the family's wealth. A flash of anger always ignited inside her when she thought of how many times they'd had to borrow money to either fund one of her father's new ventures or to pay their debts when those ventures failed . . . as they constantly did.

But not this time. This time she had demanded her say. At twenty-one, an adult in the eyes of the law, she felt it was time to make a stand. Initially she believed her father would condemn her rights to be involved in their financial future but instead he'd acted relieved, as though sharing the burden deflected some of the blame. Her mother had no head for business, no inclination to help. It was easier to whine about it when it all went wrong. Hilary was sensible but lacked the drive to succeed and was content to amble through life without making a ripple.

'Are you frightened, Pippa?' Hilary glanced at her and then stared straight ahead. The muffled sounds of the town drifted on the air and the trees thinned out as houses appeared.

'About what?'

'Our future? Will we marry one of these colonial-born men or will all this be a spectacular failure and we'll go home in disgrace begging for our bread?'

'I'm tired of begging, of being humiliated.' Pippa narrowed her eyes and stared at her sister. 'This endeavour will not fail. *I* won't allow it to. The land we buy, the stud we build will flourish because *I* will be involved.'

'How can you be so sure everything will be as we wish it?' Hilary looked at her with sympathy. 'You are not a man.'

Pippa swore softly under breath. She hated being a woman.

# CHAPTER TWO

'Gerald, please draw the curtains. I cannot possibly suffer the sunlight for another moment.' Esther Noble waved her white, lace-edged handkerchief towards her husband. 'To suffer such heat in late October is intolerable! Spring they call it? More like a living hell on earth. I'll never forgive you, Gerald, never.'

Gerald Noble merely nodded towards their maid standing behind the sofa on which Esther reclined. Cissie, the only servant to have accompanied them on the voyage, hurried to his wife's bidding. He looked at his wife, the wife who was no longer young. Her whole countenance showed her displeasure at being made to endure such heat and humidity in this foreign land. Not one pleasing comment had been voiced by her since their departure from England some one hundred and twenty days ago. She made it quite clear, to all who would listen, that her husband had taken leave of his senses by making his family trek to the other side of the world to a land of heat and savages.

He resumed his occupation of studying numerous maps placed before him. The maps were vital to his plans for building the finest horse stud in the colony. Good pastures and adequate water were a necessary requirement. The position had to be perfect. So much depended on every decision he made. Sweat beaded on his forehead. He would make this project successful or die in the attempt.

'And this lemon water, who can honestly say it's cold?' Esther held up the tall glass in her hand. 'Nothing is ever served cold in this godforsaken place. Unless, of course, it's our dinner.' She rose from the sofa and paced before him like an irritable pea hen.

'I will send for more lemon water, dearest.'

She rounded on him, her small brown eyes narrowing. 'I don't want *lemon water*. I want to go home!'

Gerald gave her a grave look. 'We cannot go home.'

'And where does that fault lie?'

Shame filled him. 'On my shoulders.'

'Exactly!'

'We can have a good life here, I promise you.'

'Huh.' Esther puffed out her ample chest and stared him down. 'Your promises are often empty.'

Gerald tried to smile with reassurance, but knew his expression resembled more a timid mouse caught in a cat's paw. He *must* argue his point, he must. He knew she no longer respected his decisions. Therefore he had to show that this time everything would be better, that *he* would do better. 'I have a good feeling about this country. I feel renewed, young once more.'

'Young?' Esther's eyebrows shot up to her hairline. 'I don't want you young again, repeating all the mistakes you've already made,' she spat. 'Look where that got us.'

Gerald squirmed. 'Just a figure of speech, dearest.'

'And our daughters, where will they fit into this backward colony? How will they find husbands of note here?'

'Quite easily, my dear.' Gerald relaxed, knowing he was to redeem himself with his next piece of news. 'I have been granted an audience with the Governor of New South Wales.'

'Really? Then let us pray to the Almighty, that you do not muddle it.' Esther returned to the sofa. With a sigh of the condemned, she picked up her glasses and placed them on her nose before opening her small book of poetry. She peeped over the book. 'When is it to be?'

'I shall receive a summons presently no doubt.'

Esther tutted and turned her shoulder to him.

The incessant humming of a small black fly that circled above his balding head annoyed Gerald. He folded away his maps and reached for his lemon water. Over the rim of his glass he watched his wife of twenty-three years. Had she always possessed that sour expression? Had she ever laughed with him? Yes. Long ago, she'd been happy, in love with him. . . .

Their depleted fortune was his fault and as a husband and father he had failed dismally. Therefore, he should not judge poor Esther too hard, for she had given him two beautiful and intelligent daughters. He would have been pitied by society far more indeed if he had begot two plain and stupid daughters.

Gerald rose and walked over to the open window on the other side of the room. Pushing aside the cream net curtains, he stared down at the busy street below. Thankfully, this side of the hotel was quieter than the front. This particular window held a remarkable view of the ever-growing city flowing all the way down to the great expanse of water that made up the beautiful harbour. The light breeze, captured at this first-storey height, lifted Gerald's few damp strands of hair. He brushed his hand over his bald spot and sighed. *Am I too old to start again?*

A noise from the door leading to the hallway diverted him. A smile lifted the corners of his mouth as his two daughters, Phillippa and Hilary, entered the room. Both were tall and slender with fine bones and a gracefulness pleasing to the eye. In fact, not many a man was immune to their particular beauty and by far there was many a woman given to envy at the sight of them.

That such loveliness was a product of him often stunned him into silence. He had heard people whisper behind their hands at how it was a wonder that two such daughters could come from two such parents. For the Noble twins were indeed nothing like their parents. Both girls possessed thick dark-blonde hair with golden highlights that caught the light from a candle or the rays of the sun. More striking than their hair were their dusky, velvety-brown eyes framed by long, thick, brown eyelashes. The differences in character and temperament also caused comment.

Placing her parcels on a small table by the door, Hilary went to Esther and took hold of her hand. 'We rushed back from shopping because it was getting late and we thought you would worry. Are you feeling better now, Mother?'

'No, not at all, my dear. How am I to when we are afforded no relief from this insufferable heat?' Esther fanned herself with her handkerchief.

'You must get out of that dress, Mother.' Phillippa unpinned her bonnet and threw it on a chair. She poured out two glasses of lemon water and handed one glass to Hilary. 'Why not dress in cotton or linen? A simple blouse and a fine cotton skirt would be quite adequate. Fewer petticoats would help too. Do you still wear your flannel one?'

'Silence your outlandish tongue!' Esther blushed. 'Such talk in front of your father. I am ashamed of you.'

Exhaling noisily at her mother's refusal to be more accommodating to their new life, Phillippa sat down and picked up one of her father's maps. 'Have you seen anything notable yet, Father?'

'No not yet, Pippa dear, fortunately I am to collect another few maps this afternoon. They are from a southern district in the parish of Mittagong, which is within the county of Camden. I'm led to believe that certain areas are uncharted and the population is not many.'

'I truly do not know what you *do* expect in this land of heat, flies and dust!' crowed Esther.

Gerald rolled his eyes at his daughters but refrained from comment. Since arriving in the country, he had tried to extol its virtues to his wife but to no avail. How she would behave once they left the civilization of Sydney for the primitive bush country was anyone's guess. 'Come morning, I will journey to New Town to ascertain the worth of two mares belonging to a man recently in from out west. He answered the notices I put in two of the Sydney papers. I received his missive today.'

'Are they thoroughbreds, Father?' Pippa asked.

'Arabians apparently. They may be just what we need to add to our stock.'

Phillippa looked at her father with an odd expression. 'Arabs?'

'This hard country will need a certain breed of horse, and I think we should not be too rigid in our judgement of which breeds to specialize in. Not only will we breed top quality horseflesh for the gentleman but also good strong horses for transports. I have even considered dabbling in draught horses.' Gerald's last admission drew gasps from the women.

'Draught horses! Good Lord, Gerald, are you mad? We are not farmers, but—'

'Esther.' Gerald held up his hand to silence her. 'Draught horses are essential here. Indeed, from the talk I've heard and men I've spoken to they are very much in need of draught horses to help open up the bush for agriculture out west. Bullocks cannot do everything and are slow.'

'We know little about breeding draught horses, Father. We have had very little to do with that breed, except our own Ginger.' Pippa frowned.

'Yes, I realize that, but with the new Clydesdale mare I bought on arriving, I am sure we can breed good stock. Besides, I do not feel that they would be all that much different from breeding saddle thoroughbreds or transport horses. Indeed, it would be a challenge, would it not?' He smiled at his family.

'Mad! Quite mad!' Esther retired to her bedroom and slammed the door.

'Father, wouldn't it be much more sensible to keep to one kind of horse until we have established our credentials?' Hilary murmured.

'Even though, for a time, we bred wonderful horses back home, no one knows us here.'

Gerald rubbed his forehead with the tips of his fingers and sighed. 'Yes, yes you may be right, my dear. I must not try to run before I can walk. I fear I am rather too impatient for my own good.'

'Wait.' Pippa rose and paced. 'In the end we must breed for demand. If there are claims for draught horses, then we should not dismiss it out of hand. We must be open-minded.'

'Indeed.' Gerald nodded. 'But it is the thoroughbred used for controlling stock that is needed here. The large sheep farms don't always have time to breed their own horses and break them into the saddle. If we can build a supply ready to meet—'

A knock at the door interrupted him. On Gerald's command, a young soldier entered carrying a soft leather case. He bowed. 'Sir, I come with communications from the offices of His Excellency, Governor Sir Charles Fitzroy for a Mister Gerald Noble.'

'I am he.'

The young soldier unclasped the leather case and brought forth a red-ribboned sealed letter. He handed it to Gerald.

'Thank you.'

With another curt bow the young man left the room.

Esther's bedroom door opened and she darted to her husband's side in a flurry of swaying skirts and trailing lace. She gripped her handkerchief to her breast. 'What does it say?'

Untying the ribbon, Gerald unfolded the letter and read it in silence and then smiled. 'I have been granted an audience with the Governor tomorrow morning.'

The three women gasped at such news and all spoke at once.

'Enough!' Gerald grinned.

'Am I to accompany you, Husband?' Esther frowned. 'What should I wear I wonder?'

'No, not this time, my dear, this is business. I have waited for this letter for some time. On arriving in Sydney, or at least shortly after, I presented myself at the Governor's office to inquire about obtaining an audience. I would have failed in my duty as a husband and father to not do so. A man must make himself known to those in the position to help him.'

'Father, the man in New Town?' Pippa reminded him.

'Blast it! Of all the most inopportune times. I'll have to send a note.' Gerald scowled. He patted his daughter's hand. 'I can always rely on you to be two steps ahead of everyone else.'

Pippa slipped her hand through his arm and smiled. 'There is no need to miss the appointment with the horse dealer, Father. I shall simply go in your place. You know that there is nothing that I don't understand about horseflesh. I shall be able to tell whether they are worth purchasing.'

'On no account will you travel around this town on your own, Phillippa,' Esther cried in alarm. 'Why, the things one sees and hears. It's so wild in parts that I fear for my life the minute I leave this room.'

'Mother, I will be quite safe.'

'Of course you will, but it is not on that account I will worry.' Gerald rubbed his chin. 'I cannot let you be in the company of a horse breeder of no acquaintance. He may not be all that he seems and I would be a foolish man indeed if I let you go. It's out of the question, my dear.' He shook his head.

'Oh come now, Father, you are well aware that I do not let any person take advantage of me. More like the other way around, wouldn't you agree?' Pippa grinned.

'No daughter of mine will traipse around this wild colonial town by herself,' Esther sniffed. Disapproval etched her every feature.

'I shall accompany her, Mother.' Hilary patted her mother's hand. 'No harm will come to us if we are together.'

'I say no.' Esther's lips thinned in determination. 'It's unladylike to consort with riff-raff.'

'He says his horses are of excellent quality.' Gerald hesitated. 'It is important, my dear.'

'Absolutely,' Pippa jumped in. 'We must make the most of every chance at improving our stock. To be the best in the country we have to buy the best.'

Gerald swelled with pride. Pippa was the light of his heart. Such fire and passion. He held no doubts whatsoever about Phillippa's ability to judge good horseflesh. Indeed, at times, she proved better than himself. 'Very well then, you both may go and see this man and his horses.'

Pippa kissed his cheek and his heart melted. It had been her contagious excitement after learning about his early plans to emigrate that finally persuaded him to leave England and start again in a new country. It was for her and her children, his hope for grandsons, that drove him on to regain the heights of wealth and position that could easily be theirs if this venture achieved status and respectability and most of all fortune.

*

As the driver set the horse into a trot, Pippa studied the name and address on the note of paper her father had handed her at the breakfast table. She had purposely dressed in a conservative style of navy and grey stripes with a matching small hat of navy with two grey feathers pinned along the side. She frowned as she studied Hilary's frivolous outfit of lavender and white lace, the dainty straw hat perched on her head festooned with lavender ribbons. The last thing Pippa wanted was this fellow to think they were stupid women. She needed to show him she was serious and to prove to her father she could handle business.

Hilary sighed. 'Isn't it pleasant to be away from our rooms?'

'Yes. Time away from Mother's never-ending complaints and sour expressions is a blessing.'

'Shh, Pip, that is not nice. She cannot help it.'

'Nonsense. She doesn't even try to accommodate our new life.'

Hilary took her hand. 'Do not spoil the morning.' She turned towards the window. 'We have not been in this part of the city before. Is New Town in the country?'

Pippa nodded. 'Although, not too far out I believe.' Since arriving in the colony they had been on few outings, the odd picnic, a few theatre productions and dinners with the Hendersons. She was eager to experience anything new. 'Do you know that man I sat next to at the Hendersons' dinner party last week? Apparently, he has been south to Melbourne and he says there are parts of this country that get snow in winter.'

'Really?' Hilary looked surprised. Then her face altered, became sad. 'It might be snowing at home now.'

Pippa nudged her. 'Do not talk of England! This is our home now. Do I have to keep reminding you?'

'Sorry.'

Pippa took a deep breath, not wanting to remember England and the pain she had left behind. For a moment the image of Grant Lindfield rose, but she ignored it. He wasn't worthy of her time. She summoned up all her determination and thrust the memories from her mind. She tossed her head. 'I want to see every bit of this country. I am resolute in doing so.'

For a short time they travelled through dusty streets lined with small houses in various degrees of habitation, then the road widened.

Numerous cottages with little front gardens appeared, and plots of land opened up the area for several miles until once more the streets tapered. Narrow houses built all together in rows on each side of the road filled the view from the hansom cab's windows.

The driver reined in his horse outside The Brass Bells, a hotel in desperate need of a fresh coat of paint. Pippa and Hilary descended from the cab and looked around at the filthy litter and the assortment of children that ran barefoot across the dusty main street. The children clamoured up to them with grubby little hands held out for pennies.

Hilary clutched Pippa's arm, her expression one of despair.

'We've no money to give you so go away.' Pippa eyed the nearest boys who pushed and shoved.

The driver took off his hat and wiped his forehead clear of sweat with the back of his hand. 'Are you ladies certain you're in the right place?'

'Yes. This is the hotel named.' Pippa nodded and, lifting her chin, she gestured for Hilary to follow her.

The driver replaced his hat and climbed down from his seat. He took a step towards the hotel front door. 'How 'bout I goes in an' ask fer the fella you're after?' His gaze raked over them with a subtle hint.

'Oh, yes, do let him go in, Pippa.' Hilary took a step back in relief.

Pippa told him the man's name whom they sought and waited with Hilary as the driver disappeared inside the hotel. A few minutes later he reappeared with a man dressed in a long brown coat with fawn trousers and a dusty, wide-brimmed felt hat.

'Mr Briggs? Jonas Briggs?' Pippa frowned.

'Aye. Who may you two be then?' Briggs scowled. 'I've no time for games.'

'Noble. You answered our father's advertisement and sent a note about your quality horse stock. He cannot make your appointment and we have come in his place.'

'I don't deal with women.' The man spat chewed tobacco on to the ground at their feet making Hilary jump at such coarseness.

'And we, sir, do not deal with such ungentlemanly behaviour. Come Hilary, we are wasting our time.' She spun on her heel. 'I'm certain our money will be more agreeable to someone else.'

'Wait!' Briggs stepped forward.

Pausing, she raised an eyebrow. 'Yes?'

The man swallowed and tilted his hat back a little on his head so that he could see them better. He shrugged. 'Mebbe I could show you me horses.'

'Really, sir, I fail to see how such behaviour you have shown to us would induce me to do business with you. Good day.'

'Look, me horses are worth your time if nothin' else. They're stabled round the corner and their quality will speak for itself.' Briggs walked in the direction of the stables and, after some hesitation, Pippa and Hilary followed.

They turned into a lane and through the double wooden doors of a large stable and carriage yard. The sun penetrated half a yard beyond the opening of the stable but the rest was dim and shadowy.

Pippa halted. 'Bring them out. We will wait outside.'

A minute later, Briggs led out his two mares. In the bright sunshine their chestnut coats shone and gold tinted their copper manes. Both mares stood with their heads held high and took an interest in the yard.

Stepping closer, Pippa stroked their noses and looked into their eyes. To Hilary's gasp of consternation she also pried open their mouths. After checking their teeth and legs, she asked Briggs to pick up each of their feet and she inspected them too. For over half an hour Phillippa instructed Briggs to walk, trot and then ride the mares as she assessed their merits.

Hilary abandoned all pretence of interest and went to stand against the wall in the shade.

'So, Mr Briggs, you say both mares come from the same sire, a Barb thoroughbred stallion from Cape Town?' Pippa mused, stroking one mare's mane.

'Aye. The stallion died two years back.'

'The stallion belonged to you?'

'No, he belonged to a man I did business for.'

'Then how did you come to own such excellent mares as these?'

'They were a part of his estate and when he died they were willed to me for services rendered.' The man eyed Phillippa openly defying her suspicions.

'You have papers then, I presume?'

Briggs reached into his coat pockets and pulled out folded sheets of paper tied with black ribbon. 'Here, you'll see that all is in order.' He passed the papers over.

Pippa took a minute to read them. 'Tell me, Mr Briggs, why is it you wish to sell such fine mares, surely you could start breeding them yourself?'

'Yes, I could, but I'm goin' to America. Gold has been found in California an' I intend to get meself some.'

'I see . . .' Pippa swallowed. Her heart fluttered. She *had* to do the deal. She wanted these excellent mares but was nervous as to what price they could afford. 'Well, I will give you twenty pounds for each mare.'

'Twenty pounds?' Briggs swore. 'They're worth more than that. I want at least fifty pounds each for 'em.'

'I will not finance your trip to America for you, sir. I'll give you forty-five pounds for the pair.'

'Forty-five pounds! That's robbery. I'll take seventy-five pounds the pair.'

Pippa raised her chin and stared at him. Her heart thumped like a drum against her ribs. 'Sixty-five pounds. Take it or leave it. That is the best offer you will get today and I'm not the one wanting to go to America.' She walked over to Hilary and waited for the man to make up his mind. The horses were worth more than she offered, but this was business.

'You're a hard woman, Miss Noble,' Briggs grumbled on joining them. 'You'll do well in this colony.' He held out his hand.

She took it and cemented the deal while fighting the urge to grin. 'Hilary, give Mr Briggs our card.'

When they walked into their hotel's foyer, Pippa wasn't surprised to see her father waiting for them.

He gave them each a kiss on the cheek and then led them into a small parlour used by the guests. 'Well, my dears, how did it go?'

Pippa sat at a small table and smiled at him. 'They were quality mares, Father. I've got the proof of sale, too. So, there can be no mistake.'

'Pedigree?'

'Barb thoroughbred. I bought the pair for sixty-five pounds. A bargain.' She knew every penny had to be accounted for and suddenly wondered if she'd done the right thing. 'Did I pay too much?'

Gerald shook his head. 'If you think they are worth it then you did well. Together with our stock we will be breeding fine foals in no time.'

'And the visit with the Governor, Father?' Hilary asked. 'It went well?'

'Excellent. Excellent indeed! A great man! He was most interested in our venture and suitably impressed when I told him of our scheme to breed the finest thoroughbreds in the colony.'

'But land, Father, what did he say about that?' Phillippa leaned forward. She wanted acres and acres of land. Land meant security, a home of their own. In her mind's eye she saw rolling fields of knee-high grass and a flowing river.

'Why, that is all settled too.' He beamed. 'Six hundred acres at a very reduced price. I am extremely satisfied. I've saved a considerable amount—'

'Where?' Pippa butted in, frustrated at his lack of details.

'Where? Oh, in an area they call the Southern Highlands. It has the best climate, I've been assured. We will be situated between a village called Berrima and an area called Mandemar or some such. I'm afraid that it's primarily bushland, but we will soon have it cleared.'

'Berrima. Mandemar. Don't they sound strange but charming,' declared Hilary.

Gerald stood and escorted them from the room. 'The Governor issued me with a list of requirements. The land has to be stocked within a certain time and it's vital that we grow our own food. If we have surplus we can sell it at the markets or the government stores will buy it.'

'We shall need help, Father. We're not farmers,' Hilary said as they ascended the stairs.

'Yes, I will advertise for labouring men.'

Pippa's mind raced with plans. 'It was prudent of Cousin Lindfield to loan us his husbandry books. Plus, we can study the books I bought in London.'

'Actually, the Southern Highlands area is where one of those authors lived. Sutton Forest I do believe it's called. The Governor mentioned him as we spoke about the area.'

Surprised, Pippa nodded. 'Why yes! Mr Atkinson wrote *An Account of The State of Agriculture and Grazing in New South Wales*. This is excellent news, Father. With such talented men already living in that area, we shall have help at hand.'

Gerald patted her hand. 'He died some years ago, my dear. However, the Governor did mention of many other families there. We shan't be completely friendless.'

'That will please Mother.' Hilary smiled.

'I shall soon see if they are amiable, for I am to leave for the Southern Highlands in two days.'

Pippa spun to face him. 'Aren't we all to go?'

'There is no need at this stage, my dear.' At the door leading to their rooms, he paused and kissed their cheeks in turn. 'I must go now. I am to meet a man whose name was given to me on very high recommendation. If he is suitable then he will be our overseer.' Gerald moved towards the stairs.

'Father, wait!' Pippa hurried to him.

Turning, he gave her an indulgent smile. 'What is it?'

'I must come with you to meet this man and to go to the Southern Highlands.' She raised her chin in readiness for his refusal, but she could argue her point better than most men. 'Remember what we agreed upon?'

He sighed. 'Pippa, you know your mother does not like you being a part of my business interests, it isn't ladylike.' Her father's gaze shifted.

She stood with her hands on her hips. 'You promised. Back home in England you promised me I would be a part of everything concerning our new life here. I won't let you go back on your word.'

'Come, Pippa, do not make a scene,' Hilary urged.

Gerald gestured towards the door. 'Yes, go in to your mother.'

Pippa glared at him. 'We agreed that I would persuade Hil and Mother to emigrate without them putting up too much of a fuss and in return you would let me have a say in the business. Well, I did my part so now you must honour yours.'

'Yes, but . . .'

'You said Hilary and I will inherit the stud, therefore it is only prudent that we have a say in how it is built and run.'

'But . . .'

'You once said you would never treat us as silly mindless women.'

His bushy eyebrows rose. 'I resent that you think I do!'

She softened her stance. 'Then don't, Father.'

'Very well.' He let out a breath. 'I see I must honour our agreement. There is no use in arguing with you, though your mother will not like it.'

'Mother will get used to it.' Pippa grinned and kissed Hilary goodbye.

'Are you certain you aren't tired from your journey this morning?' He tried one last time.

'Positively bursting with energy.' She winked. Slipping her hand through her father's arm, she led him back down the stairs.

They caught the Sydney to Parramatta mail coach. Situated some fifteen miles south, Parramatta had grown rapidly since its foundation not long after the first British fleet's arrival in the country.

Pippa's second outing on the hot dusty roads did not discomfort her.

The adventurous spirit inside her made each journey enjoyable. There were not enough hours in the day to experience all this novel country offered, but by God she would try!

The coach pulled up in the wide main street outside the Dog and Bone Hotel and they alighted.

Gerald wiped the sweat from his brow with a white handkerchief. 'I'll enquire inside the hotel. He should be there.'

'Perhaps I'll wait in the shade, Father.' Pippa stepped under the spreading branches of a thick gum tree beside the hotel.

'Mr Noble?' A tall man wearing grimy working clothes made up of the usual moleskin trousers, pale shirt and wide-brimmed hat came out of the hotel and approached them.

'Yes, yes indeed, er . . . Mr Robson, is it?' Gerald held out his hand.

The man shook it. 'Rob Robson. Pleased to meet you.'

'Robson, this is my daughter, Miss Phillippa Noble.'

'Mr Robson.' Pippa nodded and held out her hand.

'Pleased to meet you, Miss Noble, but please call me Robson, that's all I answer to anyway.' He smiled and strong white teeth shone from a dusty but handsome face.

'Right now, shall we go and find somewhere to eat?' Gerald offered his arm to Pippa. 'I am absolutely ravenous.'

'Please forgive my state of dress, sir.' Robson grimaced with embarrassment. 'I have just arrived in town from the country and as yet not had time to bathe.'

'Maybe we could look at some of the shops while Robson changes, Father?' Pippa scanned the street and saw a small eatery across the way and suggested that they meet him there in half an hour.

Later, upon entering the small restaurant, they made their way over to where Robson sat. The scent of soap and the touch of a razor blade replaced the dirt and dust. He wore a cheap suit of grey woven cloth instead of the filthy riding clothes. His dark brown hair now visible without the hat was clean and combed.

They ordered their meal and talked of the state of the colony. Pippa listened to Robson talk of his work history. His responses pleased her. So far he showed intelligence.

'So your family has been in the colony for over three weeks, sir?' Robson placed his teacup back on its saucer.

Gerald swallowed the last of his cake. 'That is correct and this morning I acquired my land. It is in the Southern Highlands, do you know the area?'

Robson sat back and smiled. 'Yes, very well. I worked for some time on a land grant near Sutton Forest. It is a very fine area. The climate is excellent with good rainfall and the grazing is of superior quality once the land is cleared.'

'We are placed somewhere between the villages of Berrima and Mandemar,' Pippa said. 'Have you been there?'

'Yes, Berrima is an admirable township, but small.'

Gerald wiped his mouth with his napkin. 'I leave in two days to meet with the surveyor who is currently in the area. I want him to survey my land as soon as possible. I need to start building immediately. It is imperative the stud becomes viable at the earliest opportunity.'

'First things first, sir, if you don't mind me saying,' Robson chuckled. 'You'll be wanting a home built? Unless of course your family is to remain in Sydney?'

'No, we are not!' Pippa turned to stare at her father.

Sighing, Gerald nodded to Robson. 'Yes, a home must be at the top of the list.' He gave Phillippa a look, that spoke volumes. 'You should have been a boy.'

'It's absolutely dreadful! The middle of nowhere, that is where your father wishes us to live.' Esther stormed about her small bedroom in full steam regardless of the early hour. 'Well, I'll not go and neither will you, Hilary.'

'Mother—'

Esther swung to glare at Pippa. 'Don't talk to me! You encourage your father's ridiculous ideas.'

Hilary looked pained. 'Mother, that is not true.'

'What if something should happen to them?' Esther beseeched Hilary. 'I shall then be left alone with only you as my one remaining family member in this strange land. It cannot be borne.'

Pippa and Hilary sat on either side of their parents' bed. Pippa hid her impatience at her mother's selfish behaviour and took Esther's hands to calm her. 'Listen, Mother, all will be well. I promise.'

'You care nothing for my wants,' her mother spat. 'You are self-interested like your father.'

Ignoring the performance, Pippa took a deep breath. 'I will make an inventory of all that we need for the new house. Father has declared you will not need to leave Sydney until the house is built and all I have written on the inventory is bought and placed at our new home. Will that not be satisfactory?'

'Indeed it will not,' snapped Esther, pulling away from Pippa. 'Your father has no concern for my wishes for staying here in town, here at least there is some aspect of civilization. But out there, in the wilds, we'll be murdered in our beds, you mark my words. I just want to go home.' Exhausted by her outburst, Esther flopped on to the bed beside Hilary and cried into her handkerchief.

Hilary shrugged her shoulders at Pippa and patted their mother's back.

'I have to finish packing,' whispered Pippa, which only increased her mother's tears.

Pippa left the room and crossed to the bedroom she shared with Hilary. A thick material bag was on the bed and a partially packed trunk sat on the floor. From the wardrobe she took out her stout riding boots. She sat on the bed, slipped off her house shoes and placed them and her boots in the trunk. After closing and locking the lid, she then tugged on her soft kid boots. In the mirror atop the washstand, she checked her appearance as she pinned on her straw bonnet. Her stomach fluttered in excitement and she gripped her hands against her chest. She couldn't help grinning at her reflection. Adventure! At long last.

A slight knock at the door pre-empted Cissie. The maid stepped into the room carrying a freshly laundered towel and nightdress. ' 'Ere, miss, I've just got these things to go in your bag.'

'Thank you, Cissie.' Pippa smoothed the skirt of her green checked dress and blew out the candle. 'Pass me my reticule and gloves, please.'

'All set, miss?'

'Yes, I think so.' Pippa smiled. 'Can you take the bag down?' She walked to the doorway. 'Oh, and ask the hotel boy to collect the trunk.'

In the sitting-room, her father pulled the straps tight on his leather satchel. 'Ready to go, my dear?'

'Yes.'

'Good. Robson has the wagon waiting and the stable boy is holding the gig.' Gerald placed a few of his papers from the table into the breast pocket of his coat. 'You would not believe the amount of provisions Robson has put on that wagon, but he says it will all be needed.'

Esther came out of her room with Hilary behind her. 'Dearest, must you go? Can you not send the man you have hired in your place?'

'Now, my flower, we have been through this before.' Gerald promptly kissed her forehead to prevent any more of her objections.

He kissed Hilary's cheek and then made for the door. 'Come, Pippa. The sun is rising.'

'When will you be home again?' Esther demanded as she followed them down the staircase to the street and the waiting transports.

'Three to four weeks, my dear, like I've said many times.' Gerald climbed up into the gig as Robson handed Pippa up beside her father.

'Three to four weeks!' Esther's face reddened with frustration. 'I'll never forgive you for abandoning me, Gerald, never. Of all the things you've done to me this is the worst.'

Hilary come close to the gig and took Pippa's hand. 'Be careful, won't you? Come back safe.' She wiped her tears. 'We've never been apart so long before.'

Pippa leaned down and kissed the top of her head. 'I'm sorry to leave you behind,' she whispered, glancing at their angry mother.

'No, you are not,' Hilary chuckled.

Pippa laughed. No, she wasn't sorry. She straightened her shoulders just as the dawn's pink light filtered over the rooftops. Her excitement burned like a fever inside her, she could not wait to begin this journey.

# CHAPTER THREE

The weather, which had been hot and dry, turned cool. Slate-grey clouds blocked out the sun as they trundled through the settlement of Liverpool, some twenty-two miles south-west of Sydney Town.

Pippa tightened her shawl around her shoulders and gazed with interest at the few shops lining the main street. She pointed out to her father a small brick church with its surrounding graveyard. At the far end of the town they stopped at a small inn, busy with trade.

Robson rummaged in a canvas bag at his feet and produced a muslin-wrapped meal. He hurriedly took a bite from his buttered slice of bread. 'We made good time, despite the load on the wagon. Your Clydesdale mare has done well, Mr Noble. She has an easy gait. Ginger didn't like her at first but she's calmed down now.'

'Indeed yes, very well done. She was a good buy at the time. I'm well pleased.' Gerald glanced at the angry-looking sky. 'You think it wise we only spend a short time here? My daughter needs to see to her needs.'

'The horses need a rest, but yes, sir, a short time only.'

Pippa and her father went inside the inn while Robson watered the horses. After drinking cups of tea to quench their thirst and wash away the road grit in their mouths, they re-emerged to find the weather worse. A fierce wind howled down the street sending whirlwinds of dust into their faces.

Robson pointed to the black furious sky. 'Sir, we need to get going if you want to make it to Camden before this storm hits. We might have to stay the night there instead of going through to Picton.' He looked in Pippa's direction, but didn't meet her eyes.

Pippa, holding her hat on with one hand raised her eyebrows at him. 'Be assured, Robson, that I am quite able to make this trip without complaint.' He knew nothing of her stamina as yet, but she would show him.

Gerald helped her up on to the seat. 'I don't want to spend more time on the road than I have to. We'll carry on to Picton, Robson.'

Pippa adjusted her skirts and secured her parasol under the seat as the wind threatened to blow it out of her hands.

'Very good, sir, but we cannot tarry. The Razorback mountain range is hazardous at the best of times and only a fool would consider taking the journey at night.'

The threatening rain held off, but the cold wind chased them all the way to Camden. They paid the bridge toll and crossed the Nepean River before driving on through the wide main street.

Pippa looked around at the town that buzzed with people, many rushing to finish their business and be home out of the foul weather. She tapped her father's arm and pointed up the hill to the left. A large church was in the process of being built, it held a commanding position. More churches and small chapels, plus quaint cottages and shops dominated the immediate vicinity.

'It's a shame we don't know the MacArthurs.' She chuckled. 'We could stop for tea.'

'I'm sure it'll only be a matter of time, dearest, before we are known and have so much company, you'll be spoiled for choice.'

'I'm very impressed, Father. Camden is more civilized than I expected.'

Gerald snorted. 'I doubt John MacArthur would have wanted it any other way, my dear. It's a legacy to him and his family. His sons do much for the area, I've been told.'

She nodded and remembered the history of the infamous man who stirred up trouble within the fledging colony years ago. However, MacArthur also contributed greatly to the foundation of the colony's wool, wine and wheat industry. One of the many pioneers who had the courage to strike out and be counted. For a moment, Pippa forgot the awful weather and dreamed of her own desire to carve out a life, a future from this untamed land.

As they ventured away from the centre of town they followed the curve of the Great South Road and headed towards the jutting line of mountains called Razorback. As they passed the entrance to MacArthur's Belgenny Farm and Camden Park House large fat raindrops fell.

Gerald shifted his position and flicked the reins. 'Get out the sheeting, Pippa, and cover yourself.'

It took her a few minutes to unfold the canvas sheet and drape it over the both of them. At the same time the wind rose to a howl accompanied by more rain.

Robson called out between claps of thunder and, as they halted the gig, he climbed down from the wagon and rushed over to them. 'I think it best if we turn back, Mr Noble. We can spend the night in Camden.'

'What if the rains last for days and make the roads unusable? We could be stranded in Camden for weeks which will certainly disrupt my plans.'

'But if we continue we might not make it and be stuck on the range without shelter.'

Pippa leaned forward. 'The rain is light at the moment. If we hurry we could clear the mountains before the roads are rendered useless. You say Picton is on the other side?'

'Yes, Miss Noble.'

She nodded to her father. 'Then we should hurry.'

He looked at Robson. 'What's your opinion of continuing up the mountain in this weather? If we push on, what do you think of our chances at succeeding?'

Robson put his finger around the inside of his collar and shivered. Scrunching his shoulders against the weather he peered through the rain at the range. 'It'll be tough, but not an impossible climb. A decision needs to be made before it gets any later. We can't be stuck up there in the dark.'

Pippa frowned in thought. 'I guess there isn't an inn along the mountain top?'

'No, miss.'

'It's too risky,' said Gerald, sighing. 'We'd better turn back.'

'No, Father.' She grasped his arm.

'Dearest . . .'

Pippa's grip tightened, her eyes pleading. 'We can do it, I know we can. And if we turn back now, it'll delay us. That means less time to view our land.'

Gerald wiped the moisture from his eyes. 'I'll not put you in jeopardy.'

Pippa smiled and licked the rain off her lips. 'This bit of water doesn't bother me.' She leaned her shoulder against him. 'Come, Father, where is your sense of adventure?'

Groaning, Gerald gave a look of the damned to Robson.

They began the ascent, however, shortly after, the ruts and holes in the road caused Robson and Gerald to drive off the dirt track and into the bush alongside. The wheels creaked, churning up the thick mud. Before long, the rain became an unrelenting downpour, quickly turning the road into a quagmire.

Pippa pushed back her damp bonnet and peeped out from under the canvas to peer up at the huge expanse of mountain looming before them. Recent landslides had deposited earth and rock on to the road and in places new tracks were cut into the surrounding bush.

Plucking at the wet folds of her skirts, Pippa glanced at her father. His coat glistened with raindrops. 'Others are making it through.' She pointed in the direction of the winding road and in the distance through the trees they glimpsed a bullock team picking its way down the slope towards them.

The weather and heavy traffic made the main path over the range a perilous trek. The steep climb wound its way through thick scrub. At times they rounded a bend to find themselves at the very edge of the track with the escarpment falling away at dizzying heights.

As the horses strained against their harness, Pippa gripped the edge of the gig until her fingers went numb. She refused to close her eyes as the wheels slipped and skidded towards the edge of the cliff. Her relief was audible when the road veered back inland.

Despite the danger, the magnificent view between the trees of a cloud-topped valley filtered through her anxiety. She treated the elements as a test. The grey, wretched weather and the terrible road conditions paled into significance as she gazed at glorious sights of tree-cloaked hillsides and outcrops of rock formations being washed free from dust, the colours of their surroundings manifested.

Pippa jumped when a loud thunderclap heralded their final ascent. A fork of lightening split the sky making the horses toss their heads.

'Well done, Father.' She kissed him and he breathed more easily as they peaked the ridge.

'Now we must go down.' Gerald slapped the reins. 'Hold tight, my dear.'

If Pippa thought the journey up was treacherous, the passage down took the heart out of her chest. Her father rode the brake all the way, but this didn't stop the wheels from skidding in the soft mud. The rain pelted them without let up.

Turning in her seat, she watched Robson hold his pair skilfully. The loaded wagon was harder for him to handle than their light gig.

Suddenly, the front wheel on Pippa's side hit a large rock, jolting her off her seat. She screamed and reached for her father.

'Pippa!' Gerald grabbed at her skirts.

She came down with a thump. The force landed her sideways, half tipping her out of the gig. With a strength she didn't know she had, she held on to the seat. Below the cliff dropped away. Small rocks skirted down the embankment and tumbled over the edge.

'Hold on, Pippa. Don't let go.' Gerald struggled with the frightened horse. 'Steady girl, steady,' he soothed the animal.

Heaving herself up, she scrambled back into the seat, her heart beating so fast she thought it would explode. 'I-I'm fine, Father.' Her voice shook, her throat went dry and for a moment she wondered if she'd be sick.

'Sit closer to me. Link your arm through mine,' Gerald ordered, his arms straining with the effort to hold the horse.

Pippa clung to the gig's front rail, and vaguely noticed that one of her gloves now sported a good-sized tear. Taking hold of her emotions, she straightened in the seat and did as he instructed. Regardless of the rain, she felt hot and feverish from the experience.

'Farther down the track widens.' He indicated with his head to a spot in front of them. 'I can stop there.'

'No, I'm all right.' She braced herself as they bumped over a rut. Thunder roared again. 'Keep going, Father.'

When at last the road levelled out on to a grassy plain, it seemed the rain took pity on them and lessened. Weighted leaves hung low on the trees and dripped a tattoo of raindrops. They crossed a small wooden bridge. The water below it cursed and dashed over the rocks, lapping at the scarred banks.

Pippa glanced at her father and couldn't resist grinning now the shock had receded. 'Just think, we have to do it all again in a few weeks.' She couldn't help but laugh and it released their tension.

'What am I to do with you?' Gerald shook his head and chuckled.

She sniffed the air. Sharp scents of the kind she'd not experienced before tickled her nose. Pungent aromas from the native trees, only a few of which she could name, permeated the air. Now the danger was over, the excitement returned to tingle in her veins. Behind them, rumbling like an empty stomach, the thunder continued eastwards.

To the west, the clouds parted. Rays from the setting sun highlighted the little town of Picton as the gig bumped its way along the road. They were too tired and dirty to take much notice of the small township. Lanterns lit the windows of the George's Inn, and to Pippa it seemed a dry haven from the uncomfortable, wet gig seat.

Once in the yard, her father helped her down. 'How do you feel, pet?'

She shook out her saturated skirts. 'In need of a hot bath. I hope they have one. I'm cold to the bone.'

Robson joined them. 'We were lucky to escape without damage, Mr Noble.'

'Agreed.' Gerald took Pippa's arm. 'Come, a hot bath and a hot meal are in order.'

Pippa woke and gazed out of the window. Dawn filtered the night's darkness with stripes of cherry and gold. She had slept well and, refreshed, was eager to begin the day. A little sore from yesterday's journey, she dressed with some difficulty. The absence of Cissie made dressing a chore that required much patience until the innkeeper's daughter finally came and helped.

Slipping out of the inn's front entrance, Pippa walked around to the stables. Yesterday's rain had brightened the surroundings, washing away the cloak of dust and dirt. She paused to look out to the west. Daylight showed a line of clouds in the distance. The clear air filled her lungs as she breathed in deeply.

Inside the stables, she shook awake the two stable boys asleep on straw bales beside the horse stalls. The boys yawned and scratched their heads but didn't grumble as they assisted her in harnessing Gerald's mare to the gig.

She was leading Ginger, the Clydesdale, out of her stall when Robson appeared. He grinned at her and nodded, both of them knew she had made her point. She might be a woman but she was no dainty flower easily crushed.

They left Picton straight after breakfast and made good pace to Bargo some twelve miles farther south. There, Gerald halted the horse and after a whispered conversation with Robson, reported in to the local constabulary.

Puzzled, and a little annoyed at not being informed of their intentions, Pippa climbed down and stretched her legs. Along the street a bullock and his team rested under a large gum tree. Situated across the road was a small house. The front part of it indicated a shop. Entering it, Pippa paused and took note of the few items for sale. Soap, bottles of ointment, candles, shoe brushes and the like littered the shelves along the back wall.

A woman came through a doorway behind the small counter. 'Good morning.'

'Good morning.' Pippa inclined her head. 'May I buy a drink if possible?'

The woman smiled. 'Would you like a bottle of fresh ginger ale, miss? I made it yesterday.'

'Yes. Thank you.'

Gerald came into the shop, a frown worrying his forehead. 'There you are.' He waited as Pippa paid for the bottle and together they left the shop.

'You should not have left the gig.'

She paused to stare at him. 'Why?'

Flustered, her father guided her up into the gig's seat without answering. Pippa turned to him as he climbed up and took the reins. 'Why did you see the constable?'

'Simply to get our bearings.' He looked over his shoulder checking that Robson was ready to depart and then flicked the reins to set the gig in motion. 'Nothing for you to worry about.'

She crossed her arms over her chest and tilted her head at him. 'You are a terrible liar, Father. The Great South Road is the main road and, from the maps, we travel on it right to Berrima.' She sensed his hesitation and narrowed her eyes. 'At breakfast, Robson mentioned the police as I came to my chair.'

Her father shifted in his seat. 'He did, yes.'

'Well?'

Gerald patted her cheek. 'Enjoy the journey, my dear. Let us count how many different birds we can see.'

Pippa jerked away. 'Do not patronize me, please.' She looked over her shoulder at Robson following behind. Every now and then he would search the scrub on either side of the road. They were travelling fast. Why would they endanger the wagonload by moving at this pace?

'Father?'

Gerald kept his gaze on the road ahead. 'Yes, well, you see . . . there is talk, no, well, more than talk really. That is to say there have been actual sightings and evidence of . . . well . . .'

'What *is* it?'

'Bushrangers.'

Pippa stared at him. 'Bushrangers?'

'This stretch of country is known for them. This is the infamous Bargo Brush. They hide in the trees waiting for a carriage or a wagon which will be of value to them and then hold them up,' Gerald whispered, again flicking the reins. 'The constable said it has been quiet of late. However, that doesn't necessarily mean they aren't there.'

Anger flared in her. 'How could you keep such important information from me? What would I have done if we were attacked and I wasn't prepared?'

'I am sorry. I . . . we thought it best not to worry you.'

'Being ignorant of the facts worries me more.' She peered into the bush around them. At a fast trot it was difficult to pick out unusual objects. Abruptly, the virgin bush had turned into a trap. Within its shadows a hidden menace lurked.

In a smooth movement, Gerald moved his foot and with the toe of his boot nudged a rifle out from under the seat. His look held meaning and Pippa nodded. Gently, he moved to hide the weapon again.

'I have a pistol in my coat as well,' Gerald spoke between clenched teeth. 'If anything should happen to me then you get it straight away, do you understand?'

'Yes.' A shiver ran over her skin as a magpie called from a tree nearby. Every sound had to be identified quickly.

'You are a good shot. You know how to make a bullet work.'

'Yes,' she repeated. An image came to her unbidden. A cold winter's day. Snow lay deep on the ground. In the icy stillness of a grey afternoon, just as the light was fading, Pippa leaned against an elm tree and raised the rifle to sight a stag half hidden in the wood. Behind her, Grant placed his arms around her, holding the weight of the rifle. 'Be still,' he breathed into her ear. Her mind recoiled from shooting the proud stag, instead her body grew hot under her woollen coat at Grant's nearness.

Grant's mouth came closer, making her hair whisper about her ears as he talked. 'Have you sighted him?'

Pippa closed her eyes. She leaned back against Grant's chest. Turning her face up to his, she smiled. 'He is not the stag I want . . .'

Mittagong was sighted a few minutes before noon after another short, steep climb of mountain ranges. With the threat of bushrangers behind them, Pippa eagerly gazed at the little cottages and huts that at intervals lined the road to the village. Great tracts of land had been cleared and it was pleasant to see herds of cattle and flocks of sheep grazing.

Closer to the township the cottages plus a good deal of inns and shops grew in numbers. Pippa studied her father's maps. The town was situated at the northern end of a triangle with Berrima to the south-west of Mittagong.

'Do you wish to rest a while, my dear? Or go straight on to Berrima?' Gerald smiled. His relief was evident to her as the tension of journeying through the Bargo Brush slid away.

'Oh no, Father, let us go straight on to Berrima.' She grinned. 'We are nearly there. Besides, I can explore this village another day.'

'There is much to explore of this district, my dear.'

'And I cannot wait to begin.' Pippa linked her arm through his. 'Look, Father. Mittagong seems very well settled into a niche between those two large mountains. We've continually climbed since leaving Bargo. Have you noticed how the air is much cooler and the grass is greener?'

'Yes and all good grazing from what I see.'

As they left the busy little town and drove along, they noticed many men and wagons. Gerald pointed to a group of small buildings. 'That is the colony's first iron mine, the Fitzroy Iron Mine, named after the Governor himself.'

'Most impressive.'

'From the map it appears Berrima should not be far.'

The amount of traffic on the road to Berrima surprised them. After a few miles of dense bush, they rose over a hill and then levelled out before once more meandering down a slope and into the township. At intervals, bark and wooden huts dotted the roadside. Everything seemed raw. Felled trees opened up the landscape. Timber fences and buildings in different stages of construction filled her view.

Pippa's first look at Berrima made her smile. Quaint stone, brick and wooden cottages lined the main street that snaked through the town. On their right, built on a slight rise was the court house – an impressive stone structure and next to it, the horrifying Berrima gaol, the sight of which caused a shiver to tickle across her skin.

As they continued, Pippa noticed a shallow creek to the left of her before more houses and stores came to her attention. Near to the end of the village, Gerald turned right at the village green and then reined in before the Victoria Inn.

'Come, my dear, you must be all in. I know I am.' Gerald yawned as he helped her down from the gig.

'It's not yet the evening, Father. Perhaps we could walk some to stretch our legs?'

'Good lord, my dear, I'm as stiff as a board. All I want is a bed to lie on. Tomorrow will come soon enough and then we can discover the town.'

Pippa shook out her skirts and gazed around. 'It is more open than I expected. True frontier country.'

A large man wearing a white apron came out of the inn's central door. 'Welcome, welcome!' He shook Gerald's hand vigorously. 'Mr Noble and party?'

'Yes. We are here at last.'

Robson pulled the wagon to a stop behind them, but didn't climb down from his seat. 'Is there room for the wagon around the back, landlord?' he called.

'Aye, go straight 'round, there's a young lad who'll help you,' the landlord replied before leading Gerald and Pippa into the inn.

A few men drank in the taproom and they nodded respectfully as she passed. On the other side of the small hallway a quiet hum of voices filtered through from the main bar. Gerald conversed for a minute with the landlord and then they were shown to their rooms.

Pippa's bedroom, though sparse, held all she needed. She waited for her trunk to be brought up and when Robson brought it in, he was followed by a young maid who held a jug of warm water and towels. Left alone, Pippa washed and changed into a white blouse, soft grey skirt and matching short jacket. Pleased with her appearance in the small table mirror, she left her room to go down to the dining-room.

After a good meal of mutton stew and vegetables, Pippa sat back and listened to her father's plans for the following day. Outside twilight descended as they talked.

Gerald sipped his brandy. 'The good landlord told me the surveyor was not in town at present but was sure to arrive tomorrow or the day after. So, in the meantime I think it prudent to start making inquires as to the building materials available and workmen.'

'It will be a hard job ahead of us, Mr Noble. We have no idea what type of land you have bought,' said Robson.

'Why, the best land,' Gerald snapped. 'I took a great deal of effort in acquiring high-quality land with water and that is what I got.'

Pippa patted his hand, aware it was his fear of another failure that caused his outburst. 'I'm sure it is, Father. I'm sure Robson simply meant that since we have not viewed our land we should wait before hiring men and supplies so we know exactly what we need.'

'As a requirement of the purchase I have instructions that I must improve my land with buildings and stock it well. The maps I viewed with the Governor were lately drawn. He himself has seen the type of land around here,' Gerald argued. 'He assured me I would not be disappointed with the area. He often spends part of the summer in this district.'

'Yes, of course it will be splendid,' Pippa agreed, rising. 'Now, if you will excuse me, I must retire to my room and write some letters. It has been a long day for us all. I bid you goodnight.'

Both men stood, and Robson pulled back her chair for her. 'Goodnight, Miss Noble.'

'Goodnight, Robson.' Pippa smiled.

Gerald kissed her cheek. 'If you need anything my room is across from yours. Sleep well.'

'I intend to, Father, for tomorrow I mean to explore!' She laughed and went upstairs.

In her room, she pushed aside the thin curtains and stared out. Along the roadside teamsters began camping for the night. The odd bellow of a bullock echoed around the surrounding hills. The small windows of the houses threw out golden squares of light from the candles within. A humming noise from the inns lining the street became noticeable as more men joined the throng to quench their thirsts. A sudden feeling of contentment settled over her.

Here she was in a strange land, amongst a community built on the sweating backs of convicts, the ruthlessness of adventurers, the imaginations of dreamers and the strength of spirited pioneers. And, at this moment, as she stood poised on the precipice of her new life, she had never felt more in tune with her destiny. She belonged here.

# CHAPTER FOUR

Raucous birdsong greeted Pippa as she stepped from the inn and strolled up the road, intent on exploring the town before breakfast. Rumbling drays and laden horsemen riding in from outlying settlements brought the township alive. Coaches, filled to capacity with passengers and luggage, vied for road space with produce-stocked wagons leaving north for Camden, Liverpool and Sydney.

Even at this early hour, people flocked the streets to buy and sell. Children and dogs ran wild ignoring the noise, dust and the dangers of being trampled on by passing vehicles.

Pippa gathered up her skirts and sidestepped a horse deposit reeking in the morning sun. Her gaze couldn't hold all the town's images. And she knew she must adsorb the details to tell Hilary. Later she would find the time to paint the scenes that depicted Berrima. She stopped to watch two birds bicker with each other on a fence post. The soft grey and pink birds were a type she had not seen before. Pippa wished she had thought to carry her sketchbook to capture their likeness.

Ambling along, content to linger and smell the roses growing along cottage picket fences, she nodded to a woman who was banging carpets against a wall. She waited until a farmer ushered his milk cow out of her way and on to the village green before crossing the road and heading for the bakehouse, where the aroma of fresh bread tantalized her empty stomach.

Beside a small wooden cottage, a red rooster strutted in front of a gathering of hens. The hens were having none of him and Pippa smiled at his antics. A typical male.

Suddenly, she heard whimpering broken by a sniffle. Pippa paused and gazed around, looking for the source. The muffled cry came again. Intrigued, she stepped towards a large water barrel close to a cottage wall and peeked behind it. A small boy, about five or six years of age and with a shock of curly blond hair lay curled up on the ground. 'What is the matter, little one?'

The dirty face stared up at her. Carefully he stretched his leg out and showed her a cut on his knee. A narrow rivulet of crimson ran down to his ankle.

'Dear me, that must be sore. Where's your mother?'

His bottom lip quivered. 'Inside.'

'Shall we find her?'

The boy shook his head and gave her a wounded look, his chin wobbled. 'I wasn't to climb.'

She went to speak when a woman's voice called for Davy. Pippa gazed down at the boy and smiled. 'Are you Davy?'

A petite, dark-haired woman appeared around the corner of the cottage. 'Davy?' Rushing up to them, she plucked the boy from his hiding spot.

'I heard him crying.' Pippa smiled at her. 'He has a small cut on his knee.'

'Thank you.' The woman hitched the boy higher on her hip despite his age and peered at his leg. She raised his chin to meet her stare. 'Were you climbing?'

Davy nodded as fresh tears formed.

The woman glanced at Pippa and gave her a shy smile. 'I'm Mrs Millie Stroker.'

'Miss Phillippa Noble.' Pippa held out her hand, pleased when the woman shook it. 'And this brave soldier must be Davy.' She tickled the boy's ribs making him chuckle through his tears.

Mrs Stroker's grey eyes took in Pippa's ice-blue and white lace dress. 'My home is humble, Miss Noble, but you're welcome to come in for a cup of tea.'

'That would be lovely. Thank you.' She followed mother and son to the front of the cottage.

A substantial gum tree threw shadow over the house keeping the interior cool. Pippa took off her gloves and noted the basic furniture. No personal items adorned the room, it seemed devoid of all comfort.

'Please sit down, Miss Noble.' Mrs Stroker indicated a wooden chair by a crudely made table.

'Is your husband at work, Mrs Stroker?' Pippa sat and winked at Davy who sat in the opposite chair.

'Yes, yes he is. He's a fencer.'

Pippa's eyes widened and she grinned.

'I-I mean he makes fences, wooden ones. He's not a fence as in stolen goods terms . . .' She flustered, wringing her hands in her white apron.

Pippa laughed. 'It's all right, Mrs Stroker. I understood straight away what you meant.'

'Oh good, and please call me Millie.'

'Only if you call me Phillippa or preferably Pippa.'

Davy looked up from his inspection of the cut. 'May I call you Pippa?'

Millie rounded on him. 'Certainly not! Now go wash your hands and that cut. There's more dirt in there than in my potato bucket.'

Pippa smiled as Davy peeped at her from under his lashes and slunk past.

'I had best make some tea.' Millie paused at the door, her cheeks suffusing with colour. 'I-I have nothing to eat with it. I'm sorry.'

Standing, Pippa gathered up her gloves. 'You make some tea and I'll go along to the bakehouse. Shall we have cake or pie?'

Millie blinked rapidly.

'Oh, let us have both.' Pippa declared, grinning.

The noise from the taproom next door hummed into the dining-room. Logs shifted in the fireplace, sending sparks up the chimney. Pippa shifted in her chair and drummed her nails on the cream-coloured tablecloth. As a maid hurried past the door, Pippa rose out of her seat. 'Excuse me?'

The maid returned, adjusting her white lace cap. 'Yes, Miss Noble?'

'Is my father, Mr Noble about?'

'Yes, miss, I do believe he just this minute came in.' The maid looked to the door. 'I hear him now, miss.'

'Thank you.' Pippa sat down as her father entered.

'There you are, dearest.' Gerald kissed her cheek. 'Have a nice morning?'

'Yes.' She frowned and tried not to appear suspicious. 'Where have you been?'

'I have talked to a few businessmen and made inquiries about the nature of the area. I have left a note for the surveyor to contact me as soon as he arrives in town.'

Relieved that concerns of the stud rather than ill-favoured schemes or gambling had occupied his time, she relaxed. 'And Robson?'

'Well, at this minute he is scouting around for builders to come out to the property. He and I also bought sheep today. Two hundred head. Their wool will add to our income. We secured a shepherd as well.'

'Will they not eat all the grass for the horses?'

'The sheep will eat the rough, coarse grass. The horses will be hand fed until we can sow our own grass. They must have the best, of course.'

'I heard dairy cattle fare well in this area. I think it would be wise to add a small herd to our stock.'

'Totally agree, my dear.' He rubbed his hands together. 'I'm ravenous, this country air has me as hungry as a bear.'

As the barmaid brought their tea tray, Pippa shook out her napkin. 'I am so impatient to see our land, our new home.'

'It will be worth it, I promise you.' Gerald leaned back in his chair. 'Now, there is a mail coach leaving in the hour, do you wish to send a letter to your mother and sister?'

'Yes, I have one to finish.' She poured a cup of tea for them both. 'I'll go up presently and do so. I've also managed to quickly sketch the main street for them too.'

Gerald added sugar. 'Tell me, how did you spend your morning? Did you paint?'

'No, a few sketches done and that is all.' She took a sip of tea and glanced at him. 'I went for a walk and made an acquaintance, Mrs Stroker. She has a little boy. We spent a pleasant hour together.'

'That's nice, dear.'

'I enjoyed her company. Her boy is delightful.'

'Where does she live?' Interest showed in her father's eyes. 'What does her husband do?'

'She lives in a cottage at the top end of the village.' Pippa waited for his reaction.

'A cottage?'

'Yes, and her husband is a fencer.'

Gerald jerked, spilling his tea. 'A fence!'

Pippa hid a grin as she mopped up his mess. 'Fencer. The kind that keeps animals in.'

Gerald shook his head. 'Lord, you had me there. You know your mother will expect you to keep a high standard of acquaintances even though we're in the country.'

'Millie is very nice.' She poured him more tea. 'She is a reverend's daughter from Kent.'

'Indeed?'

'When her father died, Millie came out here to be a governess.'

Selecting a sandwich, Gerald looked at her under his eyebrows. 'It is a shame she is not of our class, my dear. Your mother will not accept anything less.'

Pippa shrugged. 'Nevertheless, I like her and her son.'

'Your mother needs no more encouragement in thinking this family has slipped even further down the social ladder. Try and keep her standards.'

She rolled her eyes at this and sipped her tea. 'You know that back home I had many friends and not all were of our class.'

'Yes, but that's beside the point. Here, we must do better.'

'I will continue to call on Millie, Father. This area isn't so populated that one can pick and chose their female company. Millie Stroker is a gentle woman. Her only fault is that she's reduced in circumstances and we know how that feels, don't we?'

'What a day it will be when you have a son of your own, hey Pippa?' He grinned.

Her father's quick change of subject brought a wry smile to her face. It was a ploy of his whenever he wasn't winning an argument. 'I'll not be having children, Father. You know that.'

Gerald frowned. 'Now, Pippa, you will meet another man. One who will make you forget about Grant Lindfield.'

She shifted uneasily in her chair. How she hated it whenever anyone spoke his name. It made her think of the one man she had resolved to put out of her mind for ever. The pain of loving someone who did not love her in return had dimmed, but refused to die – just like the scandal back home.

Pippa raised her chin, she couldn't let her feelings for Grant Lindfield get in the way of what she wanted to achieve in this country, here where no one knew of her shame.

Rain descended on the region, holing up the surveyor in a nearby settlement of Sutton Forest. A full week passed before their land was surveyed. Pippa spent the week visiting Millie and Davy. She enjoyed their company and learned practical ways of colonial housekeeping – lessons vital for living in the bush, for women of all classes.

At last, late on a Friday evening, just as they were to leave the sitting-room, the surveyor walked into the inn. He had left his men at the bar to quench their thirst before closing time.

'My good fellow.' Gerald stood and shook the man's hand and then introduced him to Pippa. 'You'll have a drink, of course?'

The surveyor nodded and then bowed to Pippa.

'Is our position good, sir?' She held her breath for the answer.

'A finer area of land will be hard to beat, Miss Noble. However it's a fair ride out of town, nearly eight miles in fact and no clear track of road at all.' The surveyor paused. 'The terrain is rocky and your acres are bound on each side by steep hills and gorges. Yet, down in the middle of all this is a great stretch of flat land. What you have in fact is a valley.'

Gerald leaned forward, glowing with enthusiasm. 'What about water?'

'A good creek, not very wide in parts, runs through the property. Indeed, sir, you are most fortunate. You are surrounded by crown land, which you can enquire about for grazing purposes.' The surveyor handed over a small leather pouch. 'I have put my initials in many trees to mark the boundaries, but it is all written in there. It contains copies of the maps which I will lodge at the government offices.'

'I thank you, sir.' Gerald shook the man's hand again. 'You've given us the best news we could hope for.'

After the surveyor left them, Pippa slipped her hand through her father's arm. Such happiness flowed through her, she felt light-headed. 'I cannot believe it, Father, after waiting so long, dreaming of it that now we finally have confirmation. Land, indeed a valley!'

He kissed her forehead. 'A home of our own, Pippa. Imagine it.'

Tears pricked her eyes and she struggled to talk. 'We leave tomorrow to inspect it?'

'Definitely, my dear. The sooner the better.'

A sun-drenched morning greeted the party as they headed north-west out of Berrima. Once on the outskirts of the town the bush grew thick with scrub, rendering the wagon and gig nearly useless. After eight miles of battling steep hills and rock-strewn descents, they decided to leave the transports and go the rest of the way on foot. However, this setback didn't deter them and Pippa, excited as a child at Christmas, hoisted her skirts above her ankles and strode ahead.

Stepping over grass tussocks and around jutting boulders, she jumped as startled kangaroos and rock wallabies bounded away, their thumping feet sounding like distant thunder. Flocks of white cockatoos screeched their disapproval from high in the trees.

The sharp scent of eucalyptus permeated the air and Pippa sniffed deeply, wondrously. At intervals, trees thick with blooms of yellow, which she knew to be called wattles, punctuated the grey-green landscape and gum trees let their little blooms of red dance in the breeze.

She jerked suddenly as a low branch jagged at her skirt. Her father helped to extricate the material and when her petticoat's lace hem tore, she cared little. Nothing and no one could spoil this day.

Gerald grimaced at the ruined fabric. 'You should not have come, my dear.'

'Nonsense, Father.' Pippa grinned. 'A little hardship strengthens character.'

'Mr Noble.' Robson gestured to a large eucalyptus trunk. The surveyor's initials were cut deep into the bark.

Gerald consulted his maps. 'This ridge ends another ten yards further on.'

Pippa hurried the remaining distance, nearly tripping in her haste. She stepped beyond a large tree and stopped.

Below, bathed in golden glory, lay their valley.

Tingles of excitement mixed with reverent joy sucked her breath away. She scanned the horizon of rugged hills and then gazed down at the inviting valley. It was everything she'd dreamed of and more because it was real. 'It's perfect.'

'How in God's name are we to get down there with the wagon?' Robson mumbled, breaking her spell of wonder. He walked closer to the edge and peered down at the jagged outcrops of rocks and boulders that broke up the density of the trees.

Gerald took off his hat and wiped his sweating forehead with a handkerchief. 'Maybe further along there is an easier route down.'

They walked on for another hundred yards before finding another tree with the surveyor's initials marked in it and also an arrow scratched next to them.

Robson pointed to a gentler slope and a roughly cut track snaking through the trees and scrub. 'If the surveyor went down there, then that must be the easiest way.' He frowned. 'I wonder if he took transports.'

'Likely packhorses.' Gerald studied his maps again.

Pippa walked to the edge of the slope. She paused to gauge the steepness and then reached for a nearby sapling to keep her steady as she edged her way down.

'Pippa!'

Her father's shout made her stop and glance back. 'It's all right, Father. Hold on to the trees.'

Robson and Gerald hurried towards her and gingerly made their way down to her side.

Gerald gripped her arm. 'You are too headstrong. It was a foolish thing to do.'

She tossed her head. 'I wasn't going to be left behind.'

'You'll be the death of me, girl,' Gerald panted and wiped his forehead again.

As they concentrated on getting safely to the bottom, the sounds of the bush intensified. An unseen bird made the sound of a whiplash cutting the air, flies buzzed, twigs snapped underfoot and small lizards slithered over rocks.

The track brought them out on the left side of the valley. At the bottom, the trees and scrub thinned out to grassy plains. Emerging out of the shade, the heat intensified. Pippa wished she had brought her parasol with her, but had left it in the gig so she could hold her skirts up with both hands. Sweat trickled inside her collar and dampened her bonnet. She licked her dry lips. 'Is there water close by?'

'Here, miss, I have water with me.' Robson handed her a leather-bound canteen.

'Thank you.' She stopped to drink and chuckled as the cool and pleasant water trickled down her chin. Drinking from a canteen was an art she had not yet mastered.

'Do you see that thin line of gum trees in the middle over there?' Robson pointed in front of them.

Pippa studied the ragged thin line and nodded.

'Those trees edge the creek bank.' He turned to Gerald. 'Do you see that flat rise to the right of the creek bend, Mr Noble?'

'Aye, lad, I do.'

Robson smiled. 'I think it would make an ideal homestead site.'

Gerald slapped Robson on the shoulder. 'I think you may be right, my man.'

Pippa hesitated as the two men walked on. She slowly turned a full circle, taking in the broad sweep of the valley. Acres of waist-high brown grass rippled in the infinite breeze like a long slow wave on a lazy sea.

She strolled on, enjoying the feeling of walking on her own land. She now understood the power it gave men and why they did almost anything to acquire property. They broke their backs trying to keep it viable in the hard times and, in good times, they looked to buy more. The intensity of her feelings was frightening. Her land. Her future.

She joined the men on the rise, catching the last snippets of their conversation.

'I saw a plough for sale yesterday. I'd like us to sow our grass seed as soon as possible.' Gerald pulled at a tall piece of grass and twirled it between his fingers. 'We've so much to build. You'll need to pick reliable men to help you, Robson, while I am in Sydney.'

'Yes, sir. I know a fellow, a former convict, who has just finished his ticket-of-leave. He's a hard worker, and honest, which is rare for most convicts. He goes wherever work is and I hear he's back in Berrima. He has two strong sons, too.'

'Good, good.'

'This rise should be high enough to avoid any floods,' Robson said as he paced out the area.

Gerald shielded his eyes with his hand to follow the line of the creek before them. 'This water course is a stroke of luck. We'll have fresh water on our doorstep.'

'It may dry out in a drought for it's not very deep.' Robson pointed to the opposite side. 'You'll be wanting the stables and men's quarters on the other side, Mr Noble?'

'Yes indeed.' Gerald turned and took Pippa's hand. 'What do you think my dear?'

She took a deep breath, raised her face to the sun and closed her eyes hardly able to express her feelings. 'I think we have found paradise, Father.'

Pippa placed her knife and fork on her plate, and reached for her glass of wine. 'I imagine Robson and his men have achieved much in the valley during this last week.'

Gerald touched his napkin to his mouth and frowned at the rowdy noise coming from the main bar. 'Yes, I expect so. He will be back tomorrow. His main concern this week was widening and securing a way down the slope, ready for the transports.'

'I posted a letter today to Hilary and included a few sketches of the valley. I mentioned the beauty of the area. I long to show it to her.'

'I think it will be some time before either she or your mother comes to Berrima.'

She sipped her wine. 'I have read that timber homes can be erected rather quickly.'

'You mother would never live in a timber hut, my dear.'

'I will ensure the house is comfortable for Mother. Besides, we would save money to build the house in timber. Money that could be spent on more breeding mares.'

'We will need money for more things than mares. There are building materials to be bought, wages, provisions . . .'

Pippa looked askance. 'Have we enough money for all those things after buying the land?'

'Some.' Her father's brow winkled and he lowered his gaze. 'I shall write to Howard.'

'Oh, Father, no.' Pippa sagged at the suggestion. 'We owe the Lindfields a sufficient amount already. Must we apply for more?'

'Howard's loan shall not last much longer.'

'But to keep asking for more isn't the answer either.' She pushed her plate away. 'We must bring Noble Blaze and the mares here and advertise Blaze's services immediately. We need the mares to be put into foal as soon as possible.'

Gerald put his hand up to quieten her. 'Nothing is ready in the valley.'

Pippa raised her chin. 'Then we ought to hurry or manage with what we have. I am capable of living in a tent.'

'Pippa—'

'Listen, Father, please. I have thought about this. I have written it down in my journal.' She inched closer. 'We must hurry and build a hut of some sort and stables so we can immediately live on the land. That way we'll save money on the hotel in Sydney and stable rent. It would be a considerable reduction in our expenses.'

'Now wait just a minute—'

'You have to return to Sydney and arrange for Blaze and the mares to be brought here, as well as Mother and Hilary. While you are doing that, I shall supervise the work in the valley.' She took his hand and squeezed it. 'It makes sense, Father.'

A look of horror descended over his face. 'I will not leave you here alone. It's out of the question.'

She rocked back in her seat, annoyed. 'I have Robson and Millie. I will be fine. Millie has agreed to be my companion in all things. Her husband is away for long stretches at a time. Therefore, she and Davy are alone very much. She is sensible and skilled, Father. I can rely on her to help me organize things for the valley.'

'I cannot leave you here in this inn alone. It's unthinkable. Your mother—'

'Millie and Davy will stay with me here, her husband is due to go away for work in a few days. He's to work on a property at Bong Bong and won't be back for weeks.'

Her father looked pained. 'Your mother will never forgive me if I return without you. I know I said you could be included in the running of the stud, but I had meant once it was established, not supervising workmen and staying here alone. What kind of father would I be to leave you here?'

'A sensible one!' She glared, ready to fight tooth and nail for what she wanted. 'You must stop seeing me as something fragile.'

'You're a woman!'

'Yes, but does that make me brainless? No! I'm twenty-one, not a child in the nursery.' She realized she'd raised her voice and quickly took a breath to calm down. 'You know me, Father, for what I am. I thought, no, truly *believed* you understood me, understood that some women are strong, intelligent and nothing at all weak.'

'I do.'

'Then prove it. Go against your fellow man's ridiculous notions of womanhood and prove that you see me, a woman, as someone capable.'

He shook his head in defeat. 'I don't have to prove it. I know you are capable. It's not me, it's society that I'm protecting you from. Do you want to be seen as a 'she-devil', as somebody unfeminine? A social outcast?'

'Why would I be? Just because I stay here and build a home for us all?' She slumped back in her chair. 'Women have been the backbone of civilization for centuries, Father, only men refuse to acknowledge it.'

'And some *women* refuse to acknowledge it too. It is their evil tongues which will brand you as unacceptable, and that's what I want to avoid.' He sighed, his expression tired. 'Why must you strain against the boundaries, my dear? Sometimes you go too far.'

'Because, as you always say, I should have been a boy. Then I could enjoy freedom in the way only men can.'

Silence stretched between them until Gerald shifted in his chair and looked at her. 'Stay if you wish. It's obvious that the work must continue and I must return to Sydney.'

Pippa gazed at him and noticed the fine lines around his tight, bluish lips. 'Are you all right, Father?'

He nodded and gave a wry smile. 'Indigestion. Arguing with you over the dinner table isn't healthy.'

She rose and stepped to his side. Placing a kiss on his cheek, she squeezed his shoulders. 'I promise not to take risks and to behave myself.'

He raised his bushy eyebrows. 'That would be the first time.'

# CHAPTER FIVE

Pippa stood in the simmering heat and waved to the departing gig, smiling as her father turned for one last salute.

'How long do you think he will be gone for, miss?' Robson asked as they turned to walk inside the inn.

'A month, maybe more. My mother will create a fuss and cause delays. Also, father needs to secure supplies . . .' She paused by the staircase. 'Are you leaving today for the valley?'

'Yes, miss, unless of course you need me?'

'No, no.' She placed her hand on the banister. 'I will see you in a week.'

He twirled his hat in his hands. 'Are you certain you will be safe here?'

Pippa grinned. 'Indeed, Robson. I have Millie, and Father has talked with the innkeeper so I shall have my own watch guard.'

'Well, if you do require me, just send a man to the valley.'

'Thank you.'

'Very well, miss. Good day to you.'

'Keep safe.' Pippa strolled up the staircase and into her room. She unpinned her straw hat, threw it on to the bed, then walked to the small writing desk placed under the window. She gazed at her latest sketch. It was of Davy, fishing down by the river. She had sent many sketches to Hilary, hoping to show her the natural beauty of the area. Soon, she wished to set up her easel and paint the wild flowers. Perhaps if she could complete enough paintings she could send them back to England and sell them. The extra income would be welcomed. The thought of England and money made her think of the Lindfields – Grant especially. He was in India now, an officer in the Queen's army, leaving his ageing father Howard alone in the great house in the country. The house that, if fate and bloodlines had decreed differently, would have been her father's, but instead they were the poor relations, the ones who, when times were tough, went begging for loans.

How it irritated, shamed her whenever her father asked for money from Howard Lindfield. Oh, it was all done very jovially, as though it was a standard joke that her father's latest venture had doomed like his others. But not this time, there'd be no failure in Australia and one day they would return to England and show them all that the Noble family had risen again to the heights they were born to. She'd show Grant that she'd been worthy to love. A sharp rap at the door interrupted her musing.

'Yes, come in.'

The inn's cleaning maid rushed in. 'Oh, Miss Noble!'

'Yes, what is it?' Pippa frowned.

'Downstairs is a little boy asking for you. I think he is Millie Stroker's lad. He's crying.'

Pippa dashed past the maid, across the landing and downstairs. Davy stood in the entrance wiping a dirty sleeve across his wet eyes.

'Davy! What is the matter, my pet?' She crouched down and held his shoulders. 'Have you come here by yourself? Where's your mother? Did you lose your way?'

'Mother . . .' He threw himself against her, nearly toppling them both to the floor.

Pippa stood, taking his hand. 'Come, darling, I will take you home.' She asked the maid to fetch her hat.

Halfway up the main street, she looked down at his tear-stained face. 'Your mother will worry about you, my little man. You mustn't wander off by yourself.'

'Mother is helping Father.'

She frowned. 'Your father is home?'

Davy glanced up at her, sniffling. 'He's sick.'

Pippa's throat constricted. She forced a tight smile and squeezed his hand lightly.

At the cottage, Pippa's heart lurched at the gathering at the front door. The silent crowd sent shivers along her spine. They parted to let her and Davy through. Inside, she paused to let her eyes adjust to the dimness after the harsh sunlight outside.

A woman stood by the fire stirring a large pot nestled on the flames. She inclined her head towards the bedroom. 'Millie's in there. Best not let the boy go in.'

Pippa nodded and then bent to Davy. 'Darling, will you go out the back and pick me some flowers? I will join you in a minute.'

He walked away, his finger stuck in his mouth and his blue eyes wide.

The scene in the bedroom sent a jolt of alarm through her. Upon the bed lay the bloodied and ruined body of James Stroker; a man she had never met, except through Millie's stories.

Stepping beside Millie, who sat by the bed pressing towels on to the wounds, Pippa placed her hands on her new friend's shoulders.

'Have you seen Davy?' Millie's voice seemed to come from somewhere else so detached did she sound.

'He is safe.' Pippa swallowed the bile that rose to her throat as she gazed at James Stroker, who struggled for every breath. 'W-what happened?'

'A bull gored him. He was fixing a broken fence for a man down the road. The bull was meant to be tied up, but became free and enraged. James didn't get out of the way in time. It was only meant to be a quick job to do before he left for Bong Bong . . .'

Stroker groaned and writhed, causing his wounds to bleed profusely. Millie tried to staunch the spurting blood with another towel.

'Has the doctor been sent for?' Pippa rushed around to the other side of the bed, picked up a damp cloth and, after a moment's hesitation, wiped away seeping rivers of blood.

'The doctor can't be found, he could be anywhere. He has a large area to oversee.' Millie pushed her hair back with her wrist, then pressed a wad of cloth into a hole in James's chest. The blood flowed over her hand. 'They've sent for a woman, Mary Donnelly, who lives on the road to Sutton Forrest, for she is as good as a doctor, but I . . . I think it will be too . . . late.'

'Isn't there anyone else?' Pippa dumped her soiled cloth into a bucket near the bed and reached for a fresh cloth. She had never witnessed death this close before and this man's opened chest made her feel ill. She blinked and took a deep breath, only the stench of blood filled her nose and she heaved.

'Perhaps . . . a needle and thread . . . or . . .' Millie backed away from the bed, her hands dripping red.

'Why doesn't someone help us?' Pippa cried, frightened to take the pressure off the wound as another rivulet of blood seeped down James's ribs.

'James . . .' Millie kept backing away towards the door. 'I'll stitch him shall I?' She looked at Pippa for confirmation before falling to the floor with a thud.

'Help!' Pippa called out through the door and then rushed to gather Millie up into her arms. 'Millie!'

The woman from the other room stood at the door wiping her hands on her apron. 'I'll be off now then.'

'What?' Aghast, Pippa shook her head. 'No, you cannot go. I need your help.'

The woman strode into the room and helped her place Millie in a chair in the corner. She glanced at the body on the bed. 'There's nowt yer can do fer him, anyone can see that. I've helped all I can. I've got to be goin', I've left me little lass watching me baby.'

'Can you ask one of the others outside?'

'They've all gone home. Millie will need yer help now more than him on the bed.' The woman shrugged. 'There's some dinner simmerin' in the pot. The boy's out the back.' She quickly left the room before Pippa could say another word.

'Millie.' Pippa tapped her cheeks.

Millie's eyes fluttered open. 'I . . . Oh, Pippa, James . . .' Millie staggered up and Pippa helped her over to the bed.

Blood no longer oozed out of James's wounds. His chest no longer rose and fell.

'He's gone.' Millie stared at her husband, her face white. After a slight wavering, she bent and kissed his pale face. 'Goodbye, my sweet, gentle man.'

'Come.' Pippa guided her away and out of the room. She placed her in a chair by the fire, glancing up as a girl, aged about fifteen, entered through the front door.

'I'm Jane Parker from down the road. I heard there had been an accident. Is there anything I can do?'

Pippa beckoned her in, grateful to have another person in the room. 'Can you sit with her for a moment?'

'Of course.'

Pippa left them and went back into the bedroom. Flies swarmed over the body. The blood was beginning to congeal from the heat. In revulsion, Pippa threw the bloodstained blanket over James's body and hurried from the room. Millie and Davy needed her. They had no one else and, despite the awful circumstances, Pippa vaguely realized she liked to be needed.

*

The cool breeze caught the dirt thrown over the lowered coffin and blew it on to the few mourners standing by the grave.

Pippa shivered as raindrops pitted her. She grasped Davy's hand more firmly and smiled down at him. Emotion squeezed her heart when he smiled back. Poor little man.

Finally, the vicar finished his oration of James's life and the needs of God, allowing Pippa to turn Millie away from the dismal gravesite, with its ugly mound of fresh earth.

Millie took a few steps then stopped.

Pippa leaned close. 'What is it?'

'What do I do now?' Millie's grey eyes, dull with misery, mirrored the bleakness in her voice.

'We'll go have a cup of tea.'

'No, I mean about the rest of my life. I have no money, and Davy . . .'

'You aren't to worry. I will take care of you.' Pippa hugged her thin frame. 'You and Davy will come live with me.'

'With you?'

'Yes, in the valley. You were going to stay with me anyway, while Father was away, so let's make it permanent.'

Blinking, Millie frowned, trying to comprehend. 'I can work for you?'

She tucked Millie's hand through her arm and strode away from the churchyard with Davy in tow. 'I have it all worked out. I will give you a plot of land in the valley.'

'I have no money . . .'

'You don't have to pay for it. I'm giving it to you. Simple.'

'Your father—'

'Will understand.'

'I don't know, Pippa. It is a wonderful offer, but you can't give away land.'

'I can and I will. It's my payment to you for being my friend. It would please me exceedingly to have you so close.' She patted Millie's hand where it lay on her arm. The rain fell faster. 'We leave tomorrow.'

Millie's eyes widened. 'Oh, but . . .'

'No buts.'

They hurried the rest of the way to the inn as the rain became a steady shower. Once up in her room, Pippa showed Millie her drawings of the valley. Another drawing showed how Pippa imagined the stud would look in a few years' time with buildings in the middle of the valley and horses grazing with foals.

Millie glanced at the drawings as she took off Davy's coat and shoes. 'It looks really fine.'

'Look closely.' Pippa flattened the paper out on the writing desk. 'See that area there farther up from the rise? It shall be yours. It backs on to the bush forming a natural boundary.'

'I think we should wait until your father returns. He may be against this idea.' Millie turned away to place Davy's shoes under the bed.

'A one-acre plot will not be a great loss to us, Millie dear.' She frowned at her friend's reserve. 'I promise you, Father will not be concerned.'

Sighing, Millie sat on the bed beside Davy. 'It is too generous. Besides, I cannot work it by myself.'

Pippa crouched in front of her and gripped her hands. 'You shan't be doing it by yourself. You have me and, if you need to earn more money, you can always help in the house when it's built.'

'We've only known each other a short time, Pippa.'

'Well, I am sure in my feelings. You are my friend. Friends help each other.' She rose and sat beside them. 'Of course you may have somewhere else to go?'

Millie shook her head. 'I have nowhere and no one to go to.'

'Then you'll take a chance on me and my valley?'

A slow relieved smile seeped across Millie's wan face. She nodded.

Pippa gripped the side of the seat as the wagon trundled over the uneven ground. Scrub grasses scratched against the wheels in accompaniment with the squeaking load. Wind chased grey clouds across the sky, keeping the rain at bay. The trail leading to the ridgeline appeared a little more defined from her previous visit because of the last two weeks of heavy traffic. Yet, it was the track down to the valley bottom that had been totally transformed.

Robson paused the horses as they neared the descent. Fallen trees and stumps littered the area. He climbed down from the wagon and checked the ropes securing the load.

Pippa peered over the horses' heads, noting the improved path disappearing through the trees. 'You have achieved much here, Robson.'

He climbed back on to the seat and gathered the reins. 'Aye, miss. I concentrated on this track down to the valley because of the need for transports to get safely down.'

Millie, holding Davy tightly in her lap, glanced at them both. 'It is safe?'

Robson nodded. 'Indeed, Mrs Stroker, quite safe. I've had the men clearing a roadway in a gentle sweep. From here it looks like it goes straight down but it doesn't. In places we have levelled the track for twenty yards or more to take the strain off the horses going either up or down.' He clicked his tongue and urged the pair on.

In silence, they negotiated the first descent. The horses placed their feet carefully, going at their own pace. After the first slope, the track levelled off for close to fifteen yards before descending again. Pippa stared at the thick bush beside her, its shade throwing a cool blanket over them. However, at intervals, the sun streamed through gaps the men had made by removing trees.

Robson pointed to the logs edging the road. 'I think it wise to whitewash those logs, Miss Noble, to make it easier to see the track at night should the need arise.'

'Good idea.' Pippa thanked the Fates that had led this wise man to them.

A kangaroo jumped down from the high side and dashed away in front of the horses to disappear into the bush going down the slope at Pippa's side.

'Did you see him?' Davy squirmed in excitement.

Robson soothed the horses as they tossed their heads at the sharp intrusion. 'We can do without those blasted animals, Davy lad.'

Davy stared at him. 'Why?'

'Because they eat the grass which is needed for the beasts and they scare the horses into bolting when they jump out like that.'

Davy shrugged. 'I like them.'

They made it to the valley bottom without further incident. Rumbling out into the plain, Pippa scanned the middle and along the ragged tree line that marked the creek. Canvas tents dotted the distance like giant mushrooms. A flutter of exhilaration filled her as they travelled closer.

'It's a beautiful place, Pippa,' Millie murmured, eyeing their surrounds.

'It's a Noble place,' she whispered.

Robson reined in at the campsite by the creek. Two men worked on a timber building on the opposite side, while another man guided a Clydesdale dragging a log towards the structure.

Pippa gathered her skirts and climbed down before Robson had the chance to assist her. She shielded her eyes with her hand. 'What building are they working on?'

'That's the beginning of the first stable block, miss.' Robson swung Davy down before helping Millie. 'I thought it best to start on a stable first for the stallion and his mares. I didn't think your father would want Noble Blaze being hobbled out in the open every night. I have a team of men arriving tomorrow who will build a holding yard to the right of it.' He walked to the back of the wagon and untied the ropes. 'I'll set up your tent and then help the men before we lose the light.'

Pippa and Millie inspected the campsite while he unloaded the wagon. A campfire sat in the middle between the creek and the two canvas tents the men shared.

Millie poked at the ashes and embers sparkled at her. She added dry grass to it and watched it catch fire. 'There is a tremendous amount of work to do,' she murmured, looking up.

Pippa grinned. 'Yes, I know. I'm looking forward to it.'

'Does nothing deter you?' Millie smiled as she added little twigs to the small blaze.

Pippa sniffed the fresh air. 'This is my home.' She surveyed the valley and sighed. 'I will never become tired of looking at this place.'

'You will when you're cold, hungry and exhausted.'

Robson joined them, carrying a small sack. 'I'll get the fire going properly and put some water on to boil for you, miss.' He placed the sack at his feet. 'Likely you're in need of a cup of tea?'

'Thank you, Robson, but leave that. Millie and I can light a fire and make tea.'

His eyebrows rose. 'Are you sure?'

'Of course.' Pippa gathered a few sticks from the stockpile the men had made near the fire. 'You have enough to do. I do not need a butler at the moment.'

He chuckled and then glanced at Millie. 'Can you cook damper, Mrs Stroker?'

'Naturally.'

He indicated the sack. 'Flour is in there. Everything else you'll need is in the wagon or in the tents.'

Pippa threw the sticks on to the fire, watching Millie prepare the evening meal. 'Damper is bread, yes?'

'Yes, a flat bread cooked in the fire coals or in a frying pan if you have one. It's easy to make and tastes lovely. We must go for a walk tomorrow and see if we can find a hive. Wild honey tastes great too.'

'Really? I've never thought we could have wild honey. I imagined building hives later. What else can we use in the valley?'

'Fresh meat. If the men can shoot kangaroos or wild ducks.' Millie walked into the men's tents and returned with a box of cooking ingredients plus a frying pan. 'Davy, don't stray too close to the creek,' she called to him as he wandered along the creek bank.

The clang of Robson's hammer as it hit the iron tent stakes into the ground reverberated throughout the valley. It did not take him long to erect the large tent that Pippa was to share with Millie and Davy. Once the shelter was up, she and Millie took their few belongings inside it. Robson carried two cot beds and placed one on either side of the tent, leaving a central walkway. The tent was large enough for Pippa to stand upright in the middle.

As the sun descended behind the distant ridges, Pippa strolled to the creek edge and waited for the men to walk up to the campsite. An enormous tree trunk, cut in half, spanned the narrow creek bed as a bridge.

Robson stood beside her to introduce the men as they filed across. 'Miss Noble, this is Barney Goodfellow, behind him are his two sons, Peter and Colin.'

Pippa inclined her head to the short, older man. 'Pleased to meet you, Mr Goodfellow. I trust you and your sons have everything you need?'

Goodfellow doffed his cap. 'Aye, miss, indeed we have.'

'Excellent.' Pippa looked at the two young men standing behind their father. They seemed decent enough and strong. She waved towards the campfire. 'My friend, Millie Stroker and her son, Davy are staying in the valley also. Mrs Stroker has cooked damper, potatoes and there is tea. Please go about your normal routine.'

'Thank you, Miss Noble.' Barney Goodfellow rubbed his rough hands together. 'We're as hungry as a fox in a henhouse.'

She grinned and walked back to the fire. Davy rushed up to her and grasped her skirts. She placed her hand on his head and stroked his hair. A wonderful feeling of achievement and satisfaction filled her.

The sounds of the bush changed as birds quietened and crickets and other insects took up a chorus of their own. A golden light descended into the valley as the last of the sun's rays washed over them. The murmur from the men as they washed for dinner joined that of Millie's tinkering by the fire. The pleasant scene comforted Pippa in a way she had never known. Here she was, a stranger in a strange place, surrounded by wild, inhospitable bush with people she had only known a short time, yet it felt natural. Tonight, for the first time, she would eat and sit beside an open fire, sleep in a tent and do it all on her own land. She felt more alive now than ever before.

# CHAPTER SIX

Dawn filtered over the valley in hues of pink and orange, lifting the grey. The Kookaburras or laughing jackasses as the locals called them, sent out their deep-throated calls awaking the bush to a new day. Pippa opened her eyes and stared up at the canvas above her. She listened to the sounds outside the tent flap; the men stirring the fire up, putting the water on to boil, the mutters.

Three weeks had passed since her father had returned to Sydney. Three weeks, in which she'd lived in the valley and learned to cook bush food and wash her own clothes. A secret smile played on her lips as she remembered the first time she scrubbed her clothes and the simple feeling of satisfaction of a job well done when she completed the task – even if her arms had ached. Learning to cook gave her the same fulfilment. Millie patiently showed her the ways of bush life and each day she learned something new. Her mother would be horrified if she knew of her daughter skivvying like a maid, but they hadn't budgeted for the cost of servants yet. Besides, Millie and Robson did the most odious tasks, leaving her to paint and sketch and dream of what the valley would be like in the future.

Gradually, the sounds of the men's presence faded into the distance, indicating that they'd crossed the creek to start work, she threw back the blankets and climbed out of the cot. She wrapped her shawl around her nightgown, untied the flap and stepped out. The fresh, crisp air woke her fully and she stood and stretched. Overnight dew coated the grass and shimmered like thousands of diamond beads. Necklaces of wet cobwebs adorned shrubs and, on the far side of the valley, mobs of kangaroos grazed.

She walked to the fire and held her hands out to the warmth. The shade thrown by the large gum tree at the creek's edge chilled her, but the day would be hot.

On the other side of the creek and to the right, the sight of the first completed building, a stable with three stalls, gave her immense pleasure. The holding yard led off to the side of the stable and within it, Peter Goodfellow harnessed Ginger and Happy, the new draught horse. Further on, Barney gestured to Colin, who descended into the sawpit.

Movement from behind made her spin around. Robson came down the slope carrying an armload of wood. 'Good morning, miss.'

'Good morning, Robson. What are the plans for today?' She wrapped her long shawl around her tighter. Again her mother would be traumatized to know Robson had seen Pippa in her voluminous nightgown on many occasions, but privacy in a camp was limited.

Robson threw down his load and turned to survey the stables and yards. 'Now we have one stable and holding yard built, I've asked Barney and Colin to make a start on the storage hut. We'll build it beside the stable and we should have it finished in a few days. Peter and me are fencing off an acre directly behind the stable for the stallion and his mares to be turned out in during the day. We should have it finished by the end of the week hopefully.'

'Father and I wish to have the stable block in the shape of a quadrangle, with one side open or maybe a stone wall with arches for entry.'

Robson nodded. 'The mason and his team can do that, although they are coming to start on the house, as it is the priority. In fact, they should be arriving any day.'

Pippa laughed. 'You have been saying that for three weeks now. I seriously doubt he'll turn up at all.'

'Yes, well the canny little Irishman is known for his temper and tantrums.'

'As long as he works well, that is all that matters.'

Robson added more wood to the fire and set the water can over it. 'He is the best in the district and highly sought after.'

'So he is worth his money?'

'Absolutely, miss.'

Pippa nibbled her thumbnail. 'Has my father mentioned . . .' She hesitated, not knowing whether to breach the sensitive subject of money to Robson.

He looked up as if reading her thoughts. 'At the end of the month I will need to pay the men.'

'Yes, of course.'

'Will your father be back by then?'

'I should think so, yes.'

'Pippa!' Davy ran over to them. 'There was a really big black spider in the tent. Mother killed it with your shoe.'

'Goodness!' She pretended to be shocked, but seeing large spiders was becoming commonplace now.

Davy glanced at the empty frying pan. 'I'm hungry.'

Grinning, she ruffled his hair. 'Very well. Let me have a few moments to dress.'

After breakfast, Pippa decided to make a vegetable garden. She paced the area out on the west slope of the rise. As she and Millie dug over the earth, the sun warmed their backs.

Millie straightened and wiped the sweat off her forehead. 'Why are you doing this, Pippa?'

'What do you mean? We need vegetable gardens.'

'Naturally, but why are *you* doing it? You are not a labourer.'

Pippa leaned against her shovel. The question surprised her. 'I guess I feel the need to play my part in making this stud.'

'You can do that without getting your hands dirty. You are a lady.'

She shrugged, unable to answer for a moment. 'In England we became very poor. We had a grand house that my ancestors had rented from our distant cousins the Lindfields for generations. We had money, respectability, beautiful possessions.' Pippa stared out over the valley, thinking of all the things they had lost, but she had lost much more than material possessions, she had lost Grant.

'My grandfather started to lose our fortunes through bad investments. My father tried to stem the tide but it was too great and then he gave up trying, turned to gambling and lost everything. We had to leave our house and servants. For the last few years we had to live in rented rooms in strange towns as Father tried, unsuccessfully, to regain what he'd lost.'

'It must have been an awful tragedy.'

She nodded, dug the shovel into the earth and lifted a clod with more force than before. 'I never want to feel that way again. The loss, the devastation of leaving behind everything that had been ours, hasn't left me. I doubt it ever will.'

'That is understandable.'

'Howard Lindfield loaned father money to start anew.'

Millie bent and pulled grass clumps out of the turned soil. 'So you used it to come out here?'

'Father had the notion to come to the colonies and make our

fortunes again. I encouraged him. . . .' She paused and watched a worm wriggle back into the disturbed earth. 'I could not abide staying there, to suffer the whispers and pity of visitors who came to see how dire our situation was.'

Millie closed the space between them and laid her hand on her shoulder. 'You do not have to work like a skivvy to make this place successful.'

Pippa sighed. 'Yes I do, for then I will know it has been done. I need the control. Never again will I leave my future to another to manage.'

'But that is our lot as women.'

'It's not for me.' She gave a wry smile. 'My father has told me all my life that I should have been a boy because of my waywardness, but I can't help it. Hilary delights people with her piano playing, her singing, her beautiful embroidering and gracious poise. I have none of those skills, except for painting, but I can ride, shoot and discuss world events better than most men. It is who I am and I cannot change that.' She looked down at the row of turned soil. 'If Mother or Hilary wanted a vegetable garden they would have rightly asked Robson to do it or dragged one of the men away from their work to do it. Whereas I, well, I simply take a shovel and make one.'

'Don't be ashamed of your uniqueness.'

'I'm not.' Pippa grinned. 'I have my family to do that for me.'

'I guess the nature of the country means that most women out here, whether they are high or low born have to, at some time, get their hands dirty.'

'Mother, Mother!' Davy waved from down by the creek. 'Someone is coming!'

Pippa shielded her eyes from the harsh sun and looked in the direction of the track leading down to the valley floor. A wagon trundled towards them, but the distance made it hard to recognize the owner. She dropped her shovel. 'Come, let us wash before they arrive.'

She and Millie hurried down the slope to the camp and within minutes had washed their faces and hands. Pippa untied her grubby apron and threw it on to the small stump used as a seat by the fire. She tidied her hair as best she could but was conscious of sweat-dampened tendrils sticking to her neck and cheeks.

The wagon rumbled closer and she could pick out male occupants.

'Who are they?' Davy came to stand beside her.

'We shall soon see, little man.' She counted six men in the wagon. 'Run and get Robson, darling. Tell him the mason has arrived.' She tapped his shoulder and he rushed off.

The wagon driver halted his horse a few yards from the campsite and the five men in the back jumped down. The driver took his time to climb down from his seat and walk over to her. He was of small stature, with bandy legs, which made him walk with a rolling action. He swept off his dusty hat, revealing a balding head and bowed stiffly. 'Good day to yer, miss.'

Pippa inclined her head. 'How do you do?'

'Grand, thank yer. I'm here ter see Mr Noble or Robson. I'm Jim O'Reilly, master stonemason.'

'I am Miss Noble. My father has yet to return from Sydney.' She glanced over her shoulder as Robson crossed the creek.

Jim spun his hat around in his hands and gazed about him. His weather-beaten face had aged him before his time. 'Has the rock arrived, Miss Noble?'

Before she could reply, Robson joined them and shook hands with the mason. 'Good to see you, Jim.'

'Got yerself a fine position here have yer, lad?' Jim's face creased into a grin. 'Better than the old Foggity place, I'll bet.'

Robson chuckled. 'Indeed.'

Jim looked about. 'So, where's the rock, man?'

'It's not yet turned up. It's as late as you.'

Pippa stepped forward. 'What rock, Robson?'

'For the house, miss.'

Pippa raised her eyebrow. 'Father has bought stone?'

'Of course, miss.'

'But why?' She flung her arms out wide. 'We are surrounded by stone. Great slabs of rock litter the valley. We have it in abundance. There is no need to buy it.'

Jim cleared his throat. 'The rock here hasn't been quarried, Miss Noble.'

Frustration mounted in her. 'It simply needs to be dug up and cut. You are a mason, surely you and your team can do that?'

Jim shifted his weight from foot to foot. 'Me and my men aren't ruddy miners, miss, excusing the language.' He twisted about and gestured to the men, who quickly jumped back into the wagon.

Robson swore under his breath, but Pippa heard him. His face hardened. 'Now come on, Jim. We can work this out. The building of the house will keep you in work for many months.'

'I ain't digging up no rock, laddo!'

Pippa clenched her hands, fighting back her anger. 'You will be paid extra for your labours.'

'Miss Noble, I don't mean any disrespect, but what you're asking is impossible.'

'Why is it? If you need more men, Robson will hire more and bring them in. I need you to start on the house immediately. We already have a carpenter here and once he's finished the stable buildings and a hut for my family, then I want him to start work on the main house, but he can't do that if we have no mason.'

Jim slammed his hat against his thigh. 'This is a big undertaking.'

'Are you not up to the task?'

His face grew red. 'I can do anything I put my mind to!'

Pippa inclined her head. 'Excellent. Your men can camp on the far side of the slope. After my men have built the family hut, then they'll build a hut for the men. I don't expect you all to sleep on the ground for a long period of time and I will do all I can to make sure your stay here is comfortable.' She walked away with her head high and hoped her gamble paid off. Jim started grumbling to Robson but she couldn't make out his words. Oh well, if they left now there wasn't a lot she could do about it. Her mother would just have to live in a timber hut longer than she thought she would. Millie and Davy stood beside the tent and they followed her inside it.

Millie hid her smile behind her hand. 'Oh, Pippa. Your father will be furious that you've offered them more money.'

Pippa gave an undignified sniff. 'He'll not be as furious as I when he does return.' She flopped on to the cot. 'I cannot believe he ordered stone when we have it here in the valley. Why buy something we already own? He continues to throw good money after bad. I'll cancel the order and deal with the consequences.'

'Will it cost a lot for the mason?'

Pippa sighed and rubbed her forehead. 'An elegant house will take a long time to build and drain all our resources if we aren't vigilant. However, it has to be done, for Mother will not settle for anything less. At least we can save money by quarrying our own sandstone.'

Millie sat down beside her. 'It seems so extravagant to start building a stone house, taking into account your financial situation.'

'Agreed. Which is why we must advertise Noble Blaze straight away. He is the only thing we have to earn us a regular income. If it had been left up to me, we'd all live in a timber house for years, but my parents won't consider it. They insist on setting the high standards that they lost back home, but this venture will fail if we do not act in a sensible manner.'

'You mentioned sheep before in Berrima, when are they to arrive?'

'Who knows? Everything happens at a snail's pace in this country.' Pippa huffed and swatted at an annoying fly near her face.

'You are tired, my dear, and have too much to think about.' Millie rose. 'Lie down for an hour.' She paused as the noise of the wagon rumbled away from the camp.

Pippa groaned. 'There goes the mason.'

'Shush now, sleep for a while. It's too hot to worry about anything right this minute.' Millie pushed her down to lie on the cot. 'Davy, come outside and let Pippa rest.'

She sighed and closed her eyes. The heat sapped her strength and the stress of building the stud tired her further. Frustration and anger still lingered. How could her father order stone when they had so many other things to buy? She understood his need to satisfy Mother's demands, but a stone house wouldn't help them if they had no farm to support it. *If only I had money . . .*

When Pippa woke, her head rang with noise. For a moment she wondered if the hounds of hell were at the tent flap. She scrambled out of the cot in a tangle of skirts and dashed outside only to jerk to a stop. On the other side of the creek, a flock of sheep bleated as two barking dogs rounded them up. Through the floating dust cloud, she made out Robson talking to a man holding a large stick. The shepherd.

The clang of iron on iron made her spin around and there on the far side of the rise Jim O'Reilly yelled at his men as they erected tents and banged stakes into the ground. *He stayed*. Beside the stables stood the skeleton frame of the storage hut and Barney, high on a ladder, passed timber to Colin who crouched on the roof joists.

'There you are, sleepyhead.' Millie and Davy laughed, stepping around the tent. Both were filthy dirty.

'The sheep are here and Jim O'Reilly stayed.' Pippa blinked to make sure she saw it all correctly.

'Yes. The shepherd came down the valley not ten minutes ago and Mr O'Reilly might grumble, but knows that he's on to a good thing here.' Millie collected a bucket and then ducked into the tent and brought out soap and towels. 'Davy and I are going to wash before I start dinner.'

'What have you been doing?'

Millie grinned and waved behind her. 'Go and have a look.'

Pippa lifted her skirts and walked up behind the tent towards the slope. As she got closer, her throat tightened. A vegetable garden, about fifteen feet by six feet, lay neatly turned over and trenched. Tears pricked her eyes. 'Oh, Millie . . .'

Later, as the sun set behind the ranges, Pippa knelt by the creek and cleaned her face, making sure the soapy water did not escape the shallow washbowl and contaminate the creek. It was a perfect evening. Golden light filled the valley except where shadows darkened hollows. She drew in a deep breath and gazed out over her home.

The shepherd had moved the flock to the end of the valley and into the edges of the timbered slopes. The land on the other side of their boundary was crown land and Robson said they should use it until either someone bought it, or a government official found out. She agreed with him completely. Why use their own grass, when the sheep could feed on crown land? They wouldn't be the first to do this and if it saved her money, then the happier she was.

The snap of a broken twig made her look around. Robson stood some feet away. 'I don't mean to disturb you, Miss Noble. I just wanted a word before I turned in for the night.'

She smiled up at him. 'Yes, of course. What is it?'

'Tomorrow, Colin and I will make a start on the foundations of the family hut. Peter has felled many trees in the last few days and once we've spent some time in the saw pit cutting the timber into lengths, it won't take long, perhaps, ten or twelve days, to erect the hut.'

'Very good, Robson. I am looking forward to occupying something other than a tent, which is a little restrictive.' She smiled.

'At first it will only be one room, but in the coming weeks we'll add to that. I thought you'd like a verandah to help with the heat?'

'Absolutely.'

He nodded and turned to go but hesitated a moment more. 'Is there anything you need before the men turn in?'

'No, thank you.'

'Well, good night then, Miss Noble.' He put his forefinger to the brim of his wide hat.

'Sleep well, Robson.' She looked past him as Davy wandered towards her from the tent.

'Are you finished, Pip?' Davy sat down beside her and dipped his hand into the creek.

'Yes, poppet.'

'Can you tell me a bedtime story?'

'Of course.'

He leaned against her. 'Mother was crying. I think she hurt her finger.'

'Hurt her finger? How?' Pippa ruffled his hair, enjoying the complete trust and friendship she received from this dear boy. She gathered up her belongings and tipped the soapy water against the large gum tree.

He shrugged.

She turned and went back up to the campfire and at the same time Millie left the tent and came towards her. Pippa, seeing Millie's red, swollen eyes, reached out and took her hand. 'Davy said you hurt your finger?'

Millie sniffed and looked away. 'Oh, it's nothing. Into bed now, Davy. I'll come in to see you in a minute.'

After Davy left them, Pippa leaned forward, knowing Millie hid the real reason for her tears. 'Millie?'

'I'm all right, Pippa, really.' Millie waved her away. 'I was just having a moment to myself and thinking about James.'

'Yes, of course. I'm sorry to pry.' Pippa stepped back. 'You must miss him awfully.'

Picking up a stick, Millie poked the fire's embers. 'No, you see, that's why I was crying, because I'm a terrible woman. I haven't been missing him as much as I should.' Her chin trembled slightly. 'He was a good man. Honest. Decent. And I did care for him, but he was away all the time and we hadn't married for love . . .'

'You aren't a terrible woman.' Pippa placed her hand on Millie's shoulder. 'You cannot live in the past. He would want you and Davy to be happy.'

'We are. That is the problem. I've been happy here in the last few weeks and that is wrong. I forgot about James as though he'd never existed, but I've been so grateful to have this second chance that I forgot to grieve for my son's father.'

'Though I never knew the man, I think James would understand. He would want Davy's welfare to be your most important concern.' Pippa smiled. 'Perhaps we should have Davy place flowers on his grave when we next go to Berrima?'

Millie returned her smile. 'Thank you. You are such a good friend to me.'

Pippa winked. 'I think we are good for each other.'

*

Pippa paid for Davy's sweets and handed them to him. His blue eyes wide with pleasure made her smile as they left the shop. He'd been a good boy this morning, visiting his father's grave and then being patient while she and Millie bought provisions for the camp.

A few feet from the shop's entrance, she paused and stared. A procession of convicts walked towards them in three long, dishevelled lines. Every now and then the overseer and two local constables shouted at the prisoners for dawdling, though their words had no effect for the convict men still dragged their feet, their chains jingling.

Davy stood close to her as the miserable lot passed them by. Pippa noticed the slumped shoulders and drab prison garb; all wore the look of whipped dogs. She had no wish to witness any more. Unlike most of the general population, she always felt sick at heart for the men, woman and children who endured exile from their homeland for no more than stealing a loaf of bread to feed their starving families. Long constructive talks with Howard Lindfield, a high court judge, allowed her the opinion that the ruling class had, in many cases, a lot to answer for.

Turning from the street spectacle and holding tight to Davy's hand, she went to find Millie, whom she'd left at the cobblers.

'Er, excuse me.' A man in dusty work clothes with a swag slung over his back stopped Pippa as she stepped over the narrow earth gutter running in front of the shops.

'Yes?'

The man, tall with piercing grey eyes and an angled face, swept off his hat and bowed. 'Are you Miss Noble?'

Pippa nodded, taking in his over-long copper-coloured hair. 'Yes I am.'

'I'm Neil Chalker and I'm looking for work. I was told that you've recently moved here and have land.'

'That is true, but as for work, I'm not sure . . .' Pippa glanced up and down the street looking for Robson. 'My overseer handles the hiring.'

Chalker gave her a wry smile that hinted at insolence. 'I was also told that you were in charge, maybe I was mistaken.'

Raising her chin, Pippa stared at him. 'It is Noble land and I am a Noble. Therefore, I am in charge.'

He acknowledged her with a dip of his head. 'Then are you hiring, Miss Noble?'

'What do you do?' Pippa stalled. This man was so sure of himself and too over friendly.

His smile widened and he straightened his shoulders, showing her the muscles that flexed under his battered clothes. 'I work with horses mainly.'

Pippa digested this. They needed horsemen; good stable hands and grooms. 'Do you ride?'

'Better than most.' His grey eyes darkened as he watched her.

She nodded and took a quick breath. This man had something she couldn't name, but he drew her gaze repeatedly. 'We need grooms, although our breeding horses haven't yet arrived from Sydney.'

'I can turn my hands to other things until they turn up.' His gaze never left her face and for some reason, she felt herself blushing at his words as though they held a hidden meaning.

Swallowing, Pippa cleared her throat. 'Very well, Mr Chalker. I'll give you a month's trial, starting tomorrow.'

He slowly smiled and his eyes held laughter. 'You'll not regret it, Miss Noble.'

Pippa turned away and taking Davy's hand once more, walked down the street. Shivers tingled down her spine and she didn't need to look back to know he was watching her. She was already regretting her hasty decision.

The sound of Millie's rooster crowing woke Pippa. It sounded so foreign in the valley amongst the native birdcalls. Wiping the sleep from her eyes, she yawned and stared around the hut. Its primitive form still required a little getting used to, but it was better than the tent. She and Millie now slept on a double bed and Davy had his own straw pallet.

In the six weeks since her father left, much had been accomplished. Robson pushed the men hard and the results were more then she'd hoped for. They'd established the hut on a slab of sandstone, uncovered after some shallow digging. Thin sapling tree trunks made up the walls with larger trunks used as the corner posts. Saplings created the roof's framework and large sheets of bark covered it. In turn, thin pieces of wood overlaid the bark to prevent it from blowing away.

A doorway, built in the middle of the front wall, faced the creek and the open stretch of the valley floor. On either side of the doorway were two small squares cut into the wall for windows, but, at present, like the doorway, they were enclosed with calico to keep out most of the flies.

After rising from the bed, Pippa washed and then donned a fawn-coloured linen dress, over this she wrapped a white apron of Millie's. She pulled Davy's blankets up over his shoulders and smiled at his peaceful sleeping face. Near the doorway, she paused to check for ants on the two wooden shelves. The shelves held most of the cooking utensils and some tins of ingredients like salt, sugar, tea, coffee as well as jars of jam, pickled onions and chutney. Underneath the shelves stood sacks of flour, potatoes and oats. Next to them, in small barrels, were salted beef and pork and lastly crates of fresh vegetables. All was clear of the awful insects that played havoc with the sanity of the most watchful housekeeper.

Pushing aside the weighted calico door, she went out to join Millie by the fire. 'You are up early.'

Millie nodded. 'Yes. I wanted to start washing the clothes before it got too hot.'

Sitting on a stump, Pippa reached over for the kettle and poured out some tea. Movement across the creek indicated that the men were awakening. 'I'll help you.'

'Actually if you could peel and chop the vegetables for the stew, that would be better. Then we can go for a walk later and know that dinner is all done.'

Smiling, Pippa added milk to her tea. 'Have you checked for eggs?'

Millie added strips of fatty bacon to the frying pan. 'Yes. I did it after I milked Buttercup.'

Pippa looked behind her to where Buttercup grazed. Buying the cow and chickens had been extravagant, but necessary.

'Did you finish writing your letter to your sister last night?' Millie glanced at her as she added eggs to the bacon.

'No. The candle was burning low. I shall finish it today and get Robson to post it when he goes to Berrima tomorrow. My family will want to know if I received their news about Father.'

'I hope he is much recovered now.'

Pippa nodded. 'Hilary's letter sounded positive. Father is never ill, so I believe it would have shocked them greatly to have him return and fall sick.' She broke up pieces of the fresh damper bread and her thoughts turned to her family so far away.

Hilary's letter, which arrived three days ago, had alarmed her with the news of her father's ill health, but thankfully Hilary had also enclosed money – money that Pippa desperately needed. She immediately paid the men and with the remaining amount, bought the cow, hens and food.

'You would have a lot to tell them.'

'Yes. Father will be anxious to know how we are surviving. I've told him everything.' Pippa looked around at the general state of the stud. At the moment there was no beauty. The basic stable buildings looked harsh in the morning light and, up on the rise, Jim O'Reilly's men had littered the landscape with exposed diggings, piles of rock, timber, tents and an ever-growing campsite as they erected work benches and made fires. What her mother would say about it all defied imagination.

'Look! There is someone coming.' Millie pointed to the lone horseman riding along the valley floor.

Pippa peered to see if she could make out the rider. As he rode closer, she noticed the thickset build. He was no one she knew.

The man in question pulled his horse to a stop before the clump of trees and dismounted. He took off his wide-brimmed hat, showing a crop of springy brown hair peppered with grey. Stopping in front of Pippa, he smiled and made a small bow. 'Good day to you, ladies. Please forgive my intrusion but I simply had to introduce myself to my new neighbours. I'm Meredith. Douglas Samuel Meredith, your servant, ma'am.' He bowed again.

'Pleased to meet you, Mr Meredith. I am Miss Phillippa Noble and this is my friend, Mrs Stroker.' Pippa held out her hand for him to take. 'I am most pleased that you took it upon yourself to become better acquainted with us, Mr Meredith, for I am not informed at all about our neighbours, or indeed as to whether we had any.'

'I have land to the south-west of you, Miss Noble. Over that southern ridge of yours is where my grant begins.'

'Our land begins at the top of that mount,' Phillippa turned to point out beyond the hut, 'and then includes the entire valley floor and the west, east and north-side flanks of those hills.' She couldn't help to sound proud.

'Indeed, ma'am, it is as good a spot as any I've seen. And this creek is a blessing sent straight from God himself.' Meredith grinned, stepping a small way with her towards the creek. 'An ideal situation being at the base of that mount. It will give plenty of protection from the elements.'

'We think the same.'

'And do you have family, Miss Noble?'

'Yes, I await my father, mother and sister to come from Sydney. We have recently arrived from England.'

Meredith gazed around at the busy hive of men and industry.

'You've wasted no time in establishing yourselves. What do you propose to farm?'

'We intend to build a grand stud, but alongside of that, we'll run sheep and a few cattle until the stud becomes viable.'

'A sensible plan.'

They returned to the fireside and Millie brought out two chairs from the hut. Once seated, Meredith accepted a cup of tea from Millie. 'I think you would do very well here with a stud. The climate is most suitable and there are many a wealthy gentleman and farmer who live among the villages of this district that would enjoy having quality bloodstock within a short distance of their own homes. Yes, I think you will do very well.'

Meredith stayed for another ten minutes or so before he complained of having to leave their wonderful company and head for Berrima to do business.

'Thank you so much for coming to see us, Mr Meredith, and thank you for your kind words. My father will be most pleased to know that we have a sensible man for a neighbour.' Pippa and Millie walked with him back to his horse.

'It is a pleasure, Miss Noble, to have such good quality people for neighbours myself. Many have come to toil the earth in the area, but not many have the intellect and willpower to make a success of it. So they wallow in filth and become slaves to the gin bottle until they either die or walk away and go back to the towns they had so recently left. It is a sad and sorry business.'

'I have every confidence that we shall rise above such trials.'

'I am certain of it.' Meredith smiled and then mounted his horse and donned his hat. 'I believe I could not face my wife this night if I did not extend an invitation to you and Mrs Stroker to visit my own humble home.'

'That would be most pleasurable.' Pippa liked the idea of meeting new people after her prolonged time in the bush. They made only infrequent trips into Berrima and most times, she just let Robson go while she stayed behind.

'Would tomorrow morning be convenient?'

'Yes, that would be acceptable. Thank you.'

'Good. I'll send one of my men to collect you and that will save you from riding along an unknown path. The track to our home can be treacherous. It is best to be accompanied by someone who has experience. Well, good day to you ladies, until tomorrow!'

Millie nudged her. 'A gentleman caller already. Shame he is married.'

Pippa laughed. 'Hold your tongue. I'll not be married off, thank you. Acquiring a husband is the last thing on my mind.' Only, her smile slipped as she thought of Grant. Once, she had dreamed of a husband. . . .

# CHAPTER SEVEN

Despite the jarring ride over a rough track, Pippa enjoyed the drive to the Meredith homestead. The scents of the bush, from the moist undergrowth to the strong, sharp aroma of the eucalyptus, refreshed her after weeks of heat and dust from the valley bottom.

Soon the dense bushland gave way to acres of cleared terrain. A large, log house with a verandah along the front and four steps leading down to the grass stood in the middle of the clearing.

Pippa smiled at Millie. 'The Merediths have done well for themselves.'

Three black cockatoos took flight from the gum trees and screamed out their cry, drowning out Millie's reply.

Wincing as the sound hurt her ears, Pippa laughed. 'I'll never get used to that sound.'

On drawing closer to the house, their hosts appeared from the front door and stood on the verandah. The driver stopped the cart and Meredith descended the steps to help the women down from the vehicle. 'You made it then.'

'Yes. It was a pleasant journey, thank you.' Pippa smiled.

Meredith beamed and waved his arm wide. 'Welcome to our humble abode. Please, come meet my wife, she is most delighted to have women nearby.'

Amelia Meredith, small, plump, with light brown hair and a cheery smile shook their hands. 'I am so pleased to meet you both.'

Pippa liked her immediately. 'You have a lovely home, Mrs Meredith.'

Relaxing at the Merediths' warmth and friendliness, Pippa and Millie sat in the coolness of the verandah. For an hour, they sipped tea and nibbled sweet cakes and biscuits while chatting about the state of the country and local politics.

'Would you care to have a look around the property?' Meredith asked as they finished their tea and a servant girl cleared away their cups.

The four of them first admired Amelia's vegetable garden and Pippa asked numerous questions on the success of growing different vegetables. Next, they inspected an orchard and Meredith encouraged Pippa to create the same on her land as the surplus fruit was sold to the shops in Berrima and provided a small but welcome income.

'An orchard and large vegetable garden is a must to survive out here so far away from any of the villages,' Amelia added, her voice soft.

'Yes, a successful garden is something that I will endeavour to have as well.' Pippa smiled, suddenly enthusiastic to reproduce such comforts in the valley.

'Do you have convict workers?' Meredith bent down to pick up a twig.

'We have a pardoned convict and his sons. They are good, hard-working men. I'm sure we will have more ticket-of-leave men soon, though my mother doesn't approve.'

As Meredith took Pippa away to inspect his sheep and crop fields, Millie and Amelia wandered back towards the house.

'Your husband works for Miss Noble does he, Mrs Stroker?'

Millie shook her head as they went up on to the verandah and resumed their seats. 'No, my husband recently died.'

Amelia blushed. 'Oh, forgive me. I should have thought what with you wearing black. I do apologize.'

'Please, don't feel unsettled by it. This black dress has been worn so much that it's starting to fade to grey.' Millie gave a wry smile and straightened out the black skirt. Her gaze drifted to where Pippa walked with Meredith in the far fields. Pippa's dress of apple-green silk had been packed away since they left Berrima for the valley, but when she shook it out this morning and dressed for the visit to the Merediths', Millie had realized once again how much of a lady Pippa really was, no matter how she might like to pretend otherwise.

'Miss Noble is a unique woman, she has the breeding of a lady but talks of industry like a man,' Amelia said, as though reading Millie's mind.

'Yes, that is true.' Millie accepted the fresh tea that Amelia passed. 'I have never met anyone like her in my life, but she is a truly good person. She helped me as a real friend would even though we had only just met. Quite easily she could've turned her back on me and my son, but she didn't. I owe her everything.'

'You have a son?' Amelia's eyes widened.

Millie nodded. 'Yes, Davy. He's full of mischief and, thankfully, he decided that staying with Robson today, Pippa's overseer, would be more interesting than visiting.'

Amelia lowered her lashes and sighed. 'I wish I had a son. I wish that I had any child.' She raised her eyes to Millie. 'Maybe this child I carry will be strong and survive for us.' She patted the small mound of her stomach. 'Is your son your only child?'

'Yes, he is. My husband worked away a lot.' Millie played with the plain gold wedding band she wore. 'I would have liked more children.'

'Come, I want to show you something.' Amelia walked down the verandah steps and Millie followed. They went around the back of the house, past the gardens and small tool shed and further on until they reached a small area near a young weeping willow tree.

Amelia pointed to the small graves. 'I have been pregnant eight times in ten years of marriage. Two ended in miscarriages, three in still-births, one baby survived two weeks and another ten weeks. I hope to God that this child will be the one to survive to old age.'

Millie touched her arm. 'You have suffered greatly.'

'It is the lot for women, isn't it?' Amelia's expression turned grim. 'I try to keep my faith and believe it is the will of God, but there are times when I am extremely tested, almost beyond my endurance.'

'That is true for many of us.' Millie sighed.

Amelia patted her hand and then tucked it through her arm.'I would like for us to become good friends.'

Smiling, Millie led her away from the depressing sight of such tiny graves. 'I would only be too glad to have a friend such as you, and I know Pippa would feel the same.'

'You are very quiet.' Pippa looked at Millie, as they were driven home a few hours later.

'Did you notice that Amelia is pregnant?'

'No, I didn't at first, but Douglas told me later. He is desperate to have a son to inherit the farm.'

'They have a small graveyard at the back of the house, it's where they have buried their dead babies.'

Pippa frowned. 'A tragedy indeed.'

Millie drew in a deep breath. 'I know that they are not the same class as you are used to, Pippa, and your mother will no doubt wish for her own society but I still think that the Merediths could be valuable friends to all of us.'

Pippa turned to look at her. 'Do you think that I would only wish to socialize with people of my own class? Haven't I proven to you that is not so?'

'I simply meant that maybe the Merediths would not be welcome once your family returns because they are not—'

'I resent such notions, Millie! Really I do.'

'I don't mean to be—'

'I know what you mean, Millie Stroker,' Pippa snapped.

'Do not get all heated on me, Pippa,' Millie scoffed. 'I am accepting the situation.'

'There is no situation.'

'I'm afraid of what will happen when your family returns. The present arrangement of you and I living in a hut together will not suit everyone. I know that when they return I shall sleep in a tent with Davy until Robson can build us a hut on our acre, and it's of no bother to me, but will your mother wish for you to be so close to Davy and me?'

Pippa took hold of Millie's hand. 'Never be worried about our friendship. It means too much to me to let it go. Mother is aware of our friendship, I've written to her many times about you. She is pleased I have someone with me.'

'But I'm not, nor ever will be, accepted into the society your mother entertains.'

'You think that matters to me? You and Davy will always be a part of my *family*. I don't care whether you were a parson's daughter or a street urchin.' Pippa winked. 'As for the Merediths, well, they may not be the kind of people my mother is used to socializing with, but again she will simply have to get used to it or make other arrangements.'

'Do you think your family will arrive soon?'

Pippa shrugged. 'As soon as father is well enough nothing will stop him from travelling. I hope it is soon. I have so many ideas now that I've seen the Merediths' homestead. They have shown me just what can be achieved.'

Heat sizzled the valley into a shimmering haze. Christmas, New Year and January had come and gone in a blaze of hot dry weather. The creek still ran, but its flow had dwindled to only a foot deep.

Pippa soaked her handkerchief into the cool water. Wringing it out, she then placed it on the back of her neck and sighed in appreciation of the welcome coolness.

Behind her, Millie sat under the tree mixing damper dough. 'Pippa. Someone comes.'

Turning, she looked in the direction of the track and studied the vehicle as it rattled its way to them in a cloud of dust.

'Is it the Merediths?' Millie washed her hands in a bucket and joined her.

'I don't know.' Squinting in the harsh sunlight, Pippa tried to make out the occupants. 'Amelia said she'd call tomorrow and bring some of her cheese . . .' Suddenly Pippa felt it – an indescribable feeling and she knew who sat in the seat of the wagon. Gathering up her skirts, she crossed the creek's footbridge and ran towards the wagon.

The driver halted the transport some distance away and through the dust cloud surrounding it, a figure climbed down and waved.

'Hilary!'

'Pippa!'

Laughing, Pippa ran and embraced her twin like she would never let go. 'Oh, Hil, Hil! I can't tell you how glad I am to see you. I thought you all had forgotten me.' Silly tears spilled over her lashes.

'Dear Pippa.' Hilary kissed her cheeks. 'We were so worried. Father is frantic to return here.'

'How is he? Why didn't he come?'

'Yes, well, he is a little better now, but he was dreadfully sick when he arrived back in Sydney and mother was beside herself. Oh, it's been terrible. It's his heart you know. Mother and I have worried between the pair of you.' Hilary's face creased with concern as her gaze roamed over Pippa looking for traces of injury.

'You should know by now I can take care of myself.' Pippa tossed her head but smiled. 'And Father has improved? The truth now.'

'Yes. He was desperate to come with me only Mother forbade it. He isn't strong enough for the journey.'

Pippa squeezed Hilary's hands. 'I'm so happy you're here.' Then, as the dust settled, she noticed the extra man in the back of the wagon and, unbelievably, the stallion and the mares. 'You've brought the horses!' She let go of Hilary and went to them.

'Yes. It was an easy journey, which I will be for ever grateful for.' Hilary followed her and nodded to the man who jumped down from the wagon. 'This is John Lowe, a new groom Father hired and a good man. He took excellent care of the horses.'

Pippa nodded to him. 'Thank you. You'll be paid well for your diligence.'

Hilary swiped away an annoying fly. 'Father wanted them grazing on Noble land. It seemed ridiculous to pay for stabling when we have it all here. Your letters have kept him in a constant state of excitement. He cannot believe you've established so much so soon.'

'There, my good boy.' Pippa rubbed her hand along Noble Blaze's neck. 'They need to be rested well before we can start the breeding program, but the stables are ready and waiting to be filled.'

'Pippa dearest, I care little about stables at the moment. I'd much prefer to sit down and drink something cool.' Hilary turned to stare at the huts across the creek. 'Is there room for me?'

'Yes. Yes, of course!' Pippa returned and linked her arm through her sister's. 'This is your home now. Come and meet Millie and Davy. You will like them immediately.'

Hilary gripped Pippa's hand. 'There is some sad news to impart, however, it can wait until later.'

While Hilary chatted with Millie and Davy, Pippa oversaw the horses being settled into their news stalls. Chalker, the groom Pippa had hired in Berrima, offered his opinion on the quality of the horses' care and, despite Robson's order for him to tend to his own work, he hung around near Pippa, giving her advice as though she'd never seen a horse before. Finally, out of patience, she silenced him with a cold stare and left the stables.

After a simple dinner of wallaby stew, Pippa read letters from her parents. Included in the letters was money, and she made up the men's wages before giving them permission to take the wagon and go into Berrima for the night.

As dusk coated the country in gold and pink hues, the women reorganized the hut. Robson pitched a tent for Millie and Davy to sleep in, leaving Hilary and Pippa to share the double bed.

Pippa lit a candle stub, as outside, crickets started their night-time serenade. 'Earlier you spoke of some sad news you had to tell me?' She glanced at Hilary and climbed into bed.

Hilary fiddled with her hairbrush as tears sprang to her eyes. 'Yes, I do. It's been a weight on my shoulders carrying this news.'

Alarmed, Pippa took her hand. 'Whatever is it?'

'Howard Lindfield has died. Father received a letter from his solicitor.'

'No! Howard? I cannot believe it.'

'Apparently he was ill for a while.'

Pippa's throat tightened. 'But he seemed well the last time we saw him.'

'Yes, but that was so many months ago.'

'He never hinted in his letters that he was ill.'

Hilary shrugged. 'Well, no. It is not polite, is it? Father wrote to his solicitor and also sent a letter to Grant. Poor Grant.' She looked under her lashes at Pippa.

'Yes, Grant has lost his father.' Pippa picked at the blanket, fighting to keep the memories at bay. 'But then, Grant had already abandoned him.'

Hilary gasped at her harsh words. 'Oh, that is cruel and uncalled for. Grant is allowed to make his own way in the world.'

Pippa sniffed, uncaring. 'Howard idolized Grant, his only son and heir, and what did Grant do? He left him. He left his ageing father alone in that great mausoleum of a house with no one to share his days and nights with.'

'You are too hard. Howard wanted Grant to fulfil his ambitions, he encouraged him to go.'

'To escape me.'

'No . . .'

'Liar.' Pippa swallowed, remembering the all-consuming love she'd felt for Grant. 'Yes, well, Grant can now live in that great big house alone and see what it feels like, that is if he ever returns from India,' she scoffed. Her love and hate for the man bordered a very fine line.

'The solicitor mentioned that he was to come home from the East. Of course, he would need to sort out a lot of legal matters. Father said that it would be Grant's good nature which will decide how we are to live here in Australia.'

'How can that be?' Pippa glared, shocked. 'How can he be of importance to us?'

'Why, the partnership of the stud, have you forgotten that it is Howard's loan which enabled us to start again out here?'

'No, but a deal is a deal. Grant mustn't be allowed to go back on it.' She tugged at the sheets on the bed and then straightened them out again. 'I refuse to be dependent on Grant Lindfield.'

'Father does not have the money to give back now. It's all been spent here in the valley.' Hilary gazed down at the hairbrush she toyed with. 'In fact, Father has very little money at all.'

Anxious, Pippa stared. 'What do you know?'

'I do not think that there is much money left. Father hinted that he would have to make some harsh decisions as to how we will live our lives, which of course upset Mother and she insisted we go back to England, but then she met up with some old friends and has been very happy since then.'

Confused, she frowned. 'Mother met some old friends?'

'Yes, the Talbot family from Kent.' Hilary began braiding her hair. 'Apparently, they are Mother's family's friends. She lost touch with them after she married Father. The Talbots now live near the Hawkesbury River, some distance from Sydney. They have a large property and are quite wealthy. Anyway, they invited Father and Mother to stay with them until our own house is built. They are very nice and kind.'

Pippa listened in stunned silence as Hilary told her about the friendship that had again sprung up between their mother and Rose Talbot. What a wonderful coincidence that her mother had friends, perhaps now she would settle easier. 'So Father has given up the rooms in Sydney?'

'Yes, and they want us to join them on the Hawkesbury as soon as we can. It appears that the Talbots' house is large enough to accommodate us until Father—'

'I do not want to go to the Talbots'!' Pippa banged her fist on the bed. 'What about the work that has to be done here? The *valley* is our home, not the Talbots' house. What is Father thinking of?'

'It is not our place to question him, Pippa,' Hilary whispered.

'Balderdash! He knows of the dream, the dream that we share. He should be here now, ensuring it comes true. How can we make this a success if we spend our time away? Father was so keen, what has changed? Is he punishing me for wanting to stay?'

'He has been very ill, I told you. The doctors were afraid of his heart stopping completely if he didn't have complete rest. He won't get better if he's constantly worrying about you being here. You must come back with me to the Talbots'.'

'He has no need to worry about me. I've sent letters telling him how well I'm doing.'

'Yes, and we are very thankful to receive them.' Hilary took Pippa's hand. 'He has gone to the Talbots' purely to recuperate and it is only natural that our parents want us with them.'

'So you are leaving here? You haven't come to settle?'

'Well, of course I cannot, at least not yet. We cannot stay here alone.

It may be some time before Father hears from Grant and then it will depend on whether there is money to spend on such a large place as this. It may be wiser to sell and live in Sydney where Father may be of some use to the government or . . .'

Pippa blinked, unable to take it all in. How had everything suddenly become unravelled? She wished Hilary had never come. 'Stop. Not another word. I will not leave.'

'It is sensible to—'

'And nothing Father or Grant Lindfield say or do will alter that fact.' A coldness entered Pippa's heart. Abandoning the valley wasn't an option. 'I'm terribly upset that father has been ill, and of course he must rest until he is well again, but when he's better he has to return to the valley for I won't leave the stud.'

Hilary stared. 'But you must. The place will be well looked after under Robson's careful eye until a solution is reached.'

Pippa jumped out of bed, wrapped her dressing gown around her and put on her boots. As she opened the door, she turned to her sister. 'This is Noble land. I will not leave it for any reason. If I have to work this place alone and with my bare hands, I will. I'll never give it up.' She strode out of the hut.

Hilary sat quite still and stared at the closed door, a crude door made out of rough-sewn bush timber. How ugly it all was.

She sighed. How could it be possible that twins could be so different? Why didn't she ever feel so passionate about something? Why didn't she experience such highs and lows like Pippa?

Her twin had loved Grant Lindfield with a force that broke her heart and turned her mind a little when he refused her. Pippa loved this huge strange country from the moment she'd laid eyes on it as they came through the harbour heads. She was willing to give up all creature comforts and work like a navvy along side workmen to make this place come alive while the rest of her family would easily walk away from it.

*Why am I not made the same?*

Hilary rubbed her eyes, weary of all the upheaval. Why did she have to be the one who was quiet, the listener, the practical one, the one who liked the idea of marriage and babies, the one who could sit and sew or recite a verse or play the piano? All the things that bored Phillippa. Why did there have to be such diversities between twins when they looked the same? Everyone had always said Phillippa should have been born a male and, finally, Hilary agreed with them.

She lay down on the pillow and swallowed her tears, how was she to say goodbye again to her other half?

Dabbing her paintbrush with just the lightest of pressure, Pippa added the blue-grey colour to the tree trunk in her painting. She looked down at the scene below, the hive of industry in the valley, and then back to the canvas. At this height, a cool breeze lifted the intense summer heat of February. She'd walked up to the top of the ridge an hour ago to find some peace in which to paint. Behind she'd left Hilary and Millie embroidering in the shade by the creek as Davy splashed about in the shallows.

Tilting her head, she studied the painting objectively. The colours were correct on the buildings, but not the bush lining the valley slopes. The unique light and colours of the area were hard to capture. She desperately wanted to finish the painting before Hilary returned to Sydney so her sister could take it and show their father the improvements. It could be just the spur he needed to come back. If he could just step on this soil again, he'd regain his earlier enthusiasm, she just knew he would.

A twig snapped behind her and she twisted on her small stool. Chalker casually leaned against a tree, grinning. A rifle was bent over his arm.

'Why do you stand there?' She frowned. 'What do you want?'

He pushed away from the tree and strolled towards her with the air of a gentleman at ease. 'It's a beautiful day, wouldn't you agree?'

'Answer my question.'

He shrugged and stepped closer, making her stiffen. Over the months he'd been at the stud his self-assurance and opinionated manner caused problems with the other men. Robson had broken up two fights involving this man in recent weeks and his boldness with her every time they were in contact was irritating, but he did it so subtly, that later she always felt she'd imagined it. She often toyed with the idea to turn him off the property but he was an excellent horseman, a first-rate groom, who cared for Noble Blaze and the mares with the utmost attention. Good grooms were hard to find in the country. Still, he needed to be put in his place. The rumours of the arrogance of colonial men proved to be true in this man's case.

'It's my turn to shoot fresh meat.' He indicated the gun.

'Then I suggest you be on your way.' She turned her shoulder to him, but he refused to take the hint and instead took another step, until he was able to peer at the painting.

'Very good.' He lowered his head slightly to smile at her. 'You're most talented, Miss Noble,' he murmured softly, almost as a hidden caress.

Pippa swallowed, suddenly nervous of his presence, but she refused to let it show. 'Thank you, Mr Chalker. Now please be on your way.'

'Aren't you frightened?'

She snapped her head up at him, startled. 'What do you mean?'

He gave her a crooked smile. 'All alone, away from everyone down there.'

'I am perfectly safe.' Pippa lifted her chin. 'I'm within screaming distance of twenty people.'

'A savage native or a desperate bushranger could take you away or slit your throat before you'd have the chance to open your mouth.' His gaze fixed on her lips.

She held her breath, wanting to become angry, but found fear was the stronger emotion. 'Is it your intent to frighten me, Mr Chalker?'

His eyes narrowed. 'A splendid woman such as yourself should never be alone.'

'Mr Chalker, you are too free with your opinions. I believe—'

'You need a protector.'

Packing away her paints, she forced a laugh. 'I don't think so.'

'I could be your defender against the world, if you wish it.' His voice had deepened and his hand stroked the rifle. 'Would you like to have me as your champion?'

The statement caused a tenseness between her shoulders. Collapsing her easel, Pippa glanced at him and then concentrated on stuffing her equipment away into the small bag she carried, as quickly as possible. He scared her, and for the first time ever in her life she was aware of the menacing strength a man could exert over her. Her intellect was no match against his physical power. 'I must go.'

He stepped back and bowed, suddenly humble and subservient. 'Yes, of course, Miss Noble, and please tread carefully on the way down.' In an instant he was gone, striding through the trees and into the shadows.

Pippa blinked. Had she imagined it all? Had there been any threat from him towards her? The sun baked the land with unbearable heat and Pippa held her head, feeling slightly sick in the stomach. Sweat drenched her body, her bonnet was damp and limp. Did she suffer heatstroke?

Gathering her things, she swiftly descended the slope, eager to be safe within the environment of the buildings and people. Against her better judgement, she couldn't help but glance over her shoulder, and there above her, standing on an outcrop of rock, was Chalker, watching.

# CHAPTER EIGHT

Outside the Victoria Inn, noise and confusion reigned supreme as the coach readied for departure. Dogs barked, horses snorted, children yelled, babies cried, men stood in groups talking while women came and went from the shops.

Robson handed over Hilary's luggage to a coachman who then tied it amongst the other luggage on the coach roof. Over the last two days, the district had endured storms and torrential rain, turning the dirt into mud, making the smallest job tedious and sending people into fits of temper.

Down in the valley it had been no different and the harshness of living rough in the bush had not endeared Hilary to the country. The ground around the hut became squelching mud, the roof sprang numerous leaks sending rivulets of water running down the walls and drips splashing on to the bed. Rain hitting the bark roof sounded like a drum constantly banging inside their heads. They re-lit the campfire repeatedly only for it to sizzle and splat and not draw enough heat to cook anything properly. Robson wouldn't risk lighting a fire in the hut or the stables so they ate stale damper and cold stew. This unpalatable meal made Hilary gag and then cry in wretchedness.

Thinking of it now, Pippa squirmed with guilt. Her sister wasn't used to such hardships, neither was she really, but in the end, she knew she'd cope with anything as long as she was in the valley. However, Hil felt differently and yesterday, when a damp and bedraggled Millie and Davy had to abandon their soaked tent and move into the hut, it became the last straw for her twin. Hilary insisted they all go to join the family on the Hawkesbury. Pippa had refused to consider going, but knew that Hilary must.

A horn blew to let everyone know the coach was to depart. Hilary kissed Millie and Davy and turned to Pippa.

'You'll write often?' Hilary knuckled her tears away.

'What a silly question.' Pippa smiled. Their petty arguments over the last few days were forgotten as the bond and love they shared came to the fore. 'Don't forget to give Father his letter, it's important. Don't let him worry about me, but you must insist he returns here though when his health allows him. Tell him about all the improvements and how well everything looks, despite the rain.'

Hilary hugged her. 'I will, I promise.' Robson handed her up into the coach. Once settled, she leaned out of the tiny window. 'Take care of yourself, I'll be thinking of you constantly.'

'Goodbye, goodbye, Hil!'

Millie slipped her hand through Pippa's arm. 'She won't be gone for ever.'

'Yes, I know. But it shouldn't be this way. We should all be together.' Pippa sighed. 'Oh, it doesn't matter.' She put her hand out for Davy's. Together they waved and watched the coach trundle up the hill and away.

'It is Miss Noble, isn't it?'

Pippa glanced at the tall man who addressed her. He bowed and tipped his hat. His green eyes sparkled with either merriment or mischief, she wasn't sure which and she immediately wanted to smile. 'Indeed it is, sir.'

'My name is Gil Ashford-Smith, and I have been told, Miss Noble, that you are building a stud for thoroughbreds. Is that correct?'

'Yes, that is correct, Mr Ashford-Smith.' She liked the look of this gentleman with his mop of chestnut-coloured hair. His clothes were of a superior quality, likely bought in London. He carried an air about him that spoke of wealth, privilege and boyish charm.

'I have a property out at Sutton Forest, Miss Noble, and my father and I have the need to extend our horse bloodstock. We recently bought four fine thoroughbred mares from Cape Town and we were in a quandary as to who should service them, but forgive me! My manners are appalling.' He laughed at his own folly and Pippa couldn't help but smile. 'Obviously, this shouldn't be discussed in the middle of town or in front of ladies. Pray, could I extend an invitation to you and your family to visit my home, and there, in the right circumstances, I can speak with your father?'

'I'm afraid my father is away at present and may not be back for some time. At the moment, I am in charge, and I deal with all aspects of the stud. So, Mr Ashford-Smith, the discussion is very appropriate.'

She raised one eyebrow at him, daring him to challenge her on the subject.

'Well, Miss Noble, in that case may I extend the invitation to you?' He bowed and grinned, his tone jovial and his eyes alive with interest and humour. 'And I believe I would be most disappointed if you refused.'

She bit the inside of her lip to stop another grin from spreading. He was like a golden spark, brandishing the dullness from the day. 'I would be delighted. Thank you.'

Two days later, Robson brought the wagon to a halt in front of the Ashford-Smith's impressive Sutton Forest home. Gardens and lawns flowed away on either side of the circular gravel drive. The house, made of sandstone blocks, sat on a slight rise and five wide stone steps led up to the double front doors.

A liveried servant greeted Pippa at the door. After stating her name, she was soon following him along the large cool entrance hall. From the hall, she glanced into the different rooms. No expense had been spared in the decoration and furnishing of this house. She was glad to have worn one of her best dresses of blue silk with white lace at the throat and cuffs.

The servant bade her to sit in a small drawing-room while he went in search of a member of the family. Pippa didn't have much time to study the prints on the walls before Gil Ashford-Smith entered the room and bowed before her, his expression full of merriment. 'Dear Miss Noble, what a delight it is to have you here.'

'Thank you for the invitation, Mr Ashford-Smith.'

'Please, I abhor formality, it's so . . . stuffy. I insist you call me Gil. With luck, we'll shock everyone.' He winked at her as though she was a fellow conspirator. 'I do like shocking people, don't you? It's enormous fun.'

She stared at this whirlwind of a man, bursting with energy and humour. He was a living advertisement for vitality and his openness intrigued her, made her want to share his enthusiasm. 'Very well, I will call you Gil and you must call me Pippa.'

'Excellent.' He beamed. 'I'm so relieved you aren't conventional, it's terribly boring you know. I want us to become good friends. One can never have enough friends in this small colony.'

'I agree.' She blinked, his exuberance washed over her, lifting away her worries and anxieties.

'Come, you must meet my parents and sister. They are quite eager to greet you.' He held out his arm and escorted her through French doors leading directly out on to a paved terrace. 'Are you aware, of course, that you are somewhat of a sensation in these parts?'

Pippa frowned. 'Really?'

'Oh indeed. Your courage is very much admired. People say your stud will be a great asset to the district.'

As they walked across the lawn, she peeped up at him from under her bonnet. 'Is that all they say, Mr Ashford-Smith?'

'Gil.'

'Sorry, Gil.'

He paused, his green eyes laughing down at her. 'Should there be more?'

'I'm a woman building up a property, naturally gossip will abound.'

'Tremendous!' He chuckled at her shocked expression. 'I adore gossip.'

She stared at him in open amazement.

His laughter increased. 'Don't you know that the more gossip about you the better you'll be remembered? No?' He patted her hand as though she was a child. 'Never mind. I'll teach you, and before long, you'll be furious if your name isn't mentioned in certain circles.'

She pulled her hand out of his grasp. Her past had been riddled with gossip about her father's debts and then her feelings for Grant, she needed no more in her life. 'I'm afraid I don't share your joke, Mr Ashford-Smith.'

He stopped, the laughter left his face. 'You must forgive me if I've offended, Miss Noble. I forget not everyone has my sense of humour about the ridiculous, and that is what gossip is, isn't it? Ridiculous nonsense.'

'It's not nonsense if you've been on the receiving end of it.' She stepped away and wondered if she should go home. The visit was nothing what she expected, he was not what she was used to. All the men in her life had been serious, staid – this man was neither.

'I'm sorry, deeply sorry,' he sighed. 'My mother always says I'm ill-mannered, perhaps she's right. I think I've lived in the country too long and have forgotten how to curb my tongue.'

She looked up at him and his sincerity was clear. His sober expression revealed just how handsome he was now she had the opportunity to study him properly.

His eyes turned emerald with disappointment. 'I hate to think I made you feel uncomfortable. Do you wish to go home? I can make the excuses should you want to.'

Pippa shook her head and wanted him to smile again, for she preferred his jauntiness. 'Introduce me, please. I need more time to consider whether you really are ill-mannered or not.'

He stared at her a moment and then when she grinned, he broke out into laughter again. 'We will be firm friends, I just know it!'

From under a large gum tree, the Ashford-Smith family rose from their seats and greeted her with smiles as Gil introduced her.

Settling herself at the wrought iron table, Pippa made polite conversation about the weather with Gil's father, Edgar, while Tabitha Ashford-Smith, a large woman of no apparent prettiness, but with plenty of goodwill sat in her chair, her attitude playful as she bantered lightly with Gil and his sister Augusta.

Although tall, thin and plain, Augusta's energy and humour drew Pippa's attention. Gil teased in easy familiarity with his sister and their laughter filled the air. Pippa enjoyed being surrounded by happiness. For too long her family circumstances had given them nothing to laugh about.

Tabitha refilled Pippa's teacup. 'So, Miss Noble, you say your parents are living in the Hawkesbury River community at the moment?'

'Yes, that is correct. My mother has friends there.'

'Do they worry over you being out here by yourself?'

'Yes, they do. However, we have a property that needs attention and since my father has been unwell then the responsibility falls to me.' Pippa took a sip of her tea.

'But surely a man could be put in charge?' Mr Ashford-Smith sniffed in disapproval. 'I must say that allowing a daughter to stay alone on a remote property is hardly responsible of your parents.'

'Edgar!' Tabitha nearly choked on her tea. 'It is not for you to air your opinion on how the Nobles behave, my dear.'

Chastised, Mr Ashford-Smith bowed his head in Pippa's direction in apology.

'I am not entirely alone. I have a companion and recently my sister stayed at the property. I rely on my overseer completely.'

Augusta selected a tart from the cake stand. 'I think it admirable that Miss Noble is managing the business. I know it is something I could do, if the opportunity arose. In this country, many women have taken over the administration of their homes while their menfolk are away. I know of some women left alone for years as their men drive cattle over land. Indeed, I have read of women defending their homes from bushrangers—'

'That is quite enough, thank you Augusta. We all know of your reading habits. It is Miss Noble we wish to know about.' Her mother sipped her tea and addressed Pippa once more. 'Do you miss England? I imagine your mother must find it distressing to be so far away from home?'

'I believe she will adjust eventually and I don't miss England for a moment. There is too much for me to do here.'

'You must bring your mother to visit me, when she comes into the country.'

'I will, thank you. Mother would be pleased to make your acquaintance, I'm certain.'

Gil offered her a plate of macaroons. 'Do you enjoy riding?'

'Very much so.'

His smile deepened. 'Perhaps my sister and I could show you some of the countryside?'

'I would enjoy that, thank you.'

Tabitha raised her eyebrows. 'As long as you don't involve Miss Noble in your reckless escapades, Gil. You and Augusta believe me to be blind, deaf and dumb when it comes to your adventures.'

Gil laughed and twirled Augusta into the air. 'Can I help it if my sister possesses a devil's streak?'

Augusta shrieked. 'You, Gil, are the only devil around here!'

Falling to his knees, Gil pretended to be heartbroken. 'To be so slighted by my very own sister.' He swivelled on one knee to Pippa. 'Do you think I can be saved, Miss Noble?'

Pippa covered her laughter with her hand and leaned forward. 'I very much doubt it, Mr Ashford-Smith.'

Gil and his family roared with amusement.

Amidst the jollity, Pippa watched the family, liking their closeness, envying them for it. Her own family never behaved with each other so easily as the Ashford-Smiths did. Too many times they were at war over another of father's failed investments. Too many times, they were busy hiding from their creditors or moving around the country, always having to start again.

She placed her teacup on the table and stood. 'I must be on my way. I thank you all for a pleasant afternoon tea.'

'Won't you stay a little longer, Pippa?' Gil's expression was that of a little boy who had lost his toy. Augusta nodded encouragement.

'No, I'm afraid not. Much awaits me in the valley. Thank you anyway.' Pippa turned and shook hands with his parents. 'Thank you for your hospitality.'

Edgar bowed. 'Responsibility is a heavy burden, Miss Noble. Please think of us, should you ever need assistance.'

His words warmed her. 'Thank you, sir.'

Tabitha patted her hand. 'You must come again.'

'I will and I offer you the same invitation to my home, humble though it may be.'

'I have every confidence that soon it will be as grand as anything in the district, Miss Noble.' Tabitha smiled. 'You have the spirit to do it, if anyone can.'

'Augusta and I will walk you out.' Gil offered his arm.

They walked with her to the front of the house and Gil handed her up on to the wagon seat.

Augusta promptly pulled herself up and kissed Pippa's cheek. 'You'll come again, won't you? Please say you will.'

Pippa nodded. 'Yes, of course and I insist you visit the valley soon.'

'Oh, definitely. Gil and I will ride there. Is next Wednesday convenient?'

Laughing at her enthusiasm, Pippa nodded. 'That will do wonderfully.' She turned to Gil, who stepped closer and took her hand. 'Come inspect our stallion. You'll not be disappointed.'

'I intend to.' Gil grinned, his handsome face alight with an inner warmth. 'I know for certain you'll never disappoint me, Phillippa Noble.'

The blood rushed to her face at the double meaning of his words. Since Grant's abrupt exit from her life, no decent man had flirted with her and she had encouraged no friendliness, but this man had broken down her defences without her realizing it and she didn't know if she was happy about it or not. Still, she'd gained new friends this day and for that she was eternally grateful.

Gerald sat on the bed in the Talbots' Sydney home and re-read Pippa's letter. Her words conveyed her happiness in how well the stud progressed. The list of improvements done over the last three months since Christmas made him feel guilty for his lack of attendance. Without him, she had created a home. Without him, she had survived. It shamed him to think that despite his abandonment of her, she'd endured it all.

*

The vegetable gardens grow well from constant attention, Father. Over the summer, rows of sweetcorn, potatoes, carrots, onions and spinach grew well enough to feed us all. I've traded our surplus vegetables for fruit trees of apples, pears, lemons and peaches with a man in Berrima.

Last week, Millie built a trellis alongside the hut, which we've planted with two young grape vines, and in desire for some colour, we've also planted seeds of marigolds near the front door. Do not laugh at us!

Douglas Meredith, bless the man, allowed us to borrow a team of bullocks and a plough. Robson got the men to start ploughing up the far fields of the valley ready for the following spring sowing of grass seed and hay crops. Another room has been added to the hut, which became the bedroom and we feel light-headed at all the space! The fowls have doubled in number. A pigpen and sows now add to the livestock, too.

I've begun to make friends with local merchants and land-holders. Though my sincerest friends are the Merediths and the Ashford-Smiths. Gil and Augusta visit every week – sometimes twice a week – and we have much fun together riding and entertaining each other. My hunting talents constantly surprise Gil. He believes I shoot as good as any man. He makes me laugh so very much. Their company soothes my loss over my real family being so far away.

My biggest news, and what I was leaving until last to tell you is that my advertisement in the *Sydney Morning Herald* newspaper has been most successful, Father. I know you thought it a great expense, but it has paid off, I'm pleased to tell you. Did you see it? A grand advertisement about Noble Blaze and his ability to produce splendid horseflesh. Many gentlemen have written to me, inquiring about the stallion's pedigree. A stallion of his superior quality is rare this far out from Sydney and gentlemen have brought their brood mares from as far as Goulburn in the south, the Mountains in the west and a few came up from the coast. I've enclosed copied pages of transactions for you to keep, but be rest assured, Father, that I have a very detailed record here. . . .

All this she had done on her own. His depression grew. What kind of man was he to do this to his daughter? Her letters largely went unanswered unless they requested money, which he promptly denied, not because he wanted to but because he had no other choice. Simply, he no longer had any money to give her. What's more, if the stud didn't become self-sufficient soon then the next step would be to sell. It would break her heart to do so and he didn't think he was strong enough to face it should the decision be made.

Gerald gazed at his reflection in the mirror and heaved another great sigh. He didn't like what he saw. Here he was, cowardly holed up in someone else's house, refusing to be the man his daughter so desperately needed him to be.

His sudden ill health had been a huge shock, reminding him that he wasn't to be on this earth for ever. A man's mortality should never be taken lightly and that's exactly what he'd done. He'd spent his life pleasing only himself and if he'd died, what kind of life would his family have inherited? Poverty.

It was his role to care and provide for them and what a terrible job he'd done of it. Shame swallowed him whole – shame and disgust. His daughter had achieved so much while he, gutless and weak, hid in another man's home and allowed her to do all that he should.

From somewhere in the house laughter floated to him. Esther, he knew, brimmed with happiness. The time spent on the Hawkesbury with the Talbots was exactly the kind of life Esther wanted. She ate the best food, slept in the best bed and enjoyed a good social life. Everything she had given up in England had come back to her again through the generosity of the Talbots. Hilary too seemed happier and spent a lot of her time with the Talbot's son, Toby. Esther declared a marriage between the two would set them up for life.

Even now, back in Sydney, they lived in the Talbots' large house by the harbour at their expense. How did anyone expect him to try and compete against that? His pride hung in tatters. Yet again, he couldn't provide for his family. They couldn't rely on him.

Glancing down at the dressing table, his gaze rested on another letter. A much dreaded letter. He couldn't bear to touch it again, but then he didn't need to, the words were burned into his brain.

He walked over to the window, a gentle breeze blew the lace curtains and he captured them in his hands, wanting to rip them down and tear them to pieces.

Grant Lindfield. He'd be sailing into the country some time towards the end of April and requested for Gerald to meet him in Sydney.

Gerald felt ill again at the thought of it. He had one week left to decide what he would say to Grant. He guessed he could show him

Pippa's letter about the stud's improvements, but it might not be enough. He still might demand the money back. On Howard's death, all his investments went to his son and if Grant called in the loan before they could repay him, the valley would become his.

A pain squeezed Gerald's chest, bending him over with the force of it. He gasped, clutching at the windowsill. After a moment the pain receded, allowing him to breathe easier. Puffing and feeling as old as time, he stumbled to the bed and sat down once more, his legs shaky beneath him.

The dinner gong rang throughout the house. He would have to go downstairs, but he wondered if he could make it. It was no wish of his to endure another meal at another man's table.

Taking a deep breath, Gerald heaved to his feet and stood there for a moment to regulate his breathing. Slowly, he made it out of the bedroom and down to the dining-room, where both families chatted with accustomed ease. Although weak, he was thankful to make it to his chair without being noticed. As a servant placed the leek soup before him, he steeled himself not to gag.

Hilary, seated on his left, placed her hand on his. 'Are you all right, Father? You look pale.'

'Yes, my dear, I'm fine.' Gerald forced a smile even though his chest tightened and he grew hot in the face. His breathing laboured as a vice gripped his chest.

'Are you certain?'

'I-I do feel a little unwell . . . Maybe I should retire . . .' he half whispered, half groaned back to her.

Hilary helped him to his feet, causing everyone at the table to look in their direction.

'Whatever is the matter, Gerald?' Esther frowned.

'Father is feeling a little under the weather again, Mother. I shall help him to his room. Excuse us, please.'

'Here, let me help you, Hilary.' Toby stepped to her side and caught Gerald in time as his legs buckled and he collapsed against the table. The fine china rattled amid the women's shrieks.

'Call for the doctor, Father.' Toby struggled to keep them both upright.

Between Hilary and Toby, they got Gerald upstairs and into his bedroom. Hilary then left the room while Toby and a male servant undressed him and pulled his nightshirt over him. Once they had finished, she returned to sit beside the bed. 'Are you feeling a little better, Father?'

'Yes . . .' Gerald lied.

'Good.' She sat beside the bed. 'Why do you think you are sick once more?'

'Worry.'

'Worry? But why? About Pippa? She is doing very well. Her letters are very so encouraging.'

The pain in his chest lessened to a dull ache, permitting him to suck in more air. 'In part about Pippa, but not all.'

'Then what?'

'Grant Lindfield's arrival.'

'Grant?' Hilary eyes widened and she reared back. 'He's coming here?'

Gerald nodded.

'But why? I don't understand.'

He shook his head a little. 'Howard's money. The stud.' He gasped, finding it exhausting to talk.

She took his hand and held it in both of hers. 'I am sure Grant will not want it back. He will respect his father's decisions. The money was loaned in good faith and the stud will earn it back. Look how well Pippa is doing with it. We can't sell it. It would break her heart. We must believe in it as Pippa does.'

'But will Grant?'

Esther strode into the room. 'The doctor has been sent for and will be here shortly.' She stood by the bed and looked at him. 'It is most impolite to become ill in a friend's home, Gerald. I thought we were over all this? I am not amused by this display of weakness.'

He grunted, finding it hard to breathe. 'I . . . assure you . . . my dear, that I did not do it . . . on purpose.'

'I should think not, the Talbots have been uncommonly kind to us these past months.'

Hilary glared at her. 'Mother, I believe it would be best for Father if you were to move to another room for the night. I'm sure Mrs Talbot won't mind.'

'Indeed, I shall do so at once. Though I am ashamed to be the cause of such disruption.' She turned on her heel and left the room.

Hilary quickly followed her out and caught her in the hallway. 'Mother, that was incredibly rude of you. Have you no compassion at all? Father is dreadfully ill.'

Esther faltered. 'I have compassion, yes, but not towards your father, not after all these years. Did he think of me as he gambled away what money we had? Did he ever think of me, or you girls, when he made his business decisions? Did he think of me when he dragged us to the other side of the world?'

'Of course he thought of us. He wanted us to regain what we had lost.'

'What *he* lost, you mean.'

'You can't blame him for every wrong thing that has happened in our lives, Mother!'

'Why not? It's usually down to him.' Esther took a step, but quickly turned back. 'I once loved your father more than life itself, but each year, as we suffered more and more humiliation, my love died, my respect for him died. Now look at how we live.' She shook her head, the light in her eyes fading. 'We live on the charity of others, while my daughter works like a man toiling in a valley that isn't even ours and likely never will be.'

Hilary stared at the woman she thought she knew and realized she didn't know her mother at all. For a fleeting moment, she saw so much of Pippa in her mother that it scared her, but then suddenly she felt calmer and was amazed by it. Their father had inadequately ruled their lives for so long, that only now, as he weakened, did the true character of her mother appear. Pippa had always shown her strength of spirit, but not their mother and maybe it wasn't such a bad thing that at last her mother was being the stronger partner in her marriage.

Esther sighed. 'You think ill of me now, don't you?'

'I don't know what to think.'

'I've had no power over my life. Before I married, my father controlled my life, after my marriage, my husband controlled both our lives and he did it badly. Do you blame me for being hard-hearted, for being cynical?' Esther gripped Hilary's hand. 'I never want you and Phillippa to suffer as I did. You must marry a man who will provide for you, don't let love rule you.'

'Is that why you were so harsh to Pippa when she declared her love for Grant and he rejected her? You refused to speak to her for days.'

Esther raised her chin. 'Although Phillippa wouldn't agree, she is a lot like me. No one else might see it, but I do. When I was young I was terribly impulsive. I wanted your father and I got him and look where it landed me.' She straightened her shoulders. 'I've become selfish and demanding, Hilary. At times, I don't even like myself, but I refuse to allow my daughters to travel the same path I took. Ruination changes people, destroys their dreams, their ideals and leaves them hollow, bitter.'

'I think I understand.' Hilary nodded and squeezed her mother's hand. 'I had best return to Father.'

'Toby Talbot is a good man, sensible, wealthy and of stable temperament. If he asks, you should marry him whether you love him or not.'

'What if I do love him?'

'Then I have failed to protect you as I failed Phillippa. Love and marriage should never go together.' Esther turned away and entered the room opposite.

Hilary walked back to her father's room and placed her hand on the door handle. How many times had she talked with her mother? Hundreds, thousands of times. They'd spent years shopping and visiting together, sitting by the fire in winter sewing in comfortable silence and yet, never once had she seen the woman that her mother truly was.

Tears stung her eyes. She felt guilty for every joke and comment she had uttered about her mother's silly whims for she hadn't been aware, hadn't taken the time to find out that her mother's true self lay hidden beneath a grumbling exterior, an exterior that protected her from facing the misery that was her life.

Hilary took a deep breath and entered the room, knowing nothing would be the same ever again.

Pippa stepped through the front door of the Talbots' harbourside home and into Hilary's arms. 'I am here at last! How is he?'

'Better. The doctor said it was a heart seizure.' Hilary hugged her tightly again. 'I'm so glad you're here. It's been awful. I have so much to tell you.'

Separating from her, Hilary instructed a servant to collect Pippa's luggage from the hansom cab and take it up to her room. Holding Pippa's hand she led her into the sitting-room to greet the Talbots and their mother.

'Good lord, Phillippa. You look positively wild,' Esther declared with a horrified expression on her face as she kissed and hugged her.

Pippa put a hand up to her hair that poked beneath her bonnet. She knew the sun had tanned her skin and lightened her hair to near white gold. Her gowns had become worn and the one she wore today of green and black striped silk was borrowed from Augusta Ashford-Smith. 'Forgive me for not being at my best, Mother, but I have been travelling for two days.'

Once all the introductions had been made, Pippa escaped upstairs to see her father. He stirred as she entered. Quietly she sat on the chair by the bed and slipped her hand under his that rested on the blankets.

Gerald's eyes fluttered open and focused on her. He smiled. 'Pippa.'

'Sorry to wake you.' She bent over and kissed his thin cheek. He had aged so much in the months since they'd last been together. 'I came as quick as I could.'

'I'm not planning to die just yet, my dear.'

She grinned and squeezed his hand. 'I should hope not too.'

'There is something I want to tell you, that is if you haven't already been told.'

'Been told what? I haven't had the time to be told much at all.'

'I have instructed to be informed when the ship *Starlight* docks.'

'Oh? Why is this ship important?'

'Because it carries Grant Lindfield to these shores.'

Pippa gasped. Her head swam, her mind swirling. She was so shattered she could hardly think. Her heart beat a tattoo against her chest. To see him again, to hear his voice. . . .

A long time passed in complete silence as Pippa accepted the news. Grant. Here.

She shook her head, rose and stepped to the window. In the distance, a tiny sailing boat tacked along the water. So, he was to come here then, to her one place of sanctuary. Would she ever be free of him and the pain he caused her?

'Pippa.'

She swallowed. 'Why?'

'Why?'

'His father has died. He should be on his way to England not here. Never here.'

'Australia is closer to India than England is. I guess he wishes to call here first before sailing home. I suspect he wishes to know about the money Howard lent us. Alas, I am not privy to his thoughts.'

'And what will you tell him when he comes?' Her voice came as though from far away.

'That it is gone. However, I shall try and get a position with the government or some other organization and earn the money back for him until the stud shows a profit. I hope he will accept that as a gentleman and a family friend.'

'There is no need to trouble yourself, Father. I will pay him an instalment of the loan with the profit from the next wool clippings. I noticed the price of wool has risen.' She paced the floor, thinking. 'I shall make regular repayments over the next few years, perhaps in less time if able.'

'No, that won't work.'

'Yes, it will. Money is coming into the stud little by little. I'll make no more improvements and instead give all our spare cash to Grant. May I know of the amount of the loan, Father? Did Howard agree for you to pay in instalments? It can't be that much. We used our money too, so the amount cannot be too large—'

'None . . . none of my money went into purchasing the land, I used all of Howard's that he gave me.' Gerald's voice shook and tears reddened his eyes.

She backed away. 'I-I don't understand.'

'I'm sorry, Pippa. I used what money we had to buy stock and materials. I never thought Howard would die before we had the chance to pay him back. Every time he loaned me money I was never pressured to repay it quickly. We had an understanding.'

'What do you mean? The stud is Grant's? Wholly his?'

'We have one year left under the terms of the original agreement to repay the loan. If Grant calls in the loan on time and we cannot pay, the land goes to him by default. That was the agreement I made with Howard, knowing of course that he would never take the land from me. Howard knew this was my last chance to provide you all with a home. He loved me like a brother, but Grant isn't Howard.'

'One year?' she squeaked, aghast, drowning out his pathetic excuses. 'We can never pay it all back in one year!'

'I could try to acquire another loan . . .'

She looked at him, stricken on the bed, who would give him a loan now? A hideous weight crushed her chest. Blinded by shock, she stumbled and groped for the door. She fought the faint that threatened to claim her. No. It couldn't be true. Not her valley! Not his. Never his.

# CHAPTER NINE

For the next three days Pippa hardly slept or ate. She walked the length and breadth of Sydney's main streets, trying to come to terms with the news that the beautiful land she had shed blood, sweat and tears for was not Noble land, not hers to love. She couldn't bear it.

A slow burning rage filled her, ate away at her. Grant. Grant. Grant. His name was a chant in her brain, sending her mad. She was tired of him having the power to hurt her. Once again, fate had dealt a death-blow to her heart. Wasn't it enough she suffered the humiliation of loving him before and received nothing in return but his pity and people gossiping about her? Now she was to endure it all again, would have to beg again, not for his love like last time, but for the land she'd come to love in his place.

One evening, as the family sat playing cards after dinner, Pippa walked down the garden to the harbour edge. A few minutes later, Hilary joined her and together they stared out over the ink black water.

'It is May first tomorrow.' Hilary linked her arm through Pippa's. 'How strange it is autumn here and back home it is spring.'

'Yes.'

Hilary sighed. 'Don't be so glum, dearest.'

Pippa stared at her. 'How do you expect me to behave?' Her voice rose. 'Should I smile and laugh and tell funny stories when all the while I'm trying to accept that my home isn't really my home?'

'Don't shout please.'

Pippa spun away. 'I wish to more than shout. I want to scream and cry and curse.' She twisted back. 'Why, Hil? Why has he been given the opportunity to wound me all over again?'

'I don't know, darling.' Hilary stepped closer and held her. 'What are you to do?'

'I have no idea.'

'That is not like you to give up so easily.'

'I do not have anything to give up on. I have nothing.' Pippa sighed, feeling so very tired.

'If you can show Grant that you can make a success of the property, then surely he will let you go on living there and pay back the money once the year is up. You may be worrying for nothing. He may allow you an extension of the loan.'

'It is not the same.' Her heart weighed heavy. 'All that time, I thought I was building a future for us. Giving us something solid to hold on to after all the years of being unsettled due to Father's debts.'

'Grant isn't a monster. I truly believe he will allow you to continue—'

Pippa sprang back. 'Allow me? He will *allow* me? I don't want to be treated like a servant, to be at his beck and call, to have him forever looking over my shoulder!'

'Of course not, I meant . . .'

'You don't understand. I love that valley. It's a part of me. I live in a hut and eat the same type of food everyday. I battle the heat, the mud, the rain, the flies and the ridicule from my family and people of my class, yet I would do it all again a hundred times over, if I knew that it would be all mine for ever. Instead it's his! Of all the people in the world it had to be his.'

'He is not the devil, Pippa,' whispered Hilary, placing her hand on Pippa's arm.

'Yes, he is!' Pippa closed her eyes and rubbed her forehead in torment. 'He has to be for me to feel about him as I do.' She turned and walked back inside and up to her room.

The following morning, while the family took breakfast, a message arrived. The housemaid gave it to Esther. 'It's for Mr Noble, madam.'

'Pray child, then take it up to him. I have no wish for it.' Esther waved her away and proceeded to finish her meal.

Pippa, leaving the room, paused, staring at the paper in the girl's hand. 'I will give it to him.'

The maid passed it over and hurried away. Taking a deep breath, Pippa slowly climbed the stairs and knocked on the bedroom door.

At her father's bidding, she entered the room. She'd not seen him in four days, ever since he gave her the devastating news. Hilary said it was cruel not to visit his room, but Pippa couldn't face him. To be let down by her father again hurt too much. He'd scraped her too raw for her to feel any kindness towards him.

He sat propped up in bed with a breakfast tray on his lap. 'Pippa.'

She stood at the end of the bed. 'A message has come for you.'

'Open it and read it to me.'

It pleased her that her hands didn't shake as she opened the letter. 'The ship, *Starlight*, has been sighted off the coast near the Heads. They should anchor some time late this afternoon.'

'The time has come.'

Pippa straightened her shoulders and raised her chin. 'I won't give up the land. If I have to work until my hands bleed then I will. I will pay back every penny we owe him, but I *will not* give the land up even if the year agreement elapses.'

Gerald nodded. 'Very well, my dear, we shall do it together, like it should have been from the very start. I'll talk to Grant and make him aware of our plans and see if he will let us pay him the money in instalments.'

Amazed, she stared at him speechless. Could she believe him this time?

Gerald reached out his hand and she stepped alongside the bed to take it. 'I'm most terribly sorry that I put you through such distress. However, things are going to change. We will, as a family, return with you to the valley, and we shall all live there together, helping each other.'

'What about Mother?'

'Your mother will do as I say. The time has come for us to be dependent on ourselves. She will not like it, to be sure, but then we all have to make sacrifices in our lives.'

Pippa flopped down on to the edge of the bed, nearly upsetting the tray. 'What if Grant has found a way to take the land from us? What if he doesn't honour his father's agreement with you?'

'I don't see him doing that. He is a good man, or he used to be. I doubt he has changed much in the last few years he's been in India. Besides, do we not have a long-standing friendship between our two families? He will respect his father's wishes, I'm certain of it.'

'He may not have changed in the two years he's been away, but he might be changed now his father has left him a very wealthy man.'

'No, he's a gentleman. True, he is a little arrogant and conceited but that is because of who he is. Someone born into money, breeding and position cannot act like every other normal man.' Gerald lifted his hand and brushed it softly along her cheek. 'Pippa dear, I know this will be hard for you and seeing him again will not be easy.'

She shot to her feet. 'I will not cause a scene like I did last time we were in Grant's company, you can be assured of that.'

'I know.'

'I shall be very strong and who knows, I might not even feel anything for him.'

In the candlelight, Pippa gazed at her reflection in the self-standing full mirror. Her violet, short-sleeved gown tapered in at the waist and then flared out to the floor over a stiffened horsehair petticoat in yards of shimmering satin. Violet satin slippers and elbow-length white lace gloves completed the ensemble. Her hair, sun-kissed to white gold was swept up in thick tresses and held there with mother-of-pearl combs and violet satin ribbons.

She was ready to face him – ready to see if he could still cause the same effect to her heart. She secretly hoped he couldn't for she didn't think she could go through the anguish again.

They'd been best friends ever since she first noticed him at a garden party at the Lindfield's manor house. Grant had just returned from his grand tour of Europe, lasting some two years. At twenty-four he possessed an aura of sophistication that easily commandeered her fifteen-year-old heart. She won a game of croquet against him and then they played blind man's bluff with all the other guests.

The following week they went riding out over the dales and moors of his Yorkshire county. And, as the summer progressed, they spent wonderful days together and with other friends in the happy pursuits of the rich. When she and the family returned home, they continued their friendship with witty letters and funny drawings of their every-day activities. In that vein their lives continued for nearly three years, until on one winter's day close to Christmas, when the Nobles were staying with the Lindfields, Pippa came upon Grant whispering playfully in a young lady's ear at a dinner party. Something happened to Pippa that had never happened before, jealousy.

She realized Grant wasn't only her friend but a man. Suddenly, she was watching his every smile, every conversation. In sickening fascination she became aware of other women, young and old, sending him looks of clear flirtation and invitation. It made her ill and furious and confused. She swayed from wanting his sole attention and hating him for giving it to others. They quarrelled over silly things, usually stemming from her jealousy. Then abruptly Grant no longer sought her out to talk, play games or ride. He went on long trips abroad and never sent her a letter.

At her and Hilary's nineteenth birthday, Grant gave them presents. Pippa received a leather-bound writing case with her initials in gold leaf on the front. Hilary naturally gave Grant a kiss for her present and Pippa rose to do so likewise, but, unintentionally, Grant at the same time turned the other way and so instead of a friendly kiss on the cheek, they kissed full on the mouth. The sensation surprised them both. The next day, Grant called and asked her to go riding with him. The moment they rode into the woods, they reined in their horses and fell into each other's arms, and although Grant held back from making love to her in the fullest sense, she knew it would only be a matter of time before he did so, for soon she'd be his wife.

For Pippa it was all so exciting and special. She loved Grant Lindfield with a passion that frightened her. In his kisses, he awakened senses that she didn't know she owned and it overwhelmed her. His urgent responses to her naïve advances taught her of the power women can hold over men. She didn't hide the love she felt and when people speculated a forthcoming marriage between them she encouraged it. To be his wife was her greatest dream.

Then, without warning, he went away for a month. She and her family were dining at the Hall when he returned. Grant walked into the dining-room resplendent in uniform. Howard rose and proudly presented his son, Second Lieutenant Grant Lindfield of the Queen's Royal Hussars. In the morning he would sail for India.

Pippa believed she would die without him in her life. Later, she cornered him and demanded an explanation. Didn't he want her?

Grant, his expression sad, took her hand. 'I'm sorry. I don't wish to be tied with a wife and children. I want to see and experience the world.'

She didn't understand his refusal. Surely he loved her as she loved him? 'There are many army officers stationed in India with wives.'

'Yes, there are, but I don't wish to be one.'

She raised her chin. 'Will you not marry me then?'

'No. I'm sorry.'

Her hand had shot out and slapped his cheek. 'Then you can go to hell!'

The following two years of financial difficulties gave Pippa something else to think and worry about. Yet, Grant Lindfield continued to haunt her dreams, forever living at the back of her mind.

*

The warm night breeze blew through the lace curtains and Pippa turned away from the mirror and her memories to close the window. Taking a deep breath, she left the bedroom and went downstairs to greet her old love.

The grand clock in the hallway chimed seven times and Pippa's nervousness grew with every passing minute. *Let me be strong. Let me look at him and feel nothing.*

At last there came a knock and a flurry of movement as the maid answered the summons. The company paused in their talking and sipping of pre-dinner drinks. In panic, Pippa glanced at Hilary, who smiled and gave a tiny wink of encouragement.

Pippa slipped behind the other guests, many prominent Sydney people, and let her mother and father rush to the front. Her mother's squeal of welcome filled the room and Pippa looked down at her slippers, trying to still her beating heart.

His voice, clear and strong, carried to her and a shiver of remembrance overwhelmed her. Two people in front moved aside and before she was aware of it, he was standing a few feet away. Like a dumb mute, she stood and absorbed the sight of him. He looked older, thinner. His blue-black hair still shone, his dark blue eyes still sparkled with hidden amusement and his sensuous mouth had the same wry smile. He wore no uniform, instead he looked magnificent in formal dinner wear. He made every other man present look incomplete.

Grant glanced at her and then stopped to look at her fully. Their gazes locked and a silent message of greeting passed. He smiled and her chest tightened, but before she could gather her wits, Esther quickly captured his attention again. After a moment of whispered conversation, he turned back to the hallway and then gently brought forth a young lady, whom everyone had overlooked.

He slipped her dainty hand through his arm. 'Please, everyone, I thank you for your warm welcome. It is most pleasing to arrive in a new country and already feel at ease. My wife and I look forward to being a part of your community.'

Pippa blinked and frowned, wondering if she heard properly. Wife? Whose wife? Immediately, it became clear and she felt the blood leave her face.

*His* wife.

A hand clutched her elbow and Hilary rushed her through a side doorway into another room.

'Pippa, dearest?' Her tender look made Pippa wince.

'I'm . . . all right, Hil.' But she wasn't. Her whole world had shattered once more. Until now she had still held on to the infinite hope that he would declare his undying love for her. She had waited for him.

The urge to scream and cry and rally at the Fates was strong, but she fought it, knowing it would do no good. She had behaved like that the first time he'd broken her heart. She refused to do it again.

'You looked as though you were going to faint.'

'No . . . I'm not. I'm fine. I'm stronger than I look.'

Hilary gripped Pippa's hands. 'Such news must be a shock. How do you feel?'

Pippa hesitated, feeling confused, uncertain and dead inside. 'I honestly don't know.'

'Do you feel you can cope with him here?'

*Could she?* If she was honest she'd say no, she couldn't face Grant or his wife, but that would cause comment. He'd know that he still affected her and she needed to prevent that at all costs.

Straightening her shoulders, she summoned all her courage and forced a grim smile. 'I shall pretend that we have just met for the first time. I shall be witty and clever and the soul of the party.'

Hilary kissed her cheek. 'How brave you are.'

Together they re-entered the drawing-room and almost instantly Esther seized upon them. She looked closely at Pippa, her eyes sending a silent message of understanding. She leaned close to whisper in Pippa's ear, 'Leave the past in the past, dear. He can be nothing to you now.'

'Hilary, Phillippa.' Grant gave them a small bow. 'It's wonderful to see you again.' His eyes remained locked with Pippa's as he spoke.

'We are glad you arrived safely, Grant.' Hilary smiled.

The young lady standing beside Grant drew Pippa's gaze and she focused on her to stop looking at Grant. She was young, very young, no more than sixteen, with an angelic face and delicate hands and features. She wore mourning.

Grant's blue eyes became watchful and Pippa raised her chin as he made the introductions. 'Hilary, Phillippa, this is Cynthia, my wife.'

'Pleased to meet you,' Hilary and Pippa murmured together.

'My, you do look alike. You are twins?' Cynthia giggled and her sweet girly voice made Pippa's stomach turn. God! He had refused her, Phillippa Noble, for this little twit!

During dinner, Pippa toyed with her food and paid close attention to the newly weds. She learned that Cynthia was the daughter of

Grant's company commander, a Major Eric Ward, her mother a cousin to an earl. But, for all that, a great deal of shyness and lack of confidence hampered her social skills. To most she seemed no more than a child, indeed in such company she looked like one. Pippa couldn't believe Grant had married such a creature.

When the ladies retired to the drawing-room and left the men to their port and cigars, Pippa made sure that she sat close by Cynthia. She wanted to know why Grant had chosen her above anyone else.

'Have you known Grant long?' Pippa shot out the first question to Cynthia before the others had even seated themselves.

Blushing, Cynthia accepted a cup of tea from Rose Talbot. 'We met soon after his arrival in India. My father thought very highly of him and Grant often dined at our house.'

'How long have you been married?' Teacups rattled as the ladies waited for the answer.

Cynthia, clearly uncomfortable with such attention, wiped her hand on her skirt. 'It . . . it's been about three months now. We . . . married the day before my father died. It was his wish . . .'

Some of the women asked her questions about living in India and the conditions the army wives suffered. Pippa lost interest and moved away.

Rejection gnawed her insides. Why had he done it? He couldn't have been in love with a simple child. Grant was the type of man who needed a proper wife, a woman who could equal him in conversation and knowledge.

When the men joined the ladies, Grant went straight to Cynthia's side, smiling warmly, looking devoted. Sick with jealousy and hurt, Pippa poured herself a brandy from the drink's trolley and went to the window. She ached for the valley, for the sharp aroma of rain-washed eucalyptus, the sound of sawing timber, the laughter of the men, Millie's welcoming smile and Davy's tight embraces.

'You seem very far away,' Grant whispered near her ear.

Shivers of longing ran down her spine. Her heart skipped at his nearness. 'Do I?'

'Cynthia tells me you have been paying much attention to her.'

'I was being polite.'

His mouth lifted in a wry smile. 'Polite or prying? Remember I know you very well.'

'Not well enough perhaps?' She tilted her head and studied him. 'I wanted to know what kind of woman it took to make you say your vows. Instead, I realized it didn't take a woman at all, but a girl.'

His eyes narrowed and he shifted his feet slightly, the only hint that her barb had struck home. 'I have been speaking with Gerald.'

Pippa stared, ignoring the blood pounding in her ears. 'Oh?'

'Yes. He tells me that you have established a stud out to the south-west.'

She swallowed and remained silent.

'I believe that my father lent him a good sum of money to buy land.'

'I believe so,' she echoed, hating how all her hopes and dreams once more depended on this man.

'That debt is now mine.'

Her chin rose. 'You will get your money.'

Grant swirled the contents of his brandy glass around and then sipped it. 'I asked your father for more details concerning the debt and the stud. He told me to ask you since you are the one in control. Nothing much changes there, does it?'

Pippa held her breath, annoyed that her father had pinned it all on her shoulders. 'What exactly do you want to know?'

'Everything. What kind of stock do you have, what are the buildings like, if there are any? Have you been able to make any profit as yet and what problems have you encountered? What is the forecasted budget for the next five years?' Grant smiled, but the smile did not reach his eyes. He was testing her and she despised him for it. *Blackguard.*

'Do you want it verbally or do you need a written report?'

Grant grinned and as he did so, his eyes travelled sensually up and down the length of her body, making her feel hot and exposed. 'You haven't changed, sweet Pippa,' he murmured. 'You're just as beautiful and just as maddening as you always were.'

'You're just as arrogant.'

He frowned. 'Why are you so defensive?'

Glaring at him, she had the urge to run her fingernails down his face. 'I've worked hard in that valley, and I won't have you taking it from me.'

'What makes you believe I would?'

'Simply because you can.'

'You don't think much of me, do you?'

Her lips curled in contempt. 'Not any more, no.'

He took a step closer. 'Pip—'

'Go back to England, Grant, and play happy house with your child-bride and leave us alone.'

Esther glided up to them, her gaze sending a warning to Pippa. 'Grant,' she purred, 'your dear little wife has fallen asleep where she sits!' Esther brought her hands up as though in prayer. 'Such a darling she is, she must have been bone weary from the voyage.'

Grant bowed to Pippa then gave Esther a cheeky smile. 'I must get her to her bed.'

Esther blushed like a young maiden.

Irritated by their ridiculous display, Pippa couldn't help but whisper, 'It's past her bedtime. That's what happens when you marry a child.'

Grant scowled, but she merely raised her eyebrow at him and turned away. A minor victory at long last, but it felt rather hollow.

Pippa packed the last of her clothes in the small trunk and then turned for her reticule lying on the bed. Her father's health had improved considerably. At last, after four weeks away, she was going home and she was impatient to start the journey.

'There you are.' Hilary hurried into the room and folded her arms across her chest. 'Why do you insist on going back to Berrima today? We've an invitation to a dinner party tonight and I've already replied that you'll make up a number.'

'I'm sorry, Hil, but I've had enough of dinner parties, boating trips and picnics.' She groaned at the thought. 'I've stayed to please you and Mother, but the stud needs me.'

Hilary flounced on to the bed with a huff. 'Nonsense. It doesn't need you like I do.'

Pippa sighed. 'You don't require me at all. You spend all your time with Toby, Mother and Rose.' She locked the trunk and checked the room for any forgotten items. 'Father says you are to join me soon, so the time will go by very quickly.'

'Mother will never tolerate the hut.'

'It is our home. I promise you it will not always be so primitive.'

'Grant is driving you away, making you go back there so soon, isn't he?'

Pippa stopped and looked at her. 'No, he isn't. True, I am tired of seeing him and his child-wife at every function, but I crave the valley because of what it means to me.'

Hilary nodded and glanced down at her clasped hands. 'I'm sorry. I shouldn't have said such a thing. Only, I've been worried about how you're feeling with Grant here. I know the valley owns your heart, but don't let it be everything to you, Pippa.'

Pippa sat beside her. 'It's too late for that I'm afraid.'

'Do you not want to marry?'

Shaking her head, she popped up again and paced the room. 'I imagine one day a man might tempt me into marriage. However, I wouldn't be sorry if it never happens.'

'Pippa!' Hilary rushed to hold her. 'Grant is not the only man in the world.'

'He was for me for such a long time. However, I'm eradicating him from my heart once and for all. Him having a wife is helping the process. As they say, I've closed the book on all of that, so don't worry any more.' Releasing Hilary, she stepped back and tidied her hair. 'I must finish packing. I've missed the whole of May and what the weather has been in the valley. It's important to see the changes in this first year, so we're aware of what's to come next year. The altitude is higher there than Sydney and now it's . . .'

A maid knocked on the open door. 'Excuse me, miss, but Mr Lindfield has called.' She looked straight at Pippa.

Downstairs, Pippa paused at the door to gather her courage. Then, head held high, she strode into the drawing-room and found Grant flipping through a book left on the occasional table. Her stomach fluttered but she refused to pay heed to it or any other foolish sensibility regarding him. 'You wish to see me, Grant?'

He turned with a ready smile. 'Good day to you too, Pippa.'

She went to sit on a sofa and indicated for him to do the same. 'Where is your wife?'

'Shopping.'

'Do you want tea?'

'No, thank you.' He smiled wryly at her briskness, but she didn't care.

Pippa sucked in a breath and folded her hands tightly across her lap. He looked so healthy, so handsome. His blue-black hair needed a trim and she had the sudden urge to run her fingers through it. She shook her head, exasperated at being attracted to him, he who rejected her. Instead, she focused on the one issue they shared. 'Is this about the stud?'

'In part.'

She nodded and bit the inside of her lip. 'And?'

'Don't look so worried, Pippa.' He sighed. 'The stud is safe with you. I haven't come to demand full payment.'

'You haven't?' Her voice rose higher.

'No. My father made an agreement with yours and I will honour it. Naturally, I'll always be interested in its progress, but unless you come near to bankruptcy I have no intention of interfering.'

She stared, unable to believe her ears. 'The loan will be repaid in full as soon as possible.'

He waved a dismissing hand. 'There is no need to panic.'

'Nevertheless, I will make certain you are repaid as quickly as we can manage. I want the valley to be securely mine in every way.'

'Obviously, but as I say, there is no hurry. I've decided to stay in Australia for a while longer.'

Her heart sank. 'You have?'

'Yes, likely a year or two. I intend to purchase land and start up some businesses, especially mining. Raw materials such as coal, iron ore, silver, gold and many other minerals are all in great demand.'

She blinked, absorbing his words. 'You're staying here that long?'

'Yes. I've been assured that everything is well at home so I feel confident about staying for a while. Here, there are opportunities to be considered. I've given up my commission in the Queen's army and, after spending some time here, to add to my income, I'll return home.'

From nowhere, pain ripped her heart. He'd go home and start a family and she'd never see him again. No. She mustn't think of that. What he did was no concern of hers, never had been really.

Grant picked up a package from the table. 'This is for you.'

'For me?'

'Yes. My father mentioned you, Hilary and your parents in his will. I have already given Gerald and Hilary their documents and now I want to give you yours.' Grant handed her a large brown envelope. 'I do know that there is a little money as well as other personal belongings of my father's for you. He always considered you as a daughter.'

Sudden tears blinded her. Howard. He'd been a genuinely compassionate man, whom she had adored. 'Thank you. I shall treasure this.'

Grant swallowed. 'I have made mistakes in my life, Pippa, many I cannot undo.'

'Like walking away from me?' As soon as the words left her mouth she cringed. How could she stoop so low?

'Pippa—'

'Forget I mentioned it. I was wrong to do so.'

'Don't hate me for ever.'

'I don't hate you, Grant. I wish I did, it would be easier.' She tenderly ran her fingers over the package. 'Why did you marry her?'

He studied the patterned carpet for a moment before raising his gaze to her. 'Cynthia's father Eric became a very good friend of mine. She was his only child, they had no one but each other. When he became sick he asked me to take care of her. I didn't know how to do this, and she was so frightened of being left alone. After I received news that my father was ill and wouldn't live very much longer, it seemed sensible to marry her and take her back to England.'

'So you didn't love her?'

'No, not at first. However I do care about her now. I am all she has.'

Pippa nodded, feeling dejected. 'I hope you will be happy.'

'It means a lot to hear you say that, if you mean it.'

She bristled. 'I do mean it. I know I have many faults but lying isn't one of them.'

'No, forgive me.'

She glanced away. 'Once, your friendship was everything to me. And in respect of that I wouldn't want you to be unhappy. Yes, sometimes I can come close to hating you . . .'

'Well, you have always been passionate, Pippa.' He grinned.

She smiled at him, feeling easier of heart. Yes, she loved him, but the desperation was decreasing. The years apart had helped and she guessed maturity played its part too.

Grant stood, reached for her hand and kissed it lightly. 'I will come and visit you in your valley soon. Take care.' He turned and walked out of the room.

She sat staring at the place his lips had touched, wondering how she'd cope with him being so close for the next two years. Would her feelings dwindle into simple friendship? She prayed it would be so.

# CHAPTER TEN

As the cart's wheels bumped over the ruts and holes, Pippa's grin grew wider. The sun washed the valley with light. Birds soared on air currents high above and sheep darted away as the cart trundled beside the creek towards the cluster of buildings.

'It's good to be home, Robson.'

He flashed a smile. 'It's good to have you home, miss. We've missed you.'

'That's lovely to hear.' Her attention was caught by the progress of the house. 'Oh my, they've done so much!'

'Aye, miss, I made them get a move on so you'd have a surprise to come back to.'

'I'm certainly astonished, Robson, thank you.' She leaned forward in the seat to peer at the house structure rising from the ground. The walls were up and the roof slates on.

'Old Jim thinks he could have the house finished in a few days, miss. Sooner if he got more labourers.'

She nodded. 'I was bequeathed a small amount of money, Robson.' She pointed behind her to the new provisions tied into the cart. 'After buying all that I still have some money left. Hire more men. I'd like to have my home finished.'

'You have the wages, miss?'

'Yes.'

Robson pointed to a large timbered hut behind the original hut. 'That, miss, is the new kitchen.'

'Kitchen?' Amazed, she stared with growing excitement.

'Mrs Stroker couldn't cook in the rain and she promised that if the men built her a kitchen she would cook for them. The building went up in three days.'

She laughed, filled with indescribable happiness.

'Pippa!' Millie ran along the creek with Davy dashing away in front of her, waving madly.

She stood up in the seat and Robson gripped her arm to steady her as she waved back. 'Millie! Davy!'

She was home.

Later, as the sun began to slip behind the ranges and pink and coral streaked the sky, Pippa strolled up the rise to the newly built house. She wandered around, gazing at the construction, touching the stonework. The internal walls not made of stone needed to be plastered and the floorboards hadn't been laid, but to her it looked simply beautiful.

She stood in front of the house and surveyed the valley, shimmering in the golden glory of sunset. Her heart swelled with emotion. It was everything she ever wanted, ever dreamed of, and it all belonged to Grant. . . .

In the distance, the men were laughing, singing, all getting washed and changed, ready for their trip to Berrima. The horses grazed beyond the stables, sharing the wild grasses with the kangaroos which had managed to slip through or jump over the rail fences. Noble Blaze strutted a few paces along one of the fences, displaying his intentions to the brood mares on the other side.

A shout echoed and in a flurry of activity the men piled into two carts and drove out of camp and towards the end of the valley. Chalker waved to her from the stable block, alerting her to the fact he'd remained behind, but even his audacity couldn't diminish her joy of being home.

Pippa smiled as Millie walked towards her and handed her a cup of tea.

'They'll enjoy their break.' Millie indicated towards the dust cloud left by the carts.

'Yes, and I told them so, though they were more interested in their wages and my offer to them to spend two days in Berrima with a round of drinks on me.'

Laughing, Millie took a sip of tea. 'There will be some sore heads in the morning.'

'And a richer landlord at the Victoria Inn.'

'Glad to be back?'

'I never want to leave again.' Pippa grinned. 'I'm just so astounded. I was gone for a month and look at all that has been achieved. I cannot thank Robson enough. He is a good man.'

'He is that.' Millie nodded. 'He keeps the men under control and working hard whether they want to or not.'

'Was there any trouble?'

Shrugging, Millie rubbed the back of her neck. 'Not much. The groom, Chalker, likes to cause strife if he has the opportunity. I believe he has a cruel streak in him.'

Pippa scowled. She had let him get away with too much. He'd have to go. 'I'll speak to Robson about him.'

'The men are solid workers, but another woman about the place wouldn't have gone astray in the last month.'

'I can well imagine.' She chuckled. 'Did Robson look after you though?'

'Oh yes, very well indeed. Also Amelia Meredith came for a visit and Davy and I went back with her for the night, which was a welcomed break.'

'Good. You need time to yourself. You work too hard.' She tucked her hand through Millie's arm. 'Where is Davy?'

'Playing with the toy soldiers you bought him. I think he may even sleep with them.'

'As long as he's happy, that's all that matters.' Pippa gazed at Millie. 'Are you happy?'

Millie nodded and gazed out over the view. 'Very. I have a healthy son, a home, food and you. What more could I want?' Millie frowned at her. 'What about you?'

Pippa swept one arm out wide encompassing all before them and nearly spilling her tea in the process. 'I have all this, why wouldn't I be happy? Look at it, Millie. Look at the thriving little community it has become.' Then she sobered. 'And I will fight to the death to keep it.'

Millie grimaced. 'Are there problems?'

'Nothing I cannot handle. While I was away Father told me that none of our money went into buying the land. So, if we default on the repayments, the property will belong to a family friend.'

'Oh, Pippa. I'm so sorry.'

'Well, it's not how I'd like it to be, but I'll not give up. This is Noble land and it will remain that way. I just have to pay the money back as quick as I can. With half of my bequest I repaid some more of the loan, but it wasn't a lot. Hilary wanted to do the same but I know she really wanted to enhance her trousseau which is severely lacking.'

'She is engaged?'

'Not yet, but it's only a matter of time. Toby Talbot is eager to make her his bride.'

Crickets in the grass began to chorus and dusk settled over the land.

'When will your family arrive?'

Shrugging, Pippa sipped her tea. 'In a month perhaps. Father promised me he would return here as soon as his health allows. He is getting much better, but Mama is digging her heels in and claiming all sorts of excuses why she shouldn't come here just yet. I must not get my hopes up. Father's promises have been empty before.' She sighed. 'Mother's hoping Toby Talbot will propose to Hilary very soon and save her the bother of coming here at all. Poor Hilary would be newly married and have Mother living with them as well, not an ideal start to married life.'

'How would you feel if they didn't come at all?'

'Disappointed.' Pippa listened to the last of the bird calls as the sun slid beyond the range. 'They must do what pleases them. I cannot make them live here, although financially it is the better option, but whatever they choose I shall continue building up the stud. The valley is my home,' she smiled at Millie, 'and the people within it are now my family.'

Millie stiffened. 'Chalker is coming. He must want a word with you. I'll go and check on Davy.' She took the teacups and walked down the slope.

Pippa straightened and made her expression businesslike as the groom come closer. 'Did you wish to speak to me, Chalker?'

He removed his hat and stopped a few feet away. 'Yes, Miss Noble. Robson needed someone to stay behind while the men go to Berrima.'

'And that person is you?'

His rakish smile was not lost on her. 'Yes, miss it is. So, if you need anything, anything at all, just holler and I'll come running.'

She swallowed, feeling foolish at the double meanings she thought she heard in his simple words. His grey eyes narrowed as his grin spread and his stance became leisurely, which irritated her. He thought himself to be so appealing and charming. Obviously he was used to fascinating the women he met, and for some unknown reason he enthralled her in a strange uneasy way. She took a step back.

'Thank you, Chalker. I doubt I'll require you tonight.'

He bowed like some highborn gentleman. 'Well, should you change your mind, Miss Noble, you'll know where to find me.'

Pippa headed down the slope, eager to be with Millie. The man unnerved her, made her react to him in a way she was not used to. She was aware of him physically, but it was no meeting of the minds at all, more something akin to animals. She shook her head, not liking her thoughts. Was it true that women needed to be wed early to prevent them from being led astray by unchivalrous men?

She snorted in disgust. No man, no matter how hot he made her blood would lead her astray. She had the stud, the valley. It would be enough.

The horse's hoofs crunched over the frosted grass. Autumn had come and gone with no real rain. The land was dry, parched and everyone prayed for winter rains.

Pippa ducked her head under a low branch and guided Honey up from the valley floor and into the wooded slopes. The cool July morning allowed the morning mist to linger and, as they climbed higher, she looked back at the homestead peeking through the whiteness as though it floated in the clouds.

The incline levelled out for a distance and Pippa reined Honey in and gazed around. Over the past weeks she had taken to riding the boundaries of the property searching for signs of local Aboriginals. Recently, a group of natives were noticed crossing the valley. She'd given orders for them not to be harmed, even when they realized later that night that a few sheep had gone missing. Aboriginal raids weren't as frequent in this area as others, and she didn't want to start a war over some sheep. Her men were under orders not to injure them unless in danger themselves.

Pippa shifted in the saddle and the creaking leather sounded loud in the quiet of the bush. She patted Honey's neck and clicked her heels to ride on. Her new horse, bought with some of the money Howard left her, had been a good investment, being sure-footed and of sound temperament.

After an hour of riding the top of the range, Pippa turned back with reluctance. Accounts and correspondence awaited her. With luck, she'd receive no visitors today. All week she'd been terribly busy. Gil and Augusta had called with an invitation to a picnic that she'd declined because of concerns needing her attention. Old Barney Goodfellow slipped while chopping wood and cut his foot with the axe. Chalker fought with two of the masons and Jim O'Rielly threatened to take his men and leave if Chalker wasn't sacked. With quick talking and near begging Pippa had finally convinced Jim to stay, promising that Chalker would not go near his men again. She should have sacked him on the spot. However, he handled Noble Blaze better than anyone.

With the stallion their main source of income, she had to make certain her decisions were the correct ones, and that meant keeping Chalker a little longer.

Then to top it all off, a letter from Hilary told her not to expect them any time soon as Mama had accepted invitations for parties for the next three weeks. This hurt more than she cared to admit. When she left the Talbots', her father promised they would follow her soon, but now it was July and they were still in Sydney!

She sighed and thought of the positives. Three gentlemen brought their mares to be serviced. The stud fees greatly improved her situation, allowing her to pay some accounts. Her own mares were in foal, including the two mares she bought from Briggs last October. Noble Blaze was fit and healthy and with luck would continue to be so.

As Honey carefully trod back down the slope, Pippa tightened the reins, but the horse knew what she was doing and she relaxed. She looked forward to spending the day with Millie, who had been staying at the Merediths' for a week, helping Amelia with her new weak baby boy. Also, Pippa wanted to start teaching Davy how to ride the old pony she'd rescued a few days ago from the knackery in Berrima.

As they cleared the last of the trees at the bottom of the incline, Honey shied at a sudden movement leaping out from behind a tree. Pippa gripped the reins and swirled around, her heart in her throat. Her first thought was Aborigines, but instead Chalker stood there, grinning.

'Good morning, Miss Noble.' He tipped his hat ever so slightly, his smile cocksure.

Surprise and anger made her voice sharp. 'What are you doing here? Why aren't you at work?'

Chalker folded his arms, his manner relaxed. 'I am working, collecting firewood.'

Honey side-stepped again before settling. Pippa looked beyond Chalker and saw a small, empty handcart. 'Then I suggest you get about your chores, and in future do not jump out at a horse and rider. You nearly unseated me.'

'You are far too good a rider for that, miss.' His gaze roamed over her. He patted Honey's flank near Pippa's skirt, his hand inching towards her leg.

Stiffening in the saddle, Pippa glared at his insolence. 'You are on your last warning, Chalker. Robson says you tend to shirk your duties and I have noted how many times you've caused trouble with the men.'

His grin widened and the tip of his fingers pressed through her skirts to touch her calf. 'It warms me to know that you watch me.'

Pippa shivered with something close to repulsion, but not quite. She didn't understand the hold he had over her. 'Don't flatter yourself.' She jerked her leg away. 'Move back, please.'

Chalker's eyes narrowed as he looked up at her from under his hat brim. 'I was thinking you might be lonely out here. It's perfectly natural for a woman to want a man's comfort sometimes and, should you have such needs, I'd be more than willing to ease your feminine urges. Of course it would be our secret.'

Speechless, she stared at him, her mouth opening and closing. The audacity of the man's proposal whirled about in her mind. He'd actually spoken of *it*, of the silent uncomfortable attraction she would never have put into words.

Spluttering and gripping the reins, she whirled Honey about in a tight circle. 'You impertinent scum! You think I'd want you touching me?' Relief poured from her. She laughed now, seeing the absurdity of his words. She'd never have let the likes of him come anywhere near her.

He stepped back, his expression one of distaste. 'Don't deny you want me. I've seen the way you look at me, all hungry and needy.'

Pippa blanched. Had she done that? True, she'd felt her body respond to him, but had she really looked at him with hunger? Humiliation burned her cheeks. Was she repeating her past over again by consorting with the wrong man? First Grant and now Chalker. She quivered in horror. At least Grant was a gentleman, but Chalker was a workman, her labourer. Her breakfast rose to her throat threatening to choke her.

Chalker smirked. 'Women like you are always up for some bed sport. The fire in you needs to be quenched and I'm willing to do it for you. No one will know, I promise you.'

Outraged, Pippa leaned down from the saddle to sneer in his face. 'You've no idea what women like me need! Now pack you bags and get off my property. Consider yourself fired.' She jerked Honey into motion and thundered away.

At the stables, Pippa dismounted and, leading Honey by the reins, marched inside to Robson, who stood checking the feed barrels for vermin. In the corner, Colin forked cut grass into a stall. 'Robson, I've just fired Chalker. He's to leave the property within the hour. Can you see to it?'

'Absolutely, miss.' Robson stepped to take hold of Honey's bridle. 'It's not before time too, miss. He's been trouble from the first day, although he did well to hide it. I'll personally escort him to the boundary.'

'Pippa! Come look!' Davy ran into the stables. 'There's a carriage coming with two shiny black horses with white feathers on their heads.' He grabbed her hand and pulled her outside. 'A carriage!'

Intrigued, Pippa frowned at Robson as he came to stand at her side. They both stared along the valley track. Indeed a large, shiny black carriage pulled by magnificent horses rumbled beside the creek towards them.

'Who could it be?' Pippa glanced at Robson for his input.

'Nay, miss, I know of no one with such a carriage in this district.'

Davy jumped up and down clapping his hands. 'It's a prince!'

Pippa gently pushed him towards the hut. 'Go get your mother.'

She and Robson walked away from the service buildings and waited under the big gum tree near the footbridge. On the other side, Davy and Millie watched the carriage approach.

The driver halted the fine pair and drew the carriage to stop. The door was flung open and Gerald popped his head out. 'Pippa!'

Pippa's eyes widened in disbelief. 'Father?'

Gerald exited the carriage and then handed Hilary down, and then the maid, Cissie. 'We're here at last!' He shouted, reaching back into the carriage.

Hilary ran up to Pippa and hugged her. 'It's good to see you! Have we surprised you? How are you? Mama fainted! As soon as we started the descent into the valley, she screamed that we would all fall to our deaths and then fainted.'

Blinking rapidly to make sure of her vision, Pippa let Hilary's words wash over her. Her family was here! She couldn't believe it. They had sent her no word of their impending arrival. She wasn't ready. The house wasn't ready. She glanced at the bulk of luggage roped to the top of the carriage and cringed at the amount. Where ever would they put it all?

'Come, come, Esther. Pippa wishes to greet you,' Gerald cajoled his wife out of the carriage. 'You're safe now, so stop your hysterics.'

Pippa stepped forward and kissed her mother's pale cheek. 'Welcome, Mother.'

Esther, fanning herself with a white handkerchief, sniffled. 'What a journey, Phillippa, what a journey.' Slowly, she raised her head and gazed about. Her eyes widened, her mouth dropped open.

The heavy weight of guilt sunk Pippa's happiness at her family's arrival. Her mother's rigidness confirmed her fears. She hated the valley. 'Mother—'

'You . . .' Esther turned to scan the whole valley and all it contained, her eyes filling with tears. 'Gerald . . .' She blinked, her chest heaved as though she struggled to breathe. 'You brought me *here*?'

'Mother—'

'Esther—'

'How could you?' Esther's voice lowered in anger. 'I'll not spend one night in this god-forsaken backwater!' She spun on her heel, re-entered the carriage and slammed the door.

Pippa stared at her father, whose cheeks flushed beetroot. He stormed to the carriage and jerked open the door. 'Get out at once!'

Hilary silently came to Pippa's side and took her hand as, in disbelief and with acute embarrassment, they watched their parents argue and wrestle. At last, Esther emerged from the carriage, dishevelled and indignant.

'I will stay but one night, then I am returning to Sydney.' She marched past them all and crossed the footbridge. Hilary hurriedly followed her.

Sighing, Gerald walked away, around the other side of the carriage and, after a glance at Millie, Pippa went to join him.

'I'm sorry, Father. I didn't expect you. Hilary's letter said it could be another month as Mother had engagements. I tried to have the house finished, but—'

'I do not blame you in the least, dearest.' His eyes softened and he slipped his arm around her waist to hug her to him. 'In fact, I'm so very proud of you.' He gazed out over the valley, at the cluster of buildings, the horses and sheep grazing. 'What you've achieved here in such a short time is inspirational, my dear. You have the courage of a lion.'

Pippa kissed his thin cheek, aware that his ill health had taken its toll on him. 'I did it for us all, Father. This is our home now, and we'll be successful, I know it.'

'I have no doubt about it, not with you in charge.'

'Oh, but Father, I'm not in charge now you're here.'

Gerald shook his head. 'No, Pippa. This is your dream, your future.'

She stepped back, frowning. 'But it's yours too. We share it together.'

'Yes, but I don't have the youth, the energy, the heart that you do.' He shook his head and sighed. 'All I wanted to do was to make money.

You wanted to make a home.'

She touched his arm, frightened by how old and defeated he looked. 'We can do both, Father.'

He remained silent for a long time, staring out over the land.

'Please don't be dispirited, Father. We can be successful. The mistakes made in England do not have to be repeated here.'

'My health is failing, but I tend to think that is a good thing.'

'No—'

Gerald held up his hand. 'Hear me out. I insist we have honesty if nothing else after so many years of lies.' He paused and took a deep breath. 'If I were hale and hearty and a few years younger, there would be no stopping me, but, no doubt, that would have led to our ruin as it did back home.'

'Father . . .'

'I've had time to think while being bedridden and I've made a decision.' He took both her hands in his and smiled. 'The valley is yours to do with as you please. I'll sign it all over to you, with the provision that you support your sister.'

Pippa blinked. 'But what about you and Mother?'

'We shall return to England.'

'No!'

'It is best, dearest. Your mother will never settle here. She blames me for making her life miserable and she has just cause too. At least this way I can give her what she wants and that's England.'

'But Hilary and I need you. You can't leave.' Pippa squeezed his hands in desperation. 'Don't abandon us, Father. I've made this valley our home. The house will be finished soon and we will be happy I promise you. Mother will settle and make friends. She will adjust.'

'I've not done right by your mother for many years and she misses England. It is only fair to take her home.'

'You are correct about one thing, Gerald Noble!'

Pippa and her father jerked and turned as one to stare at the enraged Esther, who folded her arms and narrowed her eyes.

'It is true you've not done right by me and your daughters, but I'll be damned if I stand by and let you make more mistakes!'

Gerald took a step forward. 'Esther?'

'Don't Esther me! You have always been a stupid man. You've never known what I needed. I'll not be shipped back to England and separated from my girls. How could you think such a thing?' Her hands fell to her sides and clenched. 'You know of my hopes that Hilary will marry Toby Talbot and if all Phillippa's plans come to fruition then she will be a wealthy woman in her own right. You think I would miss all that?'

'But you've hated being in this country.'

'I hated being poor and friendless, which is what you made us!'

Gerald spread out his hands, appealing her. 'I've no words in defence.'

Esther nodded. 'Typical. Well, Gerald, we shan't be returning to England, we shan't be returning to Sydney.'

'But you said . . .'

'Never mind what I said earlier.' Esther glared.'I've seen the new house and when finished, I have no doubts at all it will be adequate and respectable. If Elizabeth MacArthur and other notable women of society can start their lives here living in huts, then so can I! Our estate will be as grand as any in the country and it'll be far more than what we'd ever have back in England.'

Pippa stared, amazed by her mother's complexities and also slightly admiring the spirit she rarely showed. 'Thank you, Mother. I promise you, you'll not be sorry for staying.'

Two days later, Pippa left the post office after collecting the family's mail. Her heartbeat raced whenever she thought of what she carried in her reticule and it became so bad that as she crossed Berrima's village green she stopped to sit on a bench seat to regain her breath.

She didn't have to open her reticule to know what the letter inside said. The words were emblazoned on her brain. After years of living with her father's misled gambling encounters, she had gone against all she believed in and taken a huge risk by investing a small amount of money in a speculation. Gil had been the one to tell her about it in passing conversation. Industry, he said, was booming after the depression of the early forties, and she amazed them both when she asked for more details before swearing him to secrecy.

If this chance paid off, she'd be able to give Grant more money towards the loan, it was the only reason why she'd taken such a desperate measure.

Taking a deep breath, she rose and headed along the main street to collect her mother and Hilary from the haberdashery store. All morning she'd watched her mother try her best not to cast disparaging remarks about the lack of goods on offer in the few shops compared to Sydney. Yet, in an astounding turn of character Esther had done her utmost to be understanding and accommodating in her new life and, as a reward for her gracious suffering, Pippa planned to introduce her to the best society the district had to offer.

As she passed a cottage, her mind on so many things, she jumped when suddenly a man stepped out of the shadows straight in front of her. His frame blocked the sunlight and for a moment she didn't know what was happening until she recognized the face under the slouched hat.

Chalker smirked. 'We meet again, Miss Noble.'

Pippa stepped back. His dismissal from the valley had been overshadowed by her family's arrival and now staring at his dirty, angry face a shiver trickled down her spine. 'Please let me pass.'

'What, nothing to say to the man you've made homeless?'

She raised her chin, her glare taking in his rough appearance. 'Scum like you often find a hole to crawl into.'

His grey eyes narrowed. 'I've always admired your spirit and I'll enjoy taming you.'

Her blood turned to ice and she hoped the fear didn't show on her face. 'You take one step closer and I'll scream so loud they'll hear me in Bong Bong!'

For a second he stilled and then slowly relaxed again. 'I won't let you get away with treating me as you did.'

'You got what you deserved. Now let me pass!' She gathered the skirts of her pale green dress and made to move around him, but his hand shot out and gripped her elbow.

He leaned close to whisper, 'This isn't the end of it. One day I'll repay you and I'll get a lot of pleasure out of having you squirming beneath me while I take my fill of you.'

He thrust her aside before they drew attention and Pippa stumbled. Chalker bowed arrogantly and strolled away.

Shaking, she hurried on, eager to put as much distance between herself and the man as possible. His threats echoed in her mind, but she knew he'd hardly have the chance to do her harm. He'd never be allowed in the valley again and she rarely went riding alone as most times Gil or Augusta accompanied her.

She expelled a breath of relief when she made it to the small shop. Inside, Hilary and their mother were paying for their purchases.

'Send the goods to the address on the card, girl.' Esther handed over her card to the shop assistant and glanced at Pippa. 'Did you buy the paints you needed?'

Pippa shook her head, not trusting herself to speak with a steady voice. The letter about her investment plus the incident with Chalker had scared her more than she liked to admit, but she couldn't worry her family, she couldn't let anything spoil their settling in process.

They walked back out into the street and headed for Victoria Inn where they were to meet Gerald.

'Why, Miss Noble!' Tabitha Ashford-Smith greeted her, as she and Gil came out of White's Inn and paused before them. No expense had been spared on the blue silk gown Tabitha wore and Esther's eyes widened.

'Good day, Mrs Ashford-Smith, Gil.' Pippa thrust all thoughts of Chalker from her mind and smiled warmly. Seeing Gil, knowing of his quiet support in everything she did was like a soothing balm on rough skin. 'I'm so glad we've come across one another. I was wanting you to meet my mother and sister.'

Pippa made all the introductions and soon Esther was chatting to Tabitha as though they'd known each other for years. Pippa believed they saw in each other a kindred spirit, judging by their excited conversation.

Gil, resplendent in an iron-grey suit, laughed at their chatter, his emerald eyes sparkling with mischief. Pippa grinned at him. After her encounter with Chalker, he represented safety. He was someone who listened and talked to her as an equal. His friendship meant a great deal to her.

Leaning close, Gil studied her face. 'No wrinkles yet.'

She pushed at him playfully. 'I should hope not!'

'Well, you are the biggest worrier I've ever encountered. Have you received a certain letter yet?'

Her smile faded and she glanced at her mother, before stepping away a little. 'Shh. Don't speak of it here, but yes I have received it.'

'Trust me, all will be splendid. Would I lead you down a ruinous path?' He pretended to be shocked and then chuckled. 'Don't answer that, I might not like what you say.'

'Much depends on this, Gil,' she whispered. 'I'm scared.'

'I will let nothing happen to you, I promise.' His warm smile reassured her for the moment. 'Besides, the amount you gambled is hardly worth the worry. I'm ashamed to include you in my business dealings on such a small sum.'

'It might be small to you, but for me it's large enough. Moreover, I've gone against all that I believe in to do this, so don't make fun of me. I feel as though my heart will give out every time I think of what I've done.'

'Nothing will happen, I promise you.' He took her hand and kissed it like a gallant knight. 'And if it did, I think I'd enjoy saving you. A damsel in distress is a role you rarely play.'

She slapped him away good-humouredly. 'What rot you do talk, Gil.'

Tucking her hand over his arm, he squeezed it gently and winked. 'So, when are we to go riding again? Or shall we take the gig to the falls?'

'Let us go to the falls and take a picnic. Mother would enjoy that and I could paint. Perhaps we could walk through the rainforest there?'

Gil patted her hand. 'Whatever you desire.'

Suddenly, amidst all the noise of the town, a coach rolled to a stop behind them and turning, Pippa gave it a fleeting look that quickly became an open-mouthed stare as Grant and his little wife climbed down.

Esther gave a squeal of delight and rushed to embrace the new arrivals before introducing them to Tabitha and Gil.

Pippa grasped Hilary's arm. 'Did you know they were coming?'

'No, at least, not today. Mother mentioned that Grant's last letter said he might call on his way back from the Goulburn district.'

'Why didn't you warn me?' She took a deep breath and collected herself.

Gil stepped closer, frowning. 'Is everything all right?'

Pippa forced a smile. 'Of course.' She turned to the others just as Grant looked her way, her day was getting worse by the minute.

Tabitha linked her arm through Gil's. 'Are you staying long, Mr Lindfield?'

Grant shrugged. 'No definite plans have been made as yet, Mrs Ashford-Smith. We've just called to visit our friends, the Nobles.' He glanced at Pippa. 'I've heard of many good things about the land around this area, some of which I'd like to see.'

'Then I insist that you all come to our home tomorrow for dinner.' Tabitha declared.

'Wonderful!' Esther clapped.

Pippa groaned inwardly as arrangements were made, and when Grant touched her arm she jumped.

He frowned, blue eyes questioning. 'What is wrong?'

'Nothing, nothing at all.'

'You are unhappy to see me?' His voice lowered. 'I thought we'd sorted all that out.'

'Not everything is about you, Grant,' she whispered back.

'Are there problems I should know about?'

'Is that all you care about, your investment?' she spat, hating him for reminding her that he had an interest in the valley. 'Just remember that I have paid back a third of the loan now and so the valley isn't all yours. And with luck I'll be able to pay the rest of it in the next few weeks.'

He moved to use his back to block the rest of the party from hearing them. 'How is that possible?'

'That's none of your business.' Wild horses wouldn't drag out of her the gamble she'd entered into and she wished she'd kept her mouth shut.

'What have you done? I have a right to know.'

She raised an eyebrow in contempt. 'I don't think you do.'

His face tightened. 'Don't play me for a fool, Pippa. Remember, you have less than a year to pay back that loan. I'm not as soft as my father and I won't simply forget or ignore money that is rightfully mine like he did on numerous occasions.'

Her stomach plummeted. 'You've changed your tune since we last spoke in Sydney. Then you placed no restraints.'

'I wasn't fully aware of your father's health problems then,' he whispered, glancing at the women still talking. 'Why did you all keep it from me? I felt like a fool when I found out. I had a right to know his heart is not good.'

She took a step back, disgusted. 'Your rights? Why is everything about you?'

'Don't treat me like an idiot. Gerald's health changes things. If he dies, that leaves just you to manage the stud.'

'Who do you think has been managing it thus far? You think I couldn't continue to?' She raised her eyebrows, wanting to scratch his eyes out. 'Don't pretend you don't know the truth of the matter. Father told you I was managing the stud when you first arrived.'

'But I thought, as a man, he had some control.' He gave a mocking laugh. 'I should've known better. You must have everything your own way.'

'I'm doing very well at the stud,' she ground out through clenched teeth.

He nodded. 'I believe it. Actually, I think you'd do a better job of it than Gerald would, but the point remains, you would be solely in charge – a woman alone. Men don't want to discuss business issues with a woman. The venture will fail and . . .'

Before he could finish his whispered tirade, Gil stepped around Grant and came to Pippa's side, smiling, but in his eyes she read his unspoken query. He clasped her elbow, giving her the strength she so desperately needed against Grant.

Gil held out his other hand to Grant. 'Mr Lindfield, I must say farewell.'

Grant looked from one to the other and then inclined his head. 'Until tomorrow then, Mr Ashford-Smith.' He moved back to the women and Pippa let out a pent-up breath.

How would she cope having Grant in her valley for a few days? The thought made her ill.

'Talk to me.' Gil bent his head closer, his gaze questioning. 'Do I need to call him out?'

'No.' Pippa smiled despite the resentment and anger bubbling in her chest. She ignored Grant's insufferable presence and slipped her hand through Gil's arm, not for the first time was she thankful to have met this brilliant man. 'I'll see you on Tuesday evening. Tell Augusta that we must have dancing after dinner.'

'You know where I am if you need me.' His tone sent her a message of concern. He brought her hand up and kissed it.

She smiled in gratitude, with Gil she didn't have to watch her every word or act to be other than who she was. 'What a lucky woman I am to have you as my dear friend.'

He hesitated for a moment, frowning, but then laughed. 'You're a very lucky woman indeed!'

# CHAPTER ELEVEN

After dipping the ladle into the bucket of fresh water, Pippa lifted it to her mouth and drank deeply. Sweat from the hot October day beaded her upper lip and forehead. She used her apron to blot the moisture away. 'Here, Millie, drink before you faint.'

'I cannot believe how hot it is today. Summer has come early I think.'

'It doesn't help that we've had such a dry winter.' Pippa sighed. 'Robson said if we don't get rain soon, we'll have to buy water and have it brought in. The creek is so shallow now. Everything is dry and brown.'

Millie dropped her scrubbing brush and kneeled back on her heels. 'He told me that the shepherd has taken the sheep farther into the bush to find another creek for them, to save this water for us.' She looked around the wooden floor now clean from spilled plaster. 'At least we're nearly finished in here.'

Pippa nodded and poked her head through the door of the next room. The walls sparkled with fresh white plaster. 'The men have finished.' She sighed and pushed a strand of hair away from her eyes. 'Soon you and Davy will have the hut all to yourselves.'

Standing, Millie shook out her black skirts and white apron. 'Yes, I'll enjoy that. The tent is wearing on me.'

Pippa gazed around the front room, still pleased that she'd made the decision to not build an upstairs floor. The money saved by keeping the house as a single storey would be beneficial to the stud. She saw no reason to go the extra expense of a double-storey house when one large, sprawling house would do the job just as well. With the plans for an upper floor abandoned, Jim wasted no time in building additional rooms and Barney shingled the extra roof space and verandah that swept around all sides. She'd paid off Jim O'Reilly and his team, and with them gone, a peacefulness settled on the valley as the other men knuckled down to their own routines.

'It is a lovely house, Pippa.' Millie smiled, ladle in hand.

Nodding, Pippa grinned and went on another tour. From the front door leading into the main room, a door led off to the right to the dining-room and from the dining-room a door on the back wall led into the study. On the left of the front room was her parents' bedroom, and at the back of the front room a door led off to another bedroom, hers and Hilary's. All rooms had their own French doors leading on to the verandahs. The house kitchen would remain a separate hut the men built for Millie because of the fire hazards.

'Phillippa,' her mother called from outside.

'What is it?' Pippa answered as she and Millie stepped out on to the verandah and were buffeted by a strong hot wind.

Esther puffed as she hurried up the slope from the hut, her knitting in her hands. 'The furniture wagon is coming!' She looked as excited as a child at Christmas. 'Oh, I do hope nothing is broken.'

'I'm sure nothing will be.' Pippa soothed, watching the cloud of dust spreading out behind the trundling cart. 'Is Hilary still walking with Davy?'

'Yes, but I see them now.' Millie pointed over to the right and down past the stables where Hilary and Davy stood tickling the ears of the two kids born a few weeks ago to the nanny goat.

'Your father said he'd be back in time for the wagon's arrival.' Esther pouted.

Pippa strolled down to the footbridge. 'Well, it's good that he's making friends and acquaintances in the district.'

Esther followed, holding her ruby skirts high with one hand. 'Be that as it may, he knew this was an important day. I'd like to move out of that hut as soon as possible, especially with this heat.'

Pippa paused to kiss her mother's flushed cheek. 'Would today be soon enough?'

'Indeed, my dear.' Her mother sighed with a smile. 'What a pleasing thought. I am rather happy with our house. Despite its strange shape, the rooms are large and airy. Mrs Ashford-Smith said exactly the same when she viewed it yesterday. I'll feel more comfortable too next time Grant comes to stay, for we'll have the house to accommodate him and Cynthia.'

Pippa sniffed with displeasure at the mention of Grant being in close proximity again. She'd only just tolerated his last visit, which thankfully was very short.

'One's house reflects one's status, you know that.' Esther peered at the wagonload. 'There is nothing more embarrassing than living in a house with small poky rooms. Do you remember my old aunt Bess? She detested tiny rooms, refused to enter one.'

'Yes, Mother.' Pippa then greeted the driver, effectively cutting off her mother's opinions of room sizes. She moved down the cart and lifted the canvas flap to view the stacked furniture. 'Oh look, the dining table. It's been so long since we saw it last. It doesn't seem to have suffered damage on the voyage over.'

'I'd demand compensation from the ship's captain if sea water had stained it.' Esther ran her finger over its polished legs. 'Everything is coated in an inch of dust.'

'It's been stored, Mother.' Pippa shook her head and craned to look at more of their belongings not seen since they were taken out of their house in England over a year and a half ago. 'There's the trunk with the china service in it.' She pointed to a brown trunk half buried beneath an assortment of chairs and bed frames.

'How lovely it will be to use it all again. I do hope nothing is broken for we could never replace it. Most of it belonged to my mother and is the only tableware we have of value really. And when are the women servants coming? Your father sent out advertisements weeks ago.'

'Next week.'

Esther folded her hands together. 'They must come soon, I want to make certain they are of a good standard before we hold our dinner party the week after. I never thought we'd be so busy.' She drew herself up straighter, pride shining in her eyes. 'I never imagined that in the country we would have such a wide range of friends as we do. Three dinner parties last week, two this week and one next week.'

Pippa sent a murmured thanks to the Fates for enabling her mother to settle into the area so well. Within days of her arrival she had received callers and after their first dinner party as a family, hosted by the Ashford-Smiths, Esther had behaved as though she'd always lived in the valley and immediately began calling on the new friends she'd made through the Ashford-Smiths.

'I'll go up to the house and decide where everything is to go.' Esther nodded, turning away.

A tug on her skirt alerted Pippa to Davy and she smiled down at him. 'Run and get the men for me, darling. We've got much to do today.' She looked back to the driver. 'You can begin unloading now. Everything is to go straight into the house up there.' She waved behind her.

'Yes, miss.'

'Pippa.'

She turned to Millie, who'd come down to help, but the look on Millie's face froze her. 'What is the matter?'

Millie looked towards the west, the entrance to the valley. 'There's smoke.'

Pippa glanced over her shoulder and frowned. A murky brown cloud hung over the top of the ranges.'Douglas must be burning off his fields.'

'On a hot windy day like today? I doubt it.'

'Miss Noble!'

She whipped around at the urgency in Robson's voice and blanched at the strain on his face. He skidded to a stop in front of her and pointed to the ridge. 'Bushfire. I've sent Colin to saddle a horse and ride up the valley to see how far away it is. But we must prepare.'

Pippa's mouth went dry. 'Bush . . . Bushfire?'

Esther hurried back to them, her hand clasped against her chest. 'Oh my dear Lord. What will we do?'

Robson took off his hat and scratched his head, his expression revealing his concern. 'We must fill every bucket and wet down the buildings, starting with the grain store. I've already got Peter and Barney digging a hole to bury feed and harnesses.'

Pippa's mind went blank. He talked too fast for her to absorb his meaning. 'Robson, please, what are you saying?'

He took a deep breath and then glanced away sharply as Colin galloped across the valley floor. 'Miss, try to understand. If the fire gets into the valley it'll wipe out everything in its path. We must bury what we can. Once the fire reaches, *if* it reaches the valley ridge, we'll all have to escape. I'll get the horses saddled. The ladies must pack only their valuables.'

'Escape?' Esther swayed just as Hilary and Davy joined them.

Running his hands through his hair, Robson's eyes implored Pippa to take action, yet she couldn't move or think clearly. Bushfire. Escape. 'It-it may not even come this way, Robson.'

'I hope to God it doesn't, miss.'

She swallowed. 'But you think it will?'

He looked up at the large gum trees, their top branches swaying in the warm breeze. 'If the wind doesn't change the fire will sweep over that ridge and head straight for us.'

'But it's not summer yet. You said bushfires come in January or February.'

'Miss, we've had very little rain and dry grass will burn whether it be the middle of winter or summer. We were spared fires last year, but all it takes is one spark to set the bush alight and this wind will not help us.' He shifted from foot to foot. 'Please, miss we cannot waste time talking. We must prepare.'

'Yes, go. Do what must be done.' Pippa waved him away and turned to her family. On seeing their scared and worried expressions she hid her fear and straightened her shoulders. 'Come, we must do as Robson says. Pack lightly or bury what you cannot carry. Quickly now!'

As the others turned and ran back to the house, her mother stepped forward and gripped Pippa's arm. 'This valley, the stud is all we have, Pippa.'

'Yes, Mother.' Distracted, Pippa nodded, looking beyond her towards the scurrying men.

Esther's hand clenched Pippa's arm like a vice. 'No, listen to me!'

Pippa stared at her.

'You must not let all that we have slip from our grasp. Not now we are finally finding our way. I'd not survive another disappointment.'

'I promise I won't let that happen.'

Her mother's gaze remained fixed on hers. 'For if we lose the stud that will be the end of us. The Nobles will be finished for ever.'

'I know.' She kissed her mother and gently pushed her in towards the huts. 'Go help pack. Take only the most important things and hurry!'

Robson sprang into action. He ran about issuing orders that everyone instantly obeyed, even her mother showed extreme courage and did as she was told without complaint.

Pippa knew all kinds of fear. The fear of being turned out of their house when her father squandered all their money, the fear of being unloved and rejected by Grant, the fear of being in the middle of a vast ocean on an insignificant ship. Yet, none of this could ever eclipse the fear she was experiencing now.

Terror seemed tangible, as though she could taste it, reach out and touch it. Normally, she was never one to panic, hated being vulnerable, but as the wind carried the smell of smoke, her throat closed up through pure dread. Astounded by the enormity of perhaps losing everything she'd worked for, dreamed of, Pippa stood trance-like, unable to move or think. The noise and confusion around her dimmed.

'Pip.' Davy tugged at her skirts, his face pale.

For a long moment she stared at him. She didn't realize she was frightening him until his bottom lip quivered. 'Will we die, Pip?'

Wrenched out of her daze, she blinked as his words sank in. 'No . . . No, darling.' His hand inched into hers and she squeezed it tight. 'We'll be fine. I'll take care of you.'

A shout made her jump. Colin rode like the devil towards them, waving his hat in the air. Everyone stilled and then quickly joined Pippa and Davy near the creek as Colin pulled up his horse to a skittering halt before them.

'Well?' Robson demanded, his body tense.

Colin winced as he swallowed, his lips dry and face coated with dust. 'It's heading this way about four or five miles from here, maybe a mile more, but that's all.' He sagged in the saddle. 'It's coming from the direction of the Merediths' property.'

Time froze for a second and then everyone started talking at once.

Millie stared in horror at Pippa. 'Oh no. Amelia and the baby.'

'They might be safe. Don't worry.' Pippa patted her arm and then looked to Robson for direction.

He frowned, rubbing his fingertips across his forehead. 'Right, we've got to leave the valley now.'

'Can we not fight the fire, Robson?' Pippa felt her heart would explode from the pain of losing it all. 'I mean, we've got water at our feet. Can we not—'

'Miss, a few buckets of water will not stand up to a bushfire.'

Her frustration burst into anger. 'I will not lose this place! I will stay and fight.'

'Don't be silly, Pippa,' Millie scoffed. 'We'll do as Robson says. We must get out of harm's way. Nothing is worth putting yourself in danger.'

A rifle shot echoed across the valley, sending birds screeching from the trees. Pippa wheeled around to stare at the entrance into the valley but no vehicle or horseman came dashing out of the trees.

Robson scanned the slopes, shading his eyes with his hand as the sun burned down relentlessly. 'Someone needs help. It's a signal.'

A shiver of trepidation ran down Pippa's back. 'Father,' she whispered.

'No!' Esther said. 'He's in Berrima.'

Hilary, eyes wide, stepped closer to her mother. 'But what if he had started to journey home?'

'Get down off that horse, Colin.' Pippa grabbed the horse's bridle. She'd never ridden this particular gelding, Smokey, an apt name, but she wasn't concerned about that now as Colin dismounted and then legged her up on to its back.

'What are you doing, Pippa?' Millie cried.

Robson whipped off his hat and wiped his sweating brow. '*I'll* go search, miss. You stay here.'

Pippa shook her head and put her feet into the stirrups, silently thanking the Fates that Colin shared the same height, making any adjustments to the stirrups unnecessary. 'I'll be as quick as I can.'

'This is madness!' Robson gripped Smokey's bridle. 'I don't want to have two people to rescue. Now get down, miss.'

Pippa leaned down to him. 'I need you here to save my family. No one can lead them to safety but you. I trust you to keep them from harm.'

Esther stepped forward. 'Phillippa Noble, get off that animal immediately! I forbid you to leave us.'

'No, Mother. Now heed Robson's instructions. I'll be back shortly.' A distant rifle shot sounded again, and she wrenched Smokey's head around and out of Robson's hold. 'I won't be long.'

She thundered away over the valley floor. The horse, sensing her urgency, gathered speed and she merely clung to him. The scent of smoke became stronger the nearer they came to the wooded slopes. Slowing down to a trot, Pippa scanned the area. 'Anyone there? Father!'

The silence urged her on and she guided Smokey up the rough cart track. Climbing higher, Pippa called out at intervals but received no answer. The trees and thick scrub limited her view. Rounding a slight bend, she looked up at the track ahead and gasped. Thin fingers of smoke filtered through the trees. The horse, alerted to the danger, threw its head and side-stepped.

'There now. There now.' She patted his neck. 'We're all right.'

At the top of the ridge, Pippa steered Smokey to a clearing, which afforded a view over the rolling hills and deep gullies stretching out for hundreds of miles. A large smoke cloud hung low. On the horizon, a thin red fire line zigzagged over a hill. Mesmerized, she sat watching it devour all in its path.

Turning away, she directed Smokey along the track towards Berrima. Attentive to every sound, Pippa frowned as she heard a distinct noise, a rumble. Thunder? Through the canopy of branches and smoke above her she peered at the sky, but it was clear blue, not a cloud in sight. A shiver of dread crept over her as she rode on, spurring the horse into a canter.

A shout. A crack of a whip. The wagon came upon her before she knew what happened. Smokey skidded into the scrub and Pippa gripped the reins as they whirled about.

'Christ Almighty!' Douglas Meredith stood up in the wagon, trying to keep control of his wild-eyed horse. A baby's crying added to the mayhem.

Pippa rode closer to the wagon, frowning at the strange, dazed look on Douglas's face. He was standing up in the wagon, clenching the reins similar to a Roman warrior in a chariot. His clothes were damp with sweat, streaked with grime. The baby continued to cry.

'Douglas?' She swallowed her shock as he continued to stare straight ahead. Her eyes flickered to the baby in a basket on the wagon floor, wedged in between two crates. 'Douglas, where is Amelia?'

He slowly turned his head towards her, his eyes vacant. 'Gone. It's all gone. Everything.'

Pippa thought her heart would stop beating. 'W-what do you mean?'

'Fire. All gone.' Suddenly he plopped down on the seat.

'Where's Amelia?'

'She was so brave . . .'

Pippa stifled a groan of dismay. Blinking rapidly, trying to concentrate, Pippa became aware once more of the distant crackle of flames. 'Did you fire your rifle for help?'

He shook his head, grimacing as though reliving painful memories.

Taking a deep breath, Pippa nodded. 'Go on down the valley, I'll be along soon. Millie and Robson will help you. I'm just looking for Father. We heard rifle shots. Have you seen anyone?'

'The road . . . cut off . . .' A shudder shook him.

'It is?' She looked up the track, expecting the blaze to appear any minute. The smoke was thick now, working its way across the ridge. Her alarm grew. 'I must look for Father. Go down to the homestead, Douglas, please. Take the baby to Millie.' With a last glance back at him, Pippa urged Smokey into the filtering gloom.

She rode until she began to cough and her eyes smarted. The roar of the fire could be clearly heard and Smokey baulked at every movement as his terror mounted.

Cupping her hands around her mouth, Pippa called out for her father. She waited for a few minutes and then hesitantly wheeled Smokey back the way they came. With every yard they took, her sense of unease grew. Then she saw it. A torn scrap of material caught on a branch. Wrenching it free, she studied it. It was the same brown colour as her father's jacket.

Scrambling off Smokey, Pippa screamed for her father to answer her. She ran into the scrub, stumbling in haste, dimly aware that she was spooking Smokey and he was trotting away from her.

'Father! Can you hear me?'

She darted to the right, peering around large boulders and tree trunks before running over to the left where the ground sloped away. She skidded down a few yards, searching the landscape for any sign of him. Her foot dislodged a rock and she tripped, landing on her knees.

'Father!' For a moment she knelt on the ground, exhausted. Despair waited to claim her but she refused to give up. With a frustrated sigh, she stood and wearily wiped a hand over her eyes. Where was he?

A flock of white cockatoos screeched above the trees. Abruptly, a kangaroo bounded down the slope nearly crashing into her before it jumped to the right and away. Then another came thumping over the top and down beside her, and then another. An opossum scuttled by, followed by a large fat wombat and two more smaller kangaroos. Pippa stared at the exodus as the animals and birds all headed east. From the west she heard what she thought to be the splintering of wood followed by a loud whooshing sound. The fine hairs on the back of her neck rose. The fire was close.

Rushing back up to the track, she caught her skirts on a bush and paused to unhook them. The snap and crackle grew louder. Straightening, she tore her skirts free and reached the top only to stop and stare at the orange flames licking the dry grass a few feet from her. Ash and embers floated in the air like snow. Smokey had gone. Fear closed her throat.

Lifting her skirts high, she ran down the track, heading for the entrance down into the valley. Thick smoke blanketed the countryside and crept into her lungs, slowing her down and making her cough. The roar of the fire urged her to keep going. A stiff, hot wind thrashed at the treetops, swirling the ash and embers about her head. The air seemed sucked dry and, apart from the crackle of flames, the bush was eerily quiet.

Pippa ran, the sound of her laboured breathing noisy in her ears. Her eyes smarted from the smoke. She tried to ignore the fire and the danger and just concentrated on getting down into the valley.

'Pippa!'

She spun around, heart pounding. A whoop of joy filled her as Gil galloped towards her. Never had she been so glad to see anyone in her life!

He reined in beside her, reached down to grab her arm and hoisted her up behind him. Swivelling in the saddle, he cupped her face in his hand, his eyes searching her for injury. 'Are you all right? We were out of minds with worry! What a stupid, senseless thing to do. I could shake you until your teeth rattle!'

'How did you know?' She coughed and it felt like razors were cutting into her chest. 'The-the road to Berrima is closed off,' she wheezed. 'How did you get through?'

'I came into the valley from the other side. I nearly had a seizure when they told me you'd gone off. What a foolish thing to do!'

'Father is out here. I cannot leave him. I found material on a branch. I know it is his jacket.' Throat parched, she paused and leaned her head against Gil's shoulder. 'We must find him.'

'Come, my sweet girl.' He kissed her forehead. 'We've yet to get to safety. Hold on to me.'

'But Father?'

He frowned, glancing over her head at the encroaching wall of flames. 'Pippa, if we stay here, we will die.'

She jerked back. 'No. We cannot leave now. He's out here somewhere.'

'I'll take you back to the homestead and then return to search for him.'

'That will waste time. No, Gil, I must go.' She went to slide off the horse's rump, but he grabbed her tight.

'I said no!'

She struggled, spooking his horse so that it turned in circles, nearly unseating them both.

Gil wrenched the reins, growling between clenched teeth.'Hold on!'

He spurred the horse on not giving her a chance to escape. With the last of her strength, she wrapped her arms around his waist as they began their descent. Above them the ridge erupted into a fiery blaze. The fire chased them down the track, its angry, hungry roar deafening.

Without warning, a blur of brown fur leaped from the high side of the track and belted into the side of them. Pippa had the sensation of falling, heard a cry and the horse's grunt as they sailed over the edge of the track.

She landed with a wallop that stunned her and knocked the breath from her body and then she was tumbling, rolling down the valley side. She banged into a tree and it brought her to a jarring stop, where she lay confused and shocked. As her mind cleared, she noticed Gil's horse scrambling to its feet some ten yards away. Within a few seconds it was up and racing away.

'Pippa!' Gil crawled up from below her and she grabbed his hand, hugging him to her in a fierce grip.

'Dear God, tell me you aren't hurt?' He panted. His cheek was cut and blood seeped from his hairline.

Pippa couldn't feel any pain at all at that moment and put her fingers to stem the blood flow on his cheek. 'I think I'm fine, but you are not.'

He touched his face. 'It's but a scratch.'

She looked up the hillside at the fingers of orange-red, spreading down to claim them. 'We'll never outrun it now.'

Gil used the tree as an aid to stand and then helped her up. 'We must try.'

She shook her head, swamped with rising panic. 'We cannot, Gil. Look!'

He ignored her pointing finger and instead hobbled down the slope, dragging her behind him.'If we can make it to the bottom and into the creek, we'll be safe.'

A sudden pain in her side made Pippa want to retch or faint or both. She stumbled after him, hardly heeding Gil's garbled instructions. Her spine tingled with every step, fearing the flames would scorch her back any second.

Gil, limping badly now, stumbled and fell to his knees. 'Jesus wept!' He swore again violently and then pushed her away. 'Go on, Pip. Run! I'll catch up.'

Horrified, she looked from him to the line of fire eating a circle around the valley rim. Every thought flashed through her mind at a rapid rate; her father, her mother, Hilary, Millie, Davy, Robson, the men, the horses . . . They would all burn in this hateful bushfire. What had she done to deserve such punishment? A feral rage built in her chest, tearing at her mind. No!

Gil coughed, gasping. 'Go, Pip. Now!'

She shook her head, anger giving her the strength of ten. 'Get up!'

She heaved him to his feet, shoving her shoulder under his armpit, taking his weight. Together they staggered down a few feet through the filthy smoke. The intense heat drenched their bodies with sweat, making their clothes seem heavier with every step.

'Here, look.' Gil pointed to a large hole; the entry to a wombat's burrow. He shuffled over to it and dropped to his knees, scraping away the dirt at the entrance. 'Get in! Quickly now. This will save us.'

She balked even though a piece of grass flared at her feet lit by a floating ember. 'In there? I won't fit!' Frightened beyond her senses, Pippa cried, the tears hot on her cheeks.

'Yes, you will.' Gil grabbed her shoulders and pushed her down. 'This burrow is the biggest I've ever seen and we'll not waste the opportunity. These things go a long way in. We can hide out the fire in there. Hurry now. Get on your stomach!'

Sobbing, and with visions of some mad creature coming out of the darkness to claw at her, Pippa squirmed backwards on her stomach into the black hole. The cool, damp mustiness was a relief from the heat, but the sheer blackness offered no comfort.

Gil squashed in after her, pushing her by the shoulders, but all improprieties had long gone for the sake of survival. Her toes tingled at the idea of being nibbled on by a wild beast. Pippa sniffed back her fear, keeping her gaze focused on the modest area of light beyond Gil's crumpled body. They were just far enough in to be out of harm's way, but they could still see and hear the fire around the burrow's entry.

Gil searched for her hand and held it. 'We're safe, unless a wombat takes exception to us sharing his home.'

Through the darkness she sensed his smile. 'I cannot believe you made me do this.'

'Rant at me later.' He squeezed her hand. 'You all right?'

'I think so.' She sniffed again and wiped her nose with her sleeve. The smell of dank earth mixed with the scent of smoke on their clothes. 'I feel as though I can't breathe.'

'Take deep slow breaths.'

'I'm frightened.'

'I won't let anything happen to you, I promise.' His face was so close that his breath brushed her cheeks.

'Not about me, but about Father, my family and the stud.' Lying squashed inside an animal's burrow further crushed her hope. She was useless to her family in here. She couldn't fight the fire and save her home. Emotion closed her throat but she refused to cry again. *I must be strong.*

Gil shifted his feet just inside the hole, his long legs cramped up and he rubbed them. 'The wind might shift.'

A roar came from outside the hole and they both jumped as flames swept across the entrance. The smell of burning grass and twigs filled their noses. They sat in silence for several minutes waiting for the grassfire to die out.

'Once it passes completely, we'll get out and head for the creek.' Gil squeezed her hand again as though he could transfer his courage to her. 'Your man Robson will have got everyone to safety.'

'And my Father?'

'Once you are safe I'll return for him.' He paused. 'He might even have made it to safety or turned back to Berrima.'

Pippa closed her eyes and sent up a silent prayer. 'I should be out there . . .' She moved a little, trying to find a comfortable position on her stomach. 'Did the fire reach Sutton Forrest and your home?'

'No.' His voice lowered. 'We were spared. The wind was favourable to us.'

'I'm pleased,' she whispered, her shoulders sagging at the enormity of what might face her when they crawled out of this tunnel.

'You're not alone, Pip. Should the stud be torched, I'll help you rebuild it. Don't worry.'

She couldn't speak. Rebuild? She shook her head in the dimness, weary at the thought of it. No. She wouldn't rebuild – not on Grant Lindfield's land.

# CHAPTER TWELVE

When the roar of the flames died, Pippa pushed at Gil. 'Let me out! I need to get out now.'

'Wait, let me see if it's safe.' He edged to the entrance and peeked out. Spot fires littered the immediate blackened area, plumes of smoke wafted from the ruined tree trunks. Gil crawled out of the hole and then turned to assist her.

Standing upright, Pippa brushed dirt from her dress and gazed around at their smouldering world. A wallaby corpse smoked to their right and the smell of fire seemed ingrained in her every pore, tasted thick on her tongue.

'Thank God.' Gil slumped to his knees, alarming Pippa so much she stood frozen.

'W-what?'

'The wind. The wind has shifted. Look.' He pointed to the torched trees and the ones that were spared waved slightly in a dying breeze, a breeze heading north and away from her home.

'Do you think it changed before reaching the stud?' She prayed it would be true, that her family and animals were secure.

'We must hope so.' Wearily, he staggered to his feet again and limped closer. 'Come, let us go and find out.'

She shook her head, her throat so parched she could barely swallow. 'I have to find my father.'

Gil nodded and took a deep breath. 'Very well, but first we'll go to the creek and drink. With this bad leg I couldn't carry you should you collapse from lack of water.' He smiled, tucking a tendril of her hair back behind her ear and she realized that she'd lost her bonnet.

Holding each other up, they started down the incline, stumbling and staggering. Gil limped, pain tightening his face with every step.

'Is the pain bad?'

'Not a bit.' He winked.

She gave him a wry smile, knowing he lied. In silence they carried on, the horror of the fire's aftermath behind every tree. Scorched native animals, barely alive, made no effort to run away, but simply watched them go by. Unable to stand their quiet suffering, Pippa averted her gaze.

As if by magic, the blaze's destruction ended. It was as though an invisible hand had drawn a line through the bush, one side black and glowing red, the other side untouched and normal.

'The wind did change in time,' Gil murmured. He was leaning heavily on her shoulder now, his weight pressing her down.

'The creek is nearby. It erupts out of the hillside further up.' She paused by a large rock and eased him down to sit on it. 'Stay here and I'll go get the water.'

'In what?' He held his hands up. 'We've no canteen.'

'I might be able to find something.' She took a step. 'I'll use your boot if I have to.'

He laughed softly. 'You go drink and when you're done come back for me. I'll have rested enough to walk the distance.'

She nodded, but hesitant to leave him, turned back. 'You'll be all right?'

Gil reached out and took her dirty hand and brought it to his lips. 'I'm fine. Just getting my breath back. Go.'

Confident he was safe to leave for the moment, she hitched up her torn skirts and darted away. Within moments the bush had swallowed Gil from sight, but she concentrated on getting to the creek. Thirst ravaged her, but so did unease. Something she couldn't identify pressed her on and when at last she struggled to the creek's edge, she fell to her knees in relief. Using her cupped hands, she drank the refreshing, although brackish water and splashed it over her face, washing away the filth, smoke and grime. In a daze, she watched the water drip on to her once respectable dress, adding to the stains already there.

After one more drink, she heaved herself up and turned back the way she'd come. Suddenly she stilled. Moving only her eyes, she glanced at the object to her right, half hidden in the long grass. A boot.

Pippa swallowed. Cautiously, she shuffled one foot forward an inch and winced when a pebble scraped against another, the sound seemed extraordinarily loud. She couldn't take her focus off the boot. A dark brown boot, needing a polish. Another step allowed her to see more and, leaning forward, she could see over the high grass.

She whimpered, too frightened to move. 'Father?' she whispered, her breath suspended on a quivering cry.

She shook her hands, steeling herself to investigate the form attached to the boot, the form hidden from her view by dry swaying grass. Sucking in a deep breath, she crept forward, closer, closer.

Lifting her chin, ready for whatever sight awaited her, Pippa turned her gaze to the open-eyed stare of her father.

The fear, the horror left her and she raced to his side. Gently she kneeled beside his head. As light as a butterfly's touch she ran her fingers over his eyes and closed them. They would see no more. 'I'm here, Father.'

Squirming on her bottom, she managed to lift his head on to her lap. 'I'm sorry I didn't reach you in time.' With her fingertips she combed his hair and then straightened his jacket, with its torn shoulder, and made him neat. 'I did look for you. Did you not hear me calling? Why didn't you answer me?'

A tear splashed on to his cheek and she hurriedly wiped it away. When a moan escaped her, she clapped a hand over her mouth. Her chest heaved, her heart would certainly burst from the pressure building. What could she do? Panic overwhelmed her. Wildly she looked around for help, but no one was there. She felt so alone, so vulnerable. A cry bubbled up, but she fought the impulse to give in to the emotion wanting to destroy her.

She stared down at her father, who strangely looked peaceful. The truth of the situation dawned harsh and raw. Her father was dead. He'd died alone in the bush with no one to hold his hand and comfort him in his last moments. The shock of it was too much, her breathing became laboured and she screamed when a bird squawked in the branches above.

Gil! She must get to Gil, he'd help her. She eased out from beneath her father and tenderly laid him back on the grass. 'I'm going to bring Gil, Father. I won't be long, I promise.'

Pippa scrambled to her feet, tripping in her skirts, and raced through the trees, blind to everything around her.

'Pippa! I'm here.' Gil was slowly making his way to her, using a sturdy stick as a cane.

'Oh God, Gil,' she sobbed and fell into his arms. 'I found Father.'

Lying in the tin bath in her bedroom, Pippa listened to the muffled sounds of the household. Outside, twilight lingered, the hateful day still not yet ready to end. She reached for the teacup Millie had brought in and sipped the over-sweet brew. Tiredness sapped her strength, it would have been so easy to close her eyes and drift away, but she had to get out and face the ordeal waiting her attention.

A knock preceded Millie, who entered quietly and shut the door. 'How are you feeling?'

'Exhausted.'

'Mr Ashford-Smith has gone home. His father came for him in their gig. The doctor said his leg shouldn't have any permanent damage, thankfully. His poor knee is twice the size it should be. He's not allowed to walk on it for a few days. He said he'll see you at the funeral, but should you need him before then to send a note.'

'He's a wonderful man. A true friend. I couldn't have made it without him. I owe him my life.' Pippa nodded, thinking of Gil and his wonderful support made the tears gather behind her eyes, but she'd not cry again. She'd sobbed the entire time walking from the creek back to the homestead to raise the alarm, that had been her time for grieving, now she had to be strong for everyone.

'Yes, indeed. He is a rare breed, Pippa. One you shouldn't take for granted. He is the type you should marry.'

'Like Robson?' It was the first time Pippa mentioned that she was aware of the subtle connection between her good friend and her overseer, not that she minded. In a harsh world, happiness had to be found wherever available.

Millie blushed. 'Yes, like Robson.'

Pippa sighed with tiredness and misery. 'I care for Gil too much to marry him, Millie. Once a woman is married she has to change. How could I run this stud being married?'

'It might be worth a try. Is your independence so important to you? Besides, Mr Ashford-Smith would be a help not a hindrance.'

'Perhaps.' She dismissed the thought, not wanting to think about such things now. 'How are Mother and Hil?'

'Rather good, considering. Hilary is seeing the doctor out as we speak.'

'We are fortunate he was in the district.' Pippa swished the water, reliving the events of the day. 'Though there was nothing he could do for dear Father, his weak heart couldn't stand the strain of escaping the fire.'

Millie sighed, running her fingers over the black mourning dress laid out for Pippa to wear. 'Your mother spoke to Mr Ashford-Smith and his father for some time. I think they were speaking of the funeral arrangements.'

Pippa sat up straighter, the water splashing dangerously close to the side. 'Mother shouldn't concern herself with that. I'll do it all.'

'I think it helps her. She has been very brave, Pippa. She knows you've been through an awful time. Let her take some of the work from you.'

'I'm not used to mother being efficient. I expect hysterics, not this sudden strength of character. Where has it come from? She's never been one to shoulder responsibilities.' Climbing out of the bath, Pippa reached for her towel and wrapped it around her.

'You know sometimes certain people need an event to occur in their lives which makes them change.' Millie took Pippa's house slippers out from under the bed and placed them near the chair in the corner. 'May I speak plainly?'

'Of course.'

'Your mother is a capable woman, I've seen glimpses of it. Oh, she pretends to have a nervous disposition, but I think it's all make-believe, just so she can get her own way.'

Pippa frowned as she donned underwear. It was true. In England her mother had been content to watch her husband blunder from one mistake to another and was quite satisfied to sit back and berate him for it, but after coming to this country she had slowly altered her outlook. At long last, she was willing to make an effort, to take some responsibility regarding how this family survived, instead of being an idle bystander.

'What will happen now, Pippa?'

'The stud will continue, it has to for I must provide for Mother and Hilary.' She shrugged. The future appeared bleak without her father. Despite his tendency to often let them down, their lives had never been dull because of it. Through all their ups and downs he'd been there, the head of the family. However, from this time on it was up to her to rebuild the family fortune. Could she do it? Was it really possible to make the stud viable, to pay off Grant's loan, to live well and happily? How many times had she boasted she could do it herself? Had her vain bragging tempted fate? Well, whether she had or not, it was her time to show them all that she could do it. She would make this business a triumph or die in the attempt.

'You could always sell.'

'No.' The thought repulsed her. 'Besides, I want Father buried here as I will be when it's my time.'

Refolding the discarded towel, Millie sighed deeply. 'Douglas also has many decisions to make. He is a shattered man.' She stepped up to tie Pippa's corset strings. 'He was speaking to the police constable when I left him. Poor Amelia. It's so tragic, our dear friend gone too. I shall miss her.'

The Meredith tragedy. Pippa shivered as the cold black silk of the dress slid over her. Amelia had died in the fire, trying to save the house from the ravenous flames. Douglas, hurrying back from Berrima arrived in time only to save their baby son and drag Amelia's body out of the house. He couldn't revive her and as the flames swept around him, he managed to escape with the baby. His servants had fled before he arrived.

Pippa paused and glanced down at her ruined clothes by the bath. 'I never want to see that dress again. Please tell Cissie to burn those clothes.'

Millie nodded and headed for the door. 'I'll check on Davy and the baby. Thankfully the little mite is fast asleep and too young to know he's lost his mother. Dinner will be late tonight.'

'I doubt many of us can eat anyway. Would you ask Hilary to sit with Mother? I shall talk to Douglas. Though what I'm going to say I have no idea.'

'It will be difficult to comfort a man who has lost everything except his son and the days ahead will not be any easier. Douglas was out on the verandah the last time I looked.'

Pippa brushed out her hair and then tied it up with a black ribbon. After slipping on her house shoes she left her room and went out on to the verandah.

Douglas sat slumped on the step. He'd not washed and the smell of smoke clung to his blackened clothes. She stepped closer to him and gently laid her hand on his shoulder. He didn't move.

'She asked me not to go into Berrima this morning.' His low voice barely reached her. 'She said she wasn't feeling too well. But still I went.'

Sighing, Pippa sat beside him on the step, feeling helpless. 'Amelia wouldn't want you to blame yourself.'

'Then whose fault is it?' He stared out across the valley, not blinking.

'It's no one's fault. It was a fire. An accident.'

'I should have been there.'

She tried to steer him away from self-examination. 'What do you plan to do now? Rebuild?'

A spasm passed over his face. 'I think it would kill me to go back. How can I live there without her?'

Pippa looked away, over the darkening land. 'Well, there's time enough for you to decide that later. You and the baby must stay here until you have sorted out your immediate future.'

'What future do we have without Amelia?'

'Amelia once told me she had a sister in England, could she not come out here and help you for a time?'

'There is so much to think about, so many decisions.' Douglas shook his head. 'Perhaps I should go there, and give her my son to care for. I cannot see to a baby and the homestead is gone. There is so much to consider. . . .'

'Now is not the time to make hasty decisions, Douglas. No one expects you to have all the answers right away.'

He took her hand in his soot-blackened one. 'I'm sorry about your father. He was a gentleman, a good man.'

She nodded, her throat too tight to speak. She didn't want to think about her own loss, the effects were too painful.

'Will you sell up?'

Pippa swallowed. 'No. The stud means a great deal to me.'

Douglas's eyes softened. 'You've done him proud, Pippa and I know you'll continue to in the years ahead.'

Tears welled and she blinked them back. 'I hope so.'

He turned to stare blindly towards the distance and Pippa's heart turned over in response to the pitiful sight he made. Gone was the robust, jolly man who laughed and joked all the time. Before her eyes he seemed to grow old and a wave of uselessness washed over her once more. What words would soothe his loss? How easily it could have been her who had lost not just her father, but also everything. She shuddered at the thought. The stud had been spared by a twist of fate and now she must make it a grand success to honour her father. The weight of responsibility descended on her shoulders like a blanket.

The music drew the dancers to the open floor. A rainbow of colours twirled before her as men swung their partners around. Pippa stood by the French doors, where a cool midnight breeze tempered the summer heat. Christmas was only a week away and even though the family was still in mourning they had agreed that Hilary should have a party for her engagement announcement.

Pippa smiled at Hilary, who floated by in the arms of Toby Talbot. Sydney's elite filled the two floors of the harbourside mansion, whose owner Pippa couldn't even bear to look at. Grant Lindfield. He'd insisted on hosting the party, much to Pippa's disgust.

Her first glimpse of him this evening on arrival had been enough to damage her heart again. His polite courtesy towards his young wife made Pippa feel sick to her shining silver slippers. She should have pleaded a headache and remained at the Talbots' house, only that wouldn't have been kind to Hilary, whose night this was.

However, it galled her that Grant had made friends, became known and liked. The devilish part of her wanted the whole town to reject him as he'd rejected her.

The party atmosphere was lost on her. She ached to be home, but she'd bowed to pressure from her mother that she was needed on this trip into Sydney to recuperate from the tragedies of the bushfire. Then Toby Talbot had proposed to Hilary after seeking an audience with their mother and sadly Pippa felt she was losing another member of her family.

'I do believe you have been avoiding me.' Grant's whisper behind her ear sent tiny shivers along her arms.

'Why should you believe that?' She remained unmoving, keeping her gaze on the dancers as he stepped to her side.

'I haven't seen you smile all night.'

'I find it hard to smile when I buried my father only weeks ago.'

'Of course, forgive me.' He paled, his blue eyes darkened. 'Perhaps we could go for a stroll outside in the gardens and talk?'

'Perhaps not.' The thought of being alone with him was too much, would shatter her reserve. He had a way of easing people into a comfortable companionship; one where your tongue ran away with itself and revealed more than you cared to. She couldn't afford to be weak in his presence.

'Please, Pippa.'

It was so hard to resist him, always had been. With the slightest of nods and a quick glance at him from under her lashes, she allowed him to steer her out the doors and down a dimly lit pebbled path. They rounded a bend and came to a bench overlooking the harbour's black water, shimmering in the moonlight.

Grant indicated for her to sit and then did the same. 'When do you go back to Berrima?'

'Tomorrow hopefully. There is much to do and I have many responsibilities, especially now that my neighbour, Meredith, has returned to England and has asked me to be the caretaker of his property.'

'Responsibilities indeed. It must be an encumbrance sometimes?'

'It has its moments, but I only have to ride through the valley or see a foal born to know I am blessed.' The vision played in her mind, bringing a smile to her face.

'I must visit your beloved home again.'

She spun to stare at him. 'Why? Aren't you happy with your returns on the stud?'

'Indeed. I didn't mean that I wanted to inspect the accounts, for heaven's sake. I simply meant I'd like to visit, as a guest. When will you stop seeing me as the devil incarnate?'

'When I am free of your hold.'

He sighed. 'I'm very proud of you and your business abilities. I didn't expect to see some money for a time yet.'

She lifted her chin, staring out over the water. 'The quicker we pay you back the sooner the valley is mine.'

'It is yours.'

'Not yet it isn't, but it will be. One day soon.'

Silence dragged out between them for several minutes until Grant shifted on the bench and looked at her. 'Your mother wrote to me of the fire and your heroics.' He smiled. 'I could imagine you scraping into a wombat's burrow. You always were the adventurous one. Do you remember that time you jumped that impossibly high hedge while on the Asquith's hunt?' He chuckled. 'You nearly broke your neck.'

She gave an unladylike shrug and sighed dramatically. 'I couldn't let you be the only one to make the jump.'

His light laughter drifted on the breeze. 'What about the time we went swimming in the lake and you took off all your clothes.'

A grin escaped as she remembered that day. 'The water made my clothes so heavy I nearly drowned that is why I took them off.'

Grant shook his head in wonder. 'I was speechless. Never had I known a young lady to do such a thing.'

'You made me reckless.' She pushed at his arm. 'I wanted to show you that I could keep up with you and your sophisticated friends.'

He laughed. 'All my friends were in love with you, but your wildness kept them silent.'

'There was only one love I wanted.' She recoiled as soon as the words left her mouth. Now wasn't the time to dredge up old memories, old pain. It would do no good.

'I've missed you.'

Pippa stiffened. 'Obviously not enough.'

'Pip . . .'

She rose, shook out her skirts and looked down at him. The moonlight shone on his black hair. 'I want to go inside, Grant.'

He took a deep breath and nodded, slowly getting to his feet. A frown lined his forehead. 'Pippa you must understand . . .'

Shaking her head, she walked away. 'The past is long gone, Grant. I have to accept that you chose another over me. It's not been easy, but I've had time to help me.'

'My reasons—'

Her footsteps faltered slightly. 'I care naught for your reasons, not now when it is too late.' She stopped and pinned him with a glare. 'Remember though, Grant, in the years to come, that I was all yours and you turned your back on me.' She headed for the house, but he grabbed her elbow and twirled her around to him.

'What about you? Are you going to let this fester inside you like a canker? So I didn't choose you, what of it? I never said I'd marry you.'

Her temper flashed inside her brain like lightening and she welcomed it, aching to finally respond to his rejection. He'd left for India without giving her the chance. Her lips curled back in a sneer. 'No, you never said the words but you gave me hints, your actions led me to believe that I was what you wanted! You let me *hope*!' She tore her elbow out of his grasp, anger blinding her to reason. 'You knew how much I loved you, how long I had loved you. You knew and yet did nothing to soften the blow.'

'I didn't want you to love me.' His voice was low and irate. 'I never asked for you to. In the end I was longing to escape.'

'Escape? From me?' She didn't think he could hurt her anew, but he had. Suddenly she became cold, so very cold. Shivering, she rubbed her bare arms. The organ that was her heart seemed to be wounded beyond all help, as though a lance had embedded itself into her chest and was slowly turning.

Grant swore and ran his hand through his hair. 'I didn't mean it like that. What I meant was, I didn't want to be responsible for you and the love you bore me. It, and your family's circumstances, were burdens I didn't want to carry with me into the army.'

'Burdens?' Pippa whispered. She wanted to stay angry, for anger was an emotion she could find strength from to defeat him, but it wouldn't come to her aid this time. His words kept stabbing her, cutting her. Moreover, his reference to her family's circumstances, rather her father's gambling debts, filled her with the deep-rooted shame she'd always tried to hide. Now, she was mortified that the man she had loved so passionately had held such a low opinion of her family. Had, in fact, been reluctant to be associated with them. Swiftly it all became so apparent. Stepping back, she stared at him, looked past his polished coat of civility to the real man beneath. 'You are supercilious.'

'No . . .'

'You . . . you never really liked us, did you?'

'Of course I did.' He had the grace to appear shocked.

'You put up with us for your father's sake, didn't you?'

'This is nonsense, Pippa.' But his gaze didn't quite reach hers.

A small cry escaped before she clamped a hand over her mouth. She felt cheated. All those years they had been friends were wiped away on a cloud of lies. He'd exposed all their memories as falsehoods. She wanted to hide, to crawl away somewhere and care for her raw, bleeding injuries. Flashes of distorted memories came to mind, the times he'd excused himself from their company and gone off with his friends, the times he'd not called at their house when he was close by, the times he frowned whenever her father led Howard into the study for a private talk. It all came back to her now with meaning. What she hadn't understood as a girl she now understood as a woman.

When he reached out to touch her, she shied away, nearly tripping on her hem in haste to put distance between them. She couldn't fathom the look in his eyes. Oh, there was tenderness for sure, but something else. Sympathy? Pity? Bile rose to her throat, she wanted to die. With a strength she didn't know she possessed, she straightened and walked away from him and the past that was no longer true.

Inside the house, the noise and heat assailed her senses, making her dizzy. She flinched when someone laughed loudly nearby.

'Pippa?' Hilary was beside her in seconds, holding her hand, her brown eyes full of worry. 'Are you unwell?'

'I'm fine.' Pippa forced herself to say, knowing that Hilary would not stop worrying if she didn't. The familiar wave of protectiveness hit Pippa as it always did. Hilary was the softer, more delicate of the two of them and it had been Pippa's job since they could walk to protect her, shield her from anything unpleasant.

'You don't look it.'

Pippa went to deny it again when Grant's wife strolled by clinging like a limpet to the arm of an older man. Pippa's stomach churned.

Hilary, following Pippa's gaze, tutted. 'Stop, Pippa. Stop chasing after rainbows. Grant has married and you must overcome it. You've got—'

Pippa silenced her with an ice-cold glare. 'To me, Grant Lindfield is dead.'

Hilary gasped in astonishment. 'What's happened? Where were you just now?'

An eerie calm settled over Pippa's brain. All her pain dimmed, cooled and hardened into a knot of hatred. Abruptly everything was clear, in focus.

Taking a deep breath, Pippa's eyes narrowed at Grant as he entered the room. 'Do you know, Hil, that the truth doesn't always set you free? Sometimes, it is better to keep up the pretence. Grant Lindfield will find that out to his cost. I'll make certain of that.'

# CHAPTER THIRTEEN

Esther sighed, steepled her fingers together on the desk and waited as Phillippa paced the room, kicking out her skirts at every turn. Soon, she knew, her daughter would explode. Phillippa's short temper had become even easier to ignite in the six months since Gerald's death. She looked pale and far too thin.

She glanced at Grant, sitting casually but his eyes were narrowed on her daughter. He was here alone, visiting for the week and the atmosphere was thick with tension. Phillippa was polite to him and no more. They had talked business last night but other than that they spoke rarely.

Her gaze switched to Robson standing beside the desk. The man looked concerned and he had reason to. His news hadn't been good. That another labourer had left for the gold fields hit them hard, for he was the eighth man to slink off in the night in as many weeks. They couldn't run the stud without manpower.

She heaved another deep sigh that sounded loud in the room. The labourer's defection had sent her into a melancholy mood. She missed Hilary. Oh she was pleased she had married Toby and lived happily in Sydney, yet she did miss their little chats. She could talk to Hilary, but not to Phillippa. Strangely enough she didn't miss Gerald as much as she thought she would. A woman should miss her husband after he's gone, but then he'd never been the kind of man that had deserved her undying devotion. He'd caused her too much suffering and embarrassment for that.

Not for the first time she wondered what the last months would have been like if he still lived. Would they have grown to such prosperity and be in the position they were at the present? She doubted it. Phillippa was the driving force of the family now, not him. Their daughter worked terribly hard to give them a good life, a respectable life. No more did they have to run from creditors, move house or hide from pitying friends.

Beyond Phillippa's pacing, through the window, Esther gazed at the valley. They'd done well to position the house so pleasantly. As always the view gave her satisfaction. Out there was security. Mares and their foals grazed in white fenced fields. In the distance, sheep studded the cleared sides of the valley. Closer still, lush lawns and gardens grew down the slope to end at the creek.

A servant scuttled by the window. In the quick flash she saw, she thought it to be Eve. She heard Millie and the cook talking in the next room, no doubt discussing the week's menu. What a fine sensible woman that Millie was, Phillippa had done well to befriend her. Esther glanced again at Robson, he was a good man, they wouldn't have done so well without him. She was glad he and Millie married a few weeks ago. They suited each other and were obviously in love. Davy needed a father too. Esther frowned. Would Davy be as close as she would get to having a grandchild? Poor Hilary still wasn't with child and they'd been married three months.

Abruptly, Phillippa's pacing blocked Esther's view again. She studied her daughter, noticing the frown she wore, that she always seemed to wear now. Something had happened to her some months ago, she didn't know what it was that changed Phillippa, but something certainly had. Not long after the fire and Gerald's death, she lost all her softness, became hard. She demanded the best from everyone and usually got it. Her Phillippa became a work demon, a strict business-women with a singlemindedness that actually frightened Esther in its intensity. Phillippa never laughed any more, the most they could hope for was a grim smile or a wry lift of her mouth. Her stiff resolve to make the stud a success had taken a toll on the happy young woman she had been.

Esther didn't understand her, she was the first to admit it. The stud gave them a steady income and, added to that, they had the yearly wool clippings, rent from two shops Phillippa had bought in Goulburn, the profits from the half share in the timber mill in Mittagong recently bought and lastly the cattle she pastured on the vacant Meredith property. Those in England who had taunted at the Noble's bankruptcy, at their inability to rise again would be silenced if they saw them now. They lived very comfortably, so why then did Phillippa insist on looking for other ways to earn more money? It ruled her life and Esther didn't comprehend it. The Lindfield loan was getting repaid and the stud a growing success, so she hoped that perhaps now Phillippa would relax. Maybe she would think about marrying Gil Ashford-Smith and have children. The poor boy had waited long enough for certain, and was violently in love with her.

'Mother!'

Esther shook herself, realizing that Phillippa had been talking. 'Forgive me, dear, I was miles away.'

Phillippa raised an eyebrow, her face a mask of irritation. 'Indeed!' She folded her arms and tapped her foot. 'I was saying that we can no longer keep paying the outrageous wages that labourers demand. I'll not see our profits dwindle to satisfy the greed of men who end up wasting their wages in inns and brothels.'

Esther flinched at her words. Phillippa's bluntness always surprised her. 'Well, what do you mean to do?'

Grant flexed his arms and straightened in the chair. 'The gold fields are attracting not only men from this region but from the whole country and beyond the oceans. Those who don't go seeking gold know they can command high wages to landowners needing assistance.'

Pippa snorted and paced again. 'I'll not be held to ransom from workers who work no harder despite the higher rates!'

'You're acting as though the departing labourers are slighting you.' Grant shook his head. 'They aren't. They are just looking for ways to better themselves.'

'At my expense!' Pippa glared at him. 'I'll not go under due to their lack of loyalty.'

'Will you stop that infernal pacing, dearest?' Esther frowned. 'You exhaust me.' She put a hand to her heart. She never rested easy when Grant and Phillippa were in close proximity. Her daughter's unpredictable nature in regards to Grant kept everyone who knew her on edge, waiting for her to do something untoward. Thankfully, the past had not repeated itself and Phillippa had done nothing to cause scandal between the two families so far.

Stopping by the window that looked out over the valley, Pippa drew breath. 'We must think of a way to compensate our expenses in wages.' She nibbled her fingernail, forehead creased in concentration. 'These damn gold diggings! They will destroy us if we aren't careful.'

Robson nodded. 'And you can't tell me that every man who goes there is finding gold. So many families will be ruined by man's greed.'

Pippa's head snapped up. 'Of course! That's the answer.' Her brown eyes shone. 'There must be men down there who have lost everything and have no employment. If we go to Melbourne and offer good wages and transport back here, then I'm certain some would grab the opportunity.'

Robson scowled. 'You want to go to the gold fields?'

'It's the only answer.'

'No, Phillippa.' Horrified, Esther shook her head and painfully rose to her feet. Today her joints ached worse than ever. 'Gold fields are unlawful places. Wild. No place for a woman. Robson will go.'

'Mother, we have very few men left here to run the stud. We cannot spare Robson.'

Esther stared at her. 'And you cannot go alone. I forbid it.'

'I've never heard of such foolishness.' Grant stood, his expression showing his surprise. 'This is utterly ridiculous, Pippa. You can't go there.'

Pippa's expression was one of triumph. 'I don't plan to go alone. I'll ask Gil to accompany me. We work well as a team and will soon have labourers back here and the stud shall go on as before.'

'I thought you two were quarrelling again?' Esther stepped from behind the desk. 'I've never known two people who argue as much as you and he do.'

'Our quarrels never last long nor are serious.' She shrugged. 'He was unhappy that I won our race from Mittagong to here.'

Esther raised an eyebrow. 'I wish you'd behave more ladylike. Also, Gil said you cheated.'

'Is it my fault he didn't nominate the route? Of course I'd choose the quicker way.'

'But through unknown bushland? You could have been lost and never found!' She shook her finger at her wayward child as Pippa started to protest. 'He had a right to be angry. Your every action worries the life out of him and us.'

'Nonsense,' she tutted and turned for the door. 'He just doesn't like to be beaten by a woman.'

'The whole district enjoys gossiping about your behaviour both in business and socially.'

Pausing, Phillippa glanced over her shoulder. 'Men gossip about me being in business because I beat them at their own game and social gossip keeps people guessing about me, which in turn helps my business interests. They really know nothing about me and if the district actually knew what I was up to they'd have a lot more to gossip about!' She gave Grant a defiant stare and left the room, with Robson following.

'You need to rein her in, Esther,' Grant murmured. 'She's too headstrong. I'm frightened by her ruthlessness in business. There are men who will not like her interference.'

'Like you?'

Grant shrugged and stepped to the door. 'My time here is short, Pippa can do nothing to hurt my interests.' With a small bow he left.

Esther walked to the window and watched her daughter stride down the path towards the creek. She hoped Gil would hurry up and propose. Phillippa was too wound up all the time. She'd always been a bit highly strung but not to this extreme. There were days when her daughter's eyes burned fever bright with some secret no one knew of. No challenge was too hard for Pippa, no task too difficult. And now she was planning to venture to the lawlessness of the gold fields.

Esther turned away from the window and worried her fingernail with her teeth. She was getting too old for all this anxiety. Looking around the room, noting the accounts on the desk, the ledgers on the shelf, it dawned on her that with Pippa gone, she would be in sole charge of the stud. For a moment panic filled her, then her heart rate steadied and her mind cleared. Never in her life had she been allowed to participate in business matters, much to her annoyance, as she was certain she couldn't have muddled it any worse than Gerald had done. Yet, now she had a chance.

She straightened her shoulders and lifted her chin. A small smile played on her lips as she left the room.

Pippa shuddered as a drop of rain slipped under her collar. The grey wash blighted the landscape and reduced visibility. Her rented horse stumbled on the muddy, rutted road. She gathered in the reins, not yet familiar with this mount. They had agreed at the start of organizing this venture that they'd not take their own beloved mounts and instead take a selection of horses from the Ashford-Smith stables in Sydney. Now she wished she'd insisted on bringing Honey.

To take her mind off the inclement weather and her wet clothes, she thought of the few days they'd spent in Sydney before sailing to Melbourne. She had managed to spend an hour with Hilary and Toby. She was delighted they were blissfully happy in their sedate way.

At times, she missed Hilary's steadying influence, but thankfully, she'd made her life so busy that Hilary's absence wasn't as acute as it might have been. Besides, she had Millie and was grateful.

Unbidden, Grant came to mind and she straightened in the saddle.

Her plan to see him ruined was gradually taking shape. He knew nothing of her revenge and she smiled inside at the thought. Let him think that she harboured no ill feelings towards him. Let him assume she believed his silly lies that he'd always been her friend. God rot him! She knew the truth and nothing would ever make her think of him in a kind way again, but she could pretend. Oh yes, she was doing exactly what he had done for years.

His infrequent visits to the valley allowed her to make veiled inquires about his investments and business dealings, which later she made sure to be secretly a part of. With Gil's help, she had already bought shares in one of Grant's companies, unbeknownst to anyone, by using an agent. At the time, it had taken all her capital, which had been difficult to hide from her mother, but she'd done it. If all her plans came to fruition, the day would arrive when she would be wealthier than Grant and ever so slowly she would begin to buy up his properties, reduce him to nothing. Her goal was Lindfield Manor in Yorkshire. One day it would be hers.

A splatter of rain dislodged from an overhead tree branch, hit Pippa's face and she jerked her mind back to the present. The wretched day matched the horrid journey since leaving Sydney harbour. They had endured stormy days at sea, being tossed around like a cork in a bucket, hugging the coastline down to Melbourne. The appalling weather, not at all summery, continued on their arrival and holed them up in their hotel for over a week before Pippa lost all patience and decided to head out for the gold fields anyway, against Gil's angry demands to stay.

She slowed the horse's stride to glimpse at her companions. Gil's handsome profile seemed to be etched in granite, so cold and detached did he look. They hadn't spoken to each other since that morning. Whereas Augusta rode hunched over the saddle in dejected misery. Pippa shook her head. Augusta had insisted on accompanying them on this journey, wanting to share the adventure. So, she had no one to blame but herself if she now found it harder than expected. Behind them rode Mick, Gil's man, leading the packhorse.

Shivering from the cold, she looked over at Gil again. She wasn't used to his silence, his indifference. She relied on his humour and good spirits to cheer her, to save her from becoming too harsh. Usually, Gil was one to never take anything seriously. He laughed away concerns with a sense of ease that impressed those who knew him. She enjoyed his company. His intelligence and caring made him a perfect friend, but lately they'd been bickering more often than not and she wasn't sure why.

Their argument this morning was regrettable, certainly, but she stood by her decision. Nothing could be gained by being cooped up in a hotel room. What was a bit of rain, for heaven's sake?

Pippa frowned and thought hard, trying to remember when they had last spent a day without some heated discussion on some subject or other. With surprise she concluded that most times, Gil started these snappy little word wars. Why? Why was he changing from her cheery friend into this man of sullenness whenever he was in her company? Their friendship had turned slightly for the worse in the last few months. Sometimes Gil went from being devoted to near hating her. None of it made sense.

'Pippa?' Gil suddenly reined in closer.

Her head snapped up and she stared at him. 'Sorry, I didn't hear you.'

'I said we should stop and make camp. I've checked the map and there isn't another inn for miles yet. We've seen no shelter for an hour. The evening is drawing in earlier with this weather.'

Nodding, she peered into the winter gloom, praying for a wayside inn to appear from nowhere. 'I guess you're right, but it shan't be a comfortable night for us.'

'No.' His green eyes narrowed at her for a moment and she expected to hear his grievances again. Instead, he twisted around in the saddle and called for Mick to search for a suitable campsite.

A short time later they reined in at a small clearing, showing evidence of an old campfire. Gil and his man rigged up a canvas sheet as a sort of shelter to cook under and erected two tents while Pippa worked hard to get a fire burning hot enough to boil water for a pot of tea.

As Gil predicted the light faded under heavy, slate-grey clouds. The fire spat and spluttered in vain against the misty drizzle, that it held any embers at all was a miracle.

Pippa shifted her weight, flexing each aching foot. There was nowhere dry to sit, could she stand all night? Glancing over at the forlorn tents being buffeted by the rain, she shivered again. Sleeping in one would be no pleasure for Gil had carried them only as a precaution. They never really expected to need them because maps and information they'd gleaned since arriving in Melbourne showed many inns on the route to the gold fields. Stupidly they were not prepared for sleeping rough.

As if to make their little camp more miserable, the wind blew again, slanting the rain in under the awning. Behind her, she heard Gil curse as he and Mick secured the horses for the night.

'I should have listened to Mama,' Augusta sniffed, pulling her coat tighter around her shoulders. 'She said I should not go with you.'

'We'll have a hotel room for tomorrow night, I'm certain,' Pippa soothed.

Augusta wiped her damp hair off her face. 'We should have kept riding and found proper shelter. It was silly to stop out here in the middle of the bush.'

'Where is your sense of adventure?' Pippa frowned at her friend's petulance. 'I never thought you'd be the one to complain about one night of being uncomfortable.'

A large sneeze erupted from Augusta, bodily shaking her. Pippa stepped closer and peered at her. A sickening thud of fear gripped her as Augusta raised watery eyes and a flushed face. In a flash Pippa felt her friend's forehead and even though her fingers were numb with cold, the heat from Augusta's face shocked her.

'I'm all right, Pippa.'

'No, you're not, by God!' Pippa pulled her so close to the fire they risked being singed. 'Why didn't you tell me you felt ill?'

'I'd only have slowed you down and become a responsibility.' Augusta swayed. 'But I seem to be getting worse.'

'You silly fool!' Pippa hugged her and then quickly pulled away to look around for Gil.

'No, don't let him know.' Augusta shook her head, eyes pleading. 'He'll worry too much, take risks. I shall be well by morning.'

'In this weather?' Pippa snorted.

'It's just over an hour's ride back to that last inn we passed.' Augusta trembled, her face grew redder. 'I could—'

'We have the tent. Why not lie down for a while? I'll make you some tea.'

'The tent is damp, everything we have is damp. No, it's best if I go back.'

Gil stepped into the circle of weak light cast by the pitiful fire. 'We'll all go back.' He looked at his sister, anger tightening his face. 'You should have told us. I am responsible for your welfare.'

'I refuse to be coddled like a child. A few sniffles won't see me perish.'

'Heaven forbid,' Gil snapped.

Thunder clapped and the rain increased, drumming on the canvas and drowning out their voices.

To be heard, Gil leaned close to Pippa's ear. 'This is your fault!'

'I didn't know she was ill.' She hissed back. 'If I'd known we'd have stayed at the hotel.'

Gil ripped his hat off and slapped it against his leg. 'You never think of anyone besides yourself. Everything must begin and end with you and your obsession to be important and unbelievably rich.'

Outraged by his surprise attack, Pippa bristled. 'How dare you!'

'Oh, I dare all right when it comes to my sister's safety.'

'I didn't beg you to accompany me, and I certainly didn't ask Augusta to come.'

'I should never have agreed to this madness.'

'Then why did you? I didn't make you, did I?'

'How could I refuse you?' His eyes narrowed, darkened to the colour of wet moss. 'You are selfish, Phillippa Noble. I've put up with it in the past, but not any more.'

'Selfish! If you call taking care of my family, of putting them first, selfish, then I am as you claim.' She raised her chin, fighting back the hurt his words caused. 'I do what I do for my family's security. For years we've struggled to maintain some scrap of decency out of the mess my father placed us in. I will never allow us to be in that situation again.'

Gil lingered a moment, his face close to hers. Some of his anger died and a look of confusion crossed his face. His gaze dropped to her lips, to her heaving chest and back to her eyes.

Pippa felt a sudden tingling in the pit of her stomach. Shocked by the sensation she drew back and quickly knelt to fiddle with a stick poking out of the fire. She knew that feeling, that awareness, she'd grown used to it over the years for she felt it whenever Grant was near.

Physical attraction.

Frowning, she jammed the stick into the embers. Why now? Why with Gil? He was her friend. She couldn't have survived the last couple of years without him. So, why now did it have to change? Oh, they had humorously flirted with each other before, when they first met, but it had been safe, trusting. Never had they exchanged such an intense look as they did just now. She didn't want it. Didn't want to feel anything but friendship for him. Why did he have to change what they had? She wasn't looking for love. It had been an emotion that near ruined her before, she wasn't too eager to experience it again. Besides, she had a business to run and nothing could get in the way of that, not yet.

Pippa shook her head and, for a moment more, ignored the brother and sister talking on the opposite side of the fire so she could gather her thoughts. Her powerful reaction to Gil must be due to the circumstances they were in; a stormy night, stranded in the bush with a sick loved one. Well, she could handle any situation. Hadn't she been tested so many times before?

'Pippa?'

She glanced up at Gil, his stance rigid, as though he could read her thoughts and she felt heat flow into her face that had nothing to do with the fire. 'Yes?'

'We'll never make it back to that inn tonight, but being out in this weather will only make Augusta worse.'

'I know.' She nodded, pushing their argument to the back of her mind. 'The best we can do is make the fire bigger to keep her warm. I can make her a seat of sorts out of my coat. It's dry on the inside.'

Gil nodded. 'Make some tea. Mick and I will try to find drier wood.' He wrapped Augusta in his coat and then stepped nearer to Pippa. 'If she gets worse, I'll blame you.' He turned and stalked out into the night.

His whispered warning lingered on the moist air. Pippa busied herself at the fire once more, finally creating a large blaze. Anger and resentment burned. How dare Gil speak to her so rudely? She would show him. She would show them all. Come morning, she'd send them home and go on alone. Once before she'd put her trust in a man, only to be fed false, but never again. She didn't need Gil Ashford-Smith with his harsh words and smouldering looks. She didn't need anyone!

# CHAPTER FOURTEEN

They spent a shivering hungry night, but at last, the sun rose, etching the sky in coral pink as though the greyness of yesterday had never been.

Pippa, after checking that Augusta still slept, escaped the tent and hurried to the horses. A short time later, she'd saddled, packed her horse and was leading it out on to the road. With the assistance of a nearby tree stump, she mounted and, with a last look back, rode away.

Anger still simmered in her chest over Gil's brusque manner last night. It wasn't her fault Augusta became ill. Well, maybe it was, but it wasn't intentional. She should have mentioned that she felt unwell before they set out in the rain. She loved Augusta like a sister and wouldn't wish her any harm, so Gil had no right to take it out on her. In fact, the time away from each other would be a blessing. The undercurrent of attraction that sprang to life last night alarmed her. They'd reached a turning point in their relationship and she wasn't certain where it was going to go from now on. Sadness filled her.

Shaking her head and dismissing those confusing thoughts, she focused on the day ahead. She hoped to reach Ballarat just after noon.

As the hours passed and the sun climbed higher, the dense bush started to share its space with the odd shanty and campsite. Wherever a creek meandered through the trees there was sure to be signs of human habitation in some basic form as men sought to find the rich mineral.

Each mile that brought her closer to the township, the more she forgot Gil and their argument and instead concentrated on her task. She had a mission to entice men to the valley to work for her, to do that she had to be the hard businesswoman she'd become, the woman who had no time to think of Gil and his behaviour, or of her own reaction.

It took the better part of the day to reach Ballarat. The recent bad weather turned the roads into mud pits, concealing the deep ruts beneath their murky surface. Many times she found it easier to ride in the scrub alongside the road, especially when passing bullock drays filled the width of the track. Soon she was overtaking many men walking, carrying their belongings on their back or pushing handcarts. All headed in the one direction, like a herd of sheep they followed the road to the diggings.

Exhausted, saddle sore and hungry, Pippa finally reined in before a wooden building situated in the middle of town, proclaiming itself to be an inn and stables. For a moment she didn't dismount and simply stared around. Ballarat was like nothing she'd ever seen. The entire place was raw, scarred. Trees and grass had given way to dirt streets, timbered huts and buildings or white canvas tents. The whole area rang with the noise of thousands of people. Everywhere she looked there were men and clamour. Hammering at the blacksmith's, fighting in the street, yelling, whistling, bartering, the rumbling of cart wheels, buildings and tents being erected.

The sense of urgency, of expectation filled the air like a soft humming. Pippa embraced it as it fired through her veins. Here was a unique madness and she loved it. Here things happened. Fortunes were made. Deals done. She wanted to be a part of it – *would* be a part of it.

'Can I help you, miss?'

Pippa looked down at a young lad standing near her right stirrup. She smiled. 'Do you work here?'

'Yes, ma'am. I'm the stable hand. We've got fine stables at the back.' He pointed behind, and Pippa noticed the untreated timber gates.

'Good. Yes, you can help me.' Pippa dismounted and winced as her back and leg muscles protested. She pulled her reticule out of the saddlebag. 'My horse needs a feed and a good rub down. Don't stint on either and I'll see you well.'

'Yes, ma'am.' He grabbed the horse's bridle.

'Tell me, will I find a decent meal and bed for the night in there?' She pointed to the inn's front door.

'There's not too many places, and that would be about the best in town.'

'I want to look around for a while. Can you let the landlord know I'll be needing his best room for at least a week?'

The boy scratched his head under the flat cap he wore. 'I'll let him know, but he's only got two rooms, real tiny they are too. Sometimes the only space he has left to rent is the floor.'

'Tell him I'll pay double the rent for a room.'

'He does have tents out the back, but the weather has made them damp.'

Pippa frowned. The last thing she wanted was another damp night. 'I'll be back in an hour to sort something out, just let him know, will you?'

She crossed the muddy street, dodging puddles and lumps of manure. Immediately, she became aware of the stares, the gawping of men who'd long forgotten how to bathe. Drunken layabouts littered the front of shanty shops, and she was hard pressed to find another woman among the flotsam tide of men.

'My, my, look what the storm tossed up, a pretty bit of treasure.' A greasy-haired man, with blackened and missing teeth, thrust himself away from a group of loitering men and stalked around Pippa, halting her progress.

'Excuse me, please.' Pippa stepped to once side, glancing at the cluster of men.

The man blocked her exit and laughed back to his friends. 'Listen to the pretty bird, sweet as can be.' He plunged his hands into his trouser pockets and grinned. 'Care to sing a tune, little bird?'

'Stop harassing me and be on your way.' Angered, Pippa dodged him again, lifting the hem of her riding habit high from the mud.

'Nice turn of the ankle too.'

'Leave her be, Reg, she's not the type to accept a quick tumble in the bushes.'

Pippa looked at the speaker and frowned as he pulled his wide-brimmed hat down low on his brow. Something about him needled the back of her mind, but she soon dismissed him as the man called Reg suddenly leered closer to her face and she reared away. 'Leave me alone!'

'Tell me, sweet bird, do you think you'll enjoy a tumble or two?'

Pippa noticed a barn-like building that broadcasted its use as a general store and hurried for it. Reg's laugh followed her and at the door she paused, turned around and gave him a cold, superior look.

She entered the dim interior and immediately stepped aside as two men, carrying crates of goods, edged past on their way out. They gave her a nod of thanks and she smiled before gazing around the unique store. From ceiling to floor, goods of all description littered every conceivable space.

She was terribly thirsty and headed for the bottles of cider near the counter. The sign showing the scandalous price made her blink in confusion. She didn't want to buy a whole case full. Lifting up a bottle she went to the tall man stacking shelves in the corner.

'Excuse me, I wish to purchase this bottle of cider.'

He turned and his gaze flickered over her length before he stepped to the counter. 'Of course, madam.'

Pippa noticed he walked with a slight limp. Something about him caught her attention. As she waited for him to clear a bundle of hammers off the surface, she studied him. He appeared to be in his thirties, fairly handsome in a rough way. He had an air of neglect about him, which intrigued her. 'You have a very full shop.'

He paused and looked at her with soft grey eyes. 'Yes. That'll be a shilling, please.'

'A shilling?' Pippa, eyes wide, looked from him to the bottle and back again. 'For one small bottle?'

He shrugged. 'It's the going rate.'

She laughed. 'How outrageous. You aren't serious?'

'Listen, lady, I've got a lot to do. Do you want the bottle or not?'

She lifted her chin at his rudeness, all merriment vanished. 'Is this your shop?'

He folded his arms, and the muscles stretched the thin material of his white shirt. 'Aye.'

She peered around, taking in the prices clearly marked on every item and also the sign above his dark head that said 'No Credit'. She raised her chin and stared into his grey eyes. 'And people pay your prices?'

His lips tightened and he shifted his weight from foot to foot, favouring his bad leg. 'Do you want the cider or not?'

Pippa tapped the fingers of one hand on the counter top, her business mind coming to the fore, calculating, assessing, looking for every opportunity to make money. 'How many stores like yours are there in this town?'

His eyes narrowed. 'One or two.'

'Is there . . '

At this point three men strode into the shop, noisily talking and laughing, slapping each other on the back. They came straight to the counter. One man flourished a piece of paper and another man pulled a leather pouch from his coat pocket. Pippa stood aside as the men performed a little ceremony of tipping the pouch upside down. A waterfall of glittering gold flecks cascaded into a small mound on the scratched timber surface.

In utter amazement Pippa stared. Gold. Real gold right in front of her.

The shortest of the men smoothed out the piece of paper beside the pile. 'Could you fill this list please, proprietor, until there's no gold left?'

With accustomed ease, the intriguing man behind the counter picked up the list and read it. 'I'll have the order completed within the hour.'

'Excellent!' Again with much laughter, the men trundled out again, voicing differing opinions of where to go next.

Pippa looked back to the man and realized he'd been watching her. A wry lift of his lips made him deeply attractive. He was mature, with the hint of silver in his dark hair and lines running from nose to mouth, but all that only added to his allure.

'Now you see why I can put those outrageous prices on my goods? Some men dig for gold. I sell the goods to help them dig for that gold. Understand the cycle now?'

Nodding, Pippa felt the need to sit down and she didn't know if it was the reaction to him or the gold in front of her. 'Is it always like that?'

He sighed deeply, selected a few gold flakes and rubbed them between his finger and thumb. 'No. Naturally, there's the ugly side to it. When men have lost everything they own except the clothes they wear. They beg for credit, try to steal from me, hold me at knife-point sometimes, anything to get them back to their diggings. Gold fever is worse than any other disease for it strips a man's dignity.' He shook himself as if dispensing a shadow, dusted his fingers over the small pile and pierced her with his gaze. 'I guess you didn't want to hear that. No doubt your husband is panning in some creek right now.'

'I have no husband.'

A spark of interest crossed his handsomely rugged face for a second before it was gone. 'Then why are you here?'

'Business.'

'Really?' He stepped back and folded his arms. His eyes narrowed with blatant suspicion. 'What kind?'

She knew what he was thinking. What kind of a business did women run in a town full of men? He'd already slated her into being a whorehouse *madam*. Pippa hid a secret smile. 'Recruitment.'

'Perhaps you can enlighten me more over a drink across the road?'

'I don't think so.' Her skin prickled as his gaze ran sensually over her. He didn't hide the fact he was interested in her for one reason only, and her traitorous body responded to the thought. She stiffened. Why was she always attracted to the most unsuitable men? The air throbbed with a mix of attraction and danger. Pippa became aware that she had no protection now she had left Gil.

Gil.

He flashed through her mind. Was it only yesterday when he had looked at her like this man was doing now?

She drew back her shoulders. *Men!* Did they all think they could take what they wanted and then throw the leftovers away like rubbish in the gutter? She'd not make the mistake again of loving a man to distraction like she had done with Grant Lindfield. Men used women and she was going to make sure from now on she used them.

The gold sparkled as the dying sun slanted through a small windowless opening in the wall. It brought her mind back to the present. She looked at the man, knowing he'd been studying her quietness, appraising her quality.

Pippa pretended to lose concentration and sauntered around the stacked, cramped aisles. 'I own a valley.'

'A valley?' He frowned.

'Yes. It's two days coach from Sydney. I need men for labour. The gold fields have lured them away. I've come to claim a few back.'

'What's your name?'

Pippa glanced up from inspecting a selection of nails. 'We have failed to perform the ritual of pleasantries required by civilized people.'

Laughter twinkled in his eyes. 'Perhaps we are not very civilized?'

'Speak for yourself, sir.'

'My name is Marshall.'

'You don't have a first name?'

'Do I need one?'

Crossing the floor to another shelf piled high with balls of twine, chisels, trowels and all manner of things, Pippa pondered on his flippancy. He wasn't a gentleman, not like Gil, but he was captivating. 'I have a good mind to set up a supply store like this myself.'

He laughed. 'Indeed? I thought you were looking for labourers?'

Ignoring him, she picked up a dusty scrubbing brush and wrinkled her nose as it dirtied her riding gloves. 'Naturally I will undercut your prices.'

The smile slipped from his face. 'You think this is a game?'

'Not at all.' She meandered around barrels filled with rakes and shovels. 'I'm sure there's more than enough to go around.' Mentally she absorbed as much information about his shop and the prices he displayed as possible.

Marshall's face hardened.'This town is no place for a gentlewoman.'

Pippa laughed softly. 'I am no gentlewoman when it comes to business, I assure you.'

He stepped forward and scooped up the mound of gold flecks and deposited them on the weighing scales behind the counter. He grabbed the piece of paper and began to collect things from shelves and stack them in a box he found from amongst the general confusion of his shop.

Amused, Pippa grinned as she watched him throwing the goods around like a spoilt child. She'd ruffled his feathers and found she enjoyed it. His cool veneer had cracked under the pressure of a business rival. She would enjoy this challenge. 'I see you don't offer credit. I think I shall in my store.'

Marshal paused in measuring out tea leaves into a small sack. 'You'll be ruined within a week if you do that.'

'I'll have conditions, don't worry.'

His grey eyes darkened to flint. 'You don't frighten me with all this talk. It'll take you months to set up, finds suppliers and money to invest . . .' He stopped, aware that none of those issues bothered her. Marshall tossed his head. 'Good luck to you then.'

She inclined her head regally. 'Thank you. Though, of course we could become partners instead.'

Silence stretched between them for so long that for the first time Pippa became aware of the town noise outside the building; wheels squelching in the mud, horses snorting, men talking, a dog barking.

'You want to be my partner?' Marshall said the words slowly, as if savouring them on his lips.

'Indeed. I believe it is a wise proposition, suitable to both our needs.'

'You have no idea of my needs,' he whispered in a tight, controlled voice.

Pippa looked into his eyes and shivered. The blood pounded in her veins. 'I think I do.'

'Don't play with me, woman. You will get burned.'

'Nonsense.' She waved him away like a bothersome fly, trying desperately to appear calm and worldly when the whole time her heart pounded like a threshing machine. 'We'll be good for each other. We both have what the other needs.'

'Are you certain about that?'

She forced herself to laugh and sound light-hearted. 'Absolutely. I have the money to expand and you have the know-how. We can build bigger better shops and make lots of money. Can you resist the opportunity to make more money?'

'The gold won't last for ever. I've seen it happen before where one minute there's a thriving town and the next minute there's nothing but weeds growing in the empty streets and the only place that's full is the churchyard.'

'Then we'll follow the gold.'

'I thought you had other business to do here?'

'I can do both.' She turned and faced the door to watch the happenings in the street. She needed a moment to compose her racing thoughts. On entering this dilapidated store her life had changed, but in what way she wasn't quite sure. The man, Marshall, heightened her senses, made her throb with physical awareness so acutely that it made her legs weak. Yet, she also felt alive with the excitement of adventure. Closing a business deal always affected her like this, however this time there was the added pleasure of meeting Marshall. She would get her men for the valley but she would also get much more.

Suddenly Marshall stood close behind her.

Pippa closed her eyes, her stomach clenched and heat invaded her loins with shocking intensity. She didn't know what it was that ailed her, that made her physically ache for him so badly, but whatever it was, she needed a cure. This time the attraction that gripped her was stronger than anything she'd felt before. With Grant and Gil she knew them and cared for them before the attraction had crept up on her. Yet, with this man, this stranger, something tangible had taken hold of her the moment she saw him. Like a fire, the yearning consumed her, obliterating the past, present and future.

'What's your name, beautiful girl?' Marshal whispered.

She turned and moistened her lips with the tip of her tongue and swallowed as his eyes widened and then darkened with heated desire. She took a breath, conscious of taking the next step. 'My name is Phillippa Noble.'

*

Inside the inn, boisterous men sang ditties and raised their jugs to celebrate their strikes. Others huddled together in corners, strategizing their next claim, and those without hope stood miserable and alone, snarling at stray dogs and people alike. All this noise reverberated against the inn's thin walls, nearly drowning out all normal conversation. Marshall managed to hear most of what the lovely Miss Noble said by leaning in close, this also gave him the added delight of being able to gaze into her dark brown eyes and smell her particular fragrance of lavender and rose.

He still tended to smile at the absurdity of talking business with this woman. Who'd have thought that his dull existence would change so completely? Within an hour of meeting her she'd managed to invade his mind and stir up unwanted and long forgotten feelings.

After yesterday's meeting, they had met again this morning at the store, where she had immediately begun talking business. At first her straightforwardness and large ideas startled him, alarmed him. Her visions and grand opinions of expansion and product monopoly filled him with awe. Yet, it was hard to think of prices, stock and figures with her so near. Miss Noble was an enchanting, sensual lady who had as much courage and fire as he himself once did, and because of this, she drew him like a moth to flame. He wanted her so badly he ached.

She was talking again, explaining her plans for development, controlling the market within the whole district. He watched her intimately, noticing the way her hands moved as she spoke, they way her eyes lit up with an internal blaze of excitement and intelligence. He liked intelligent women. They made such a difference to a man's world. Sadly, he hadn't met enough of them to make a large difference to *his* world, but he hoped to improve that situation with this one.

Yes, Phillippa Noble was an oddity, but a charming one. He'd not wanted a partner, either in private or business until she had walked into his store. He preferred his own company, trusted no one. It was safer that way.

'So, what do you think?'

Marshall blinked. Phillippa was waiting impatiently for him to answer, yet he hadn't registered the question. 'I'll not rush things.' His tactical evasion bought him some time. He needed to cool his head and other parts of his body. She was too close, too lovely and fresh.

She sat back in a huff, her eyes narrowing. 'I'll not sit and wait patiently for you to make your mind up. This is a good offer. You would be mad to refuse it, but if you do, be warned. I'll not ask again and I'll make sure I'll take the majority of your customers.'

He held up a hand. 'Steady on.' Shaking his head, he eyed her as he drank a mouthful of ale. 'Are you always so impetuous?'

'I go after what I want, yes. However, I am no fool.'

'I never doubted that for a moment.' And he didn't. In her expression he read the ambition, the compelling need to strike out and grab every opportunity that came to hand.

'Marshall, why do you hesitate? I can have money sent to me and within a month we could have travelling stores going out to all the smaller digs. At the same time we can build a better store here.'

'What about your home, your family?'

'They'll understand, they know me. My mother is aware I run the business to suit our needs and rarely questions my decisions. Besides, I'll send some men home to help them out.'

'It's not safe for you to stay here alone. Women are scarce around these parts. People will talk and—'

'And think of me as something I'm not, like you did at first?' She smiled so cheekily it made his heart twist in his chest.

'Pippa!'

Marshall swung around as a tall, smartly dressed lean fellow strode to their table and pulled her up by the wrist. In an instant Marshall was on his feet, but refrained from taking a step forward. He looked from Phillippa's shocked, pale face to the angry glittering eyes of the fellow who held her.

'Gil.' Phillippa swallowed. 'I didn't expect you.'

'Obviously,' the man named Gil snarled like a dog with a bone. 'Did you honestly expect me to not follow you?'

Marshall swore silently. He'd done it again, got himself mixed up with a woman who had 'carers'. He fished in his pockets for coins and threw them on to the table to pay for their meal. 'I'll leave you two alone.'

She tugged her wrist out of Gil's hold. 'No, Marshall. Let me explain.'

Gil jerked, his expression incredulous. 'Explain to *him*? What about *me*? How about explaining to me why you slipped away like a thief in the night?'

His shouting had quietened the room. All heads turned their way as it was rare for those with money to make a scene. Marshall swore again. Who was this fellow with the tired tautness of a man who'd done some hard riding, and what did he mean to her?

She wrung her hands, her expression tortured. 'Gil, I know—'

Marshall held up his hand. 'Miss Noble, perhaps it's best if you go outside with your friend and talk without having the entire room privy to your words. I'll pay the landlord.'

Swinging away from her, Gil snatched off his hat and glared at him. 'Who the hell are you, anyway?'

Phillippa reached out and placed her hand on Gil's arm. 'Gil, this is Marshall. We were discussing business.'

'Business?' Gil scoffed, sneering in Marshall's direction, tapping his hat against his leg. 'Don't be naïve, Pippa, I'll wager the last thing on his mind is business!'

Marshall laughed and shook his head, which only deepened the fellow's anger. He didn't care about that, unless the fellow would take it out on Phillippa, but he didn't look like he wanted to. He looked liked he wanted to shake her and then kiss her until she couldn't breathe.

Sighing, Marshall ran his fingers through his hair. Apparently he wasn't the only one to find Miss Noble desirable. 'Look, I don't care whether you believe us or not, but business is the reason we are here together.' He turned to Phillippa. 'If you think you are safe with this man, then I'll leave and see you in the morning. Good night.'

She nodded, her eyes sending her thanks. 'Come, Gil. We'll go out into the stableyard to talk.'

Once outside, Pippa checked to see if they were alone. The stable boy was nowhere in sight but a man, smoking, leaned against the stable door on the other side of the yard. She turned and went to the farthest corner where the inn's lights didn't reach but enough moonlight shone to light the area sufficiently.

She felt she should say something. Gil had every right to be angry, but he'd made a spectacle of them both in there. Lord knows what Marshall would think of this.

Abruptly, Gil pulled her against his chest and his mouth imprisoned hers. Startled, it took a moment to gather her wits. Then the shock gave way to anger and she wrenched her mouth from his and stared at him. He released her hastily as though she burned him and flung himself away.

Pippa heard his harsh breathing above the muted sounds from the inn. She placed her fingertips to her lips and realized her hand shook. Gil had kissed her. No, not kissed. That was never a kiss. That was a stamp of authority.

'I'm sorry,' Gil murmured without turning around. 'I shouldn't have done that. It was wrong, but I was incensed beyond reason.'

'I don't blame you for being angry, but don't ever do that again. You don't own me, Gil.' Pippa swallowed, hating this awkwardness between them and knowing she caused it.

'Why did you do such a foolish thing?' He bent to retrieve his hat that he'd dropped on grabbing her. 'Did you not think I would worry? What did you expect from me?'

'I thought you'd take Augusta back to Melbourne, or some town that had better shelter than a tent.'

In the shadowed light, his gaze locked with hers. 'Yes, I had to take Augusta back and find her a doctor, but during the whole time I was twisted inside with agony that something might happen to you and I wasn't there to help. Have you no thought to anyone but yourself?'

'I didn't mean to—'

'I nearly killed my horse trying to get here, hoping against hope that you were safe! I had to leave Augusta in Melbourne. Have you no feelings towards her to do what you did?'

'Of course I do! I would never want to harm her. Gil, please understand.'

'Understand?' He laughed a cruel sound that echoed in the yard. 'I've never understood you, Pip. As God is my witness I doubt I ever will.'

'I'm sorry.' It hurt her to hear him speak like this. She thought that he, of all people, knew her best, for they were the same type – impulsive risk takers. Yet, his admission added to her inner argument that marriage to him or anyone would be unwise.

He sighed and she felt his tiredness and guilt ripped her anew. She wanted to reach out to him but no longer believed she had the right. He'd withdrawn from her and she became frightened, because without his friendship, she'd be lost.

'Since you have a champion at the ready, I'll return to Augusta and when she's well enough we'll go home.'

She nodded, unable to speak to heal his hurt.

Gil lightly dusted off his hat. 'I'll visit your family. What do you wish me to say?'

Pippa swallowed. 'Nothing. I wrote a letter this afternoon and posted it. I explained what I was doing.'

'So you do know what it is you are doing? That surprises me.'

'Don't be cruel, Gil. It's not in your nature.' She fought the urge to cry, she hated to feel any weakness, but he was like a stranger to her now.

'You are certain not to return with me then?'

'Yes . . .'

'I thought so.' He turned to stare at the inn as a door opened and the innkeeper threw out a bucket of water. For an instant Gil's face was illuminated by the light from the doorway and Pippa stifled a gasp at the pain etched on his strong, handsome features.

'Gil . . .'

Slowly he turned to her again, his face once more in shadow. 'Please don't stay here, Pip. I have never begged anyone in my life, but I'm begging you now to not stay here.'

'I must.'

'Why? If it is men you want, I'll get them for you. I'll get anything you need, you know that. All you need to do is ask and I'll give you whatever you wish for.'

'I know, but I don't want to ask you for things. I can get whatever I need by myself.'

'Marry me, Pip.'

Stunned, she stared at him, frustrated that she couldn't see his face better.

He grasped her arms and pulled her closer. 'I mean it. Marry me. I love you and we'll be happy, I promise. I'll give you everything. Let us return home and marry and raise fine sons and daughters.'

Pippa raised her hand and touched his cheek, her heart breaking for this wonderful man. 'I cannot, Gil. You mean too much to me. We can't let marriage spoil that.'

'It wouldn't.'

'Yes it would, only you cannot see it.' Her voice broke as she tried to make him understand. 'You'd not give me the freedom I need.'

'That's not true.' His throat convulsed. 'Please, Pippa.'

'I don't suppose I'm ready for marriage, perhaps I never will be.' Her voice dropped to a whisper.

'I don't believe that for a minute,' he scoffed.

She shrugged one shoulder.

'Just return home with me and we'll discuss it.'

'No.'

Gil swore violently. 'Why stay here?'

'Something compels me to stay in this shanty town. I cannot explain it.'

'Business? You think you have to stay here for business, to make money?' He took her hands. 'But you don't, I'll give you whatever you need for the stud. I appreciate you want to be rid of Grant Lindfield's hold, so let me pay back the debt.'

She cringed, wishing now she'd never told him about Grant. It had been a feeble moment. They'd been out riding the valley boundary, laughing and joking, totally at ease with each other as normal. Pippa, thankful for such a friend as Gil, mentioned he was her very best companion and then found herself telling him about Grant and his false friendship and her wish to be free of him, to ruin him.

He stroked her cheek with one finger. 'I know you're independent.'

'It's not just about being independent or Grant's debt, it's . . .' She sighed, finding it difficult to express something she couldn't find words for. 'You don't understand.'

He stepped away and she felt a loss. He ran his hand over his face. 'Are you staying because of this man you've met?'

'No, not really. It's business . . .'

Gil chuckled. 'You don't sound very convincing, sweetheart.'

'It's not—'

'No more, Pip.' He bowed his head. 'I can bear no more. I've waited for you to give me the opportunity to ask you to marry me, but I've left it too late. What a fool I am. You don't want me as anything but your friend, like a brother perhaps. Whereas I . . . I've wanted you as my everything, my friend, my lover, my wife, the mother of my children.'

'Oh, Gil.' A tear trickled down her face. 'I never knew you felt that way. I didn't suspect. I thought you saw me as a sister.'

His eyes widened. 'Are you blind? I have a sister. I want a wife.'

'I'm sorry.'

'You know my feelings now. Does it make a difference?' He banged his hat against his leg. 'No, I didn't think so.'

'I wish I could give you what you want, Gil.'

'Thank you. However, we both know I'm not enough for you. You want excitement, stimulation. You thrive on adventures. I've tried to be your companion while I waited for you to see me as someone other than your cohort, but it's obvious you'll never want me in the same way I want you.'

'I never gave you reason to see me as anything other than a friend. Did I ever encourage you to believe I would one day be your wife?'

'No, but I felt we got along so well, spent so much time together, had the same interests that it would be a natural conclusion to our friendship.' He looked away. 'After your father's death I thought you'd need me, need a husband. Instead you wanted me only to help you try to destroy Lindfield.'

'I've not been looking for a husband, Gil, not after Grant.'

He gave a mocking laugh. 'I've been the biggest fool.'

She reached out to touch his arm but he jerked away. 'Gil . . .'

'Perhaps your new business partner will provide you with something I cannot. I doubt he's looking for marriage, so it should suit you admirably.'

Maddened by the insult, Pippa clenched her hands. 'Don't throw away our friendship, don't you dare!'

'Don't you see? I cannot be just your *friend* anymore!'

Ice-cold dread trickled down her spine. 'What are you saying? That we will no longer mean anything to each other?'

He stiffened. 'That's correct.'

'But I-I adore you.'

'As a brother, a friend.' He shrugged, uncaring. 'Well, it no longer matters. I'm done. I can't wait for you any more, Phillippa Noble.' He picked up her hand and kissed it softly. Straightening, he smiled in the dim light. 'Goodbye and good luck.' Taking a deep breath, he spun on his heel and marched across the yard and through the gate.

Frozen in mind and heart, Pippa watched him go, unable to speak or move or think.

# CHAPTER FIFTEEN

The noise from the hammering and sawing hurt Pippa's ears, but she put up with it because it meant advancement towards making a considerable amount of money. In the cool August weather, she navigated the construction site and entered the building. The new store was being erected behind Marshall's original shop, which had been demolished two weeks previously. The men gave her a nod of acknowledgement as she went by, holding her navy blue skirts high above the sawdust on the floor. The shell of the building had been completed just three days ago and now carpenters laboured on fitting out the inside. With a critical eye she studied their workmanship, pleased to find no fault. Working hard to ensure this business expanded and became a huge success helped to keep her thoughts from Gil.

She still could not accept that their friendship had ended so abruptly and so painfully. In the weeks since his hasty departure she had swung between tears and anger whenever she thought of that night behind the inn. Many times she had begun to write him a letter that only ended up thrown in the fire. How could she put into words the feelings she didn't quite understand herself?

Going through into the back room, Pippa gave herself a mental shake. She couldn't think of all that now. She stepped over a few planks and slid past the supply crates stacked to the ceiling. Marshall leaned over a table stuck in the corner, studying the papers that littered it. He gazed up at her with a wry grin and her stomach somersaulted. Every time she saw Marshall, her body reacted, but thankfully not her heart. Attraction without emotions was easier to deal with.

'Good morning, Miss Noble.'

'Good morning, Mr Marshall.' She smiled, playing his game. Stepping beside him, she noticed the map spread out. 'What's this?'

'I heard news this morning that two men found gold here.' He pointed to a spot an inch north of Ballarat. 'It's five miles away, perhaps six. The strike happened last week and somehow the men have kept it a secret, until now.'

'You think we should send a cart up there?'

'Absolutely.' Marshall rolled up the map and placed it to one side before pulling another sheet of paper out from under a pile. 'I've already sent word to Tom to bring the cart over. We can have it loaded before noon and Tom can make a start this evening. We're not sure about the road, but he should arrive before nightfall.'

Pippa took the list from him. 'If we send Tom north that will mean we'll be late with the southern run. We cannot let those men down. They are relying on us. If we don't arrive tomorrow as planned, they'll come into town and shop at the first store they come to, which is that latest establishment on the edge of town.' She bristled at the mere thought of their new threat. Someone had put up a tent at the side of the road leading into Ballarat and they sold all manner of things from it. Not only was this most recent competition taking the trade from them while the new shop was being built but they were undercutting their prices.

'Yes, I know, but I think it's important we make a presence at this new strike while the going is good. I'll find another driver to go south.'

Annoyed, Pippa tapped the paper against her palm. 'Who can we trust with such a task though? It was hard enough to find Tom and we only got him because he's too old and arthritic to dig anymore.'

'There's bound to be someone, don't worry. I'll speak to Tom, he might know—'

'I have the perfect solution.'

Surprised, Marshal raised his eyebrows, a knowing smile playing about his lips. 'Oh?'

'You.'

'Me?' His smile slipped.

'It's a faultless solution and it's cheaper. If you go we don't have to pay an outrageous wage.'

'What about all of this?' Marshall spread his arms out wide, indicating the store. 'There is too much to do here.'

'I'll take care of the builders.'

'I don't think that is wise.'

'Nonsense, it makes perfect sense.'

He shook his head, his left hand unconsciously rubbing his bad leg. 'I'll not leave you here alone.'

His concern touched her. 'Marshall, I've been in town for nearly five weeks. People know me now. I'll come to no harm.'

Marshall narrowed his eyes at her. 'I'll tell Tom to make this first trip north a short one. If he's back in two days, then he can immediately head south. Being a day or two late won't matter to those men.'

'You don't know that. Besides, it's the principle. We told them we would go out every second Tuesday. It makes good business sense to keep to our word.'

He pulled his watch from his trouser pocket and checked the time. 'Aren't you meant to be meeting the Darlington family at ten o'clock?'

Pippa nodded. The Darlington family, down on their luck, had agreed to travel to Berrima and work at the stud. They had two strong sons and both parents were fit and healthy. She'd met them a few times now and liked them more each time. Today they were leaving for her home and the thought filled her with a sudden desperate longing for her own family and the valley.

She wrote to her mother, Hil and Millie every week, telling them a little of her time at the diggings. Her mother had sent her a summons to return home, which she promptly ignored, knowing that she wasn't ready to go back. It was too soon to return to Berrima and face Gil. She needed more time to adsorb his words, his needs, before she saw him again. His declaration of love had turned her upside down. It changed everything she thought solid, leaving her floundering, rudderless. Why did he have to change things and why did she have to be difficult and not accept what he offered? Any normal woman would.

'You miss your family?' Marshall stepped closer and clasped her hand.

'Yes, I do.' She gazed up into his eyes, emotion closing her throat. Yet, it was easy to forget home and Gil when Marshall smiled at her.

'Why do you stay here then?' he whispered.

'I've asked myself that question every day.' She knew the answer, of course. She stayed away from her beautiful valley because of him. He was like magnet and she, a metal filing.

'Don't stay for me, Phillippa. I'm not worthy.'

'I'd like to think that was my decision.' Impulsively, she brought her hand up to smooth back the dark hair from his forehead. It was the first time she had touched him intimately. She bit her lip softly as tremors sizzled through her body.

He closed his eyes. 'What do you want of me?'

'I'm not certain . . .' Not for the first time she found herself wishing for him to hold her, kiss her, but as always he held back.

'We want different things, Phillippa.' Marshall stood motionless.

'Do we? I didn't think so.'

Marshal ran his thumb over her bottom lip and she shivered with desperate yearning. She wanted him as a woman wants a man.

He stepped back, breaking their contact. 'I can't marry you.'

Pippa blinked in surprise. 'I never mentioned marriage.'

'It's what all women want.'

'Not me.'

He frowned and put some distance between them. 'You just touched me and looked at me as a woman does when she wants a man.'

Raising her chin, Pippa stared at him to show she wasn't frightened by his words. 'That is true. So?'

The look he gave her was one of amusement. 'Sweetheart, you can't act like that around men. It does strange things to them.'

'Don't treat me as a fool, Marshall.' She folded her arms.

'You need a husband.'

Pippa stiffened. 'What did you say?'

His expression hardened. 'You need a husband. How old are you? Twenty-three or four? It's past the time you were wedded and very much bedded, my dear.'

Outraged, she glared at him. 'You are crude!'

'But I'm right, aren't I?' He winked and turned away. 'Go back to your valley and find a husband before you make a mistake you'll live to regret.'

Her whole being throbbed with awareness. Yes, he was correct, she did need a man, someone to ease the weird and wonderful yearnings that plagued her body. Some nights she'd dream about him or Gil and would wake up in a cold sweat, her body twisting in the sheets and pulsating with a need she couldn't satisfy. She wondered if she was going slightly mad.

Pippa gazed at his strong back as he pretended to concentrate on the papers on the desk, but she knew he bluffed for he rubbed his bad leg – something he did whenever he was unsettled about something. This gave her confidence to step forward and lightly place her fingers on his shoulder.

'Don't, Phillippa,' he murmured, not turning around. 'Don't take that next step with me. Save yourself for a man who will truly love you.'

'What is love?' she whispered.

'It's what I can't give you.'

'I don't believe I asked you for it.'

He spun around and tightly clasped her to him. His grey eyes darkened like storm clouds. 'I will *not* marry you.'

With her heart thumping fit to burst, she traced the outline of his lips with her fingertip. 'I don't want it . . .'

He lowered his head. 'I'm not the one for you. You're using me . . .'

'Kiss me . . .' She reached up, slipping her fingers through his midnight hair and melted against him as his lips delicately touched hers.

Marshall's groan, like that of a condemned man, made her smile, but in an instant all that fled from her mind as he crushed her to his chest, deepening the kiss until she left this world and entered another that existed only of sensations. Her hands slid across his wide shoulders and she revelled in his touch as he pushed her back over the table, kissing her exposed neck.

A loud knock on the open door made them spring apart. One of the carpenters cleared his throat. 'Sorry to disturb yer, guv, but I need yer opinion.'

Flustered, Pippa stepped towards the door. 'I-I must get back to the inn. The Darlingtons . . .' She twirled away only to stop and look back at Marshall and give him a secret smile.

Dashing out of the shop and across the street, Pippa lifted her skirts high to side-step the reeking deposits of horse manure. Concentrating on where to step stopped her thinking about Marshall's kisses, his caresses. She groaned inwardly with frustration. *That damn knock!* A blush warmed her cheeks and she frowned recalling Marshall's accusation that she was using him. He was right, of course. She wanted to know the relations shared between a man and woman without the bondage of marriage. Gil's image came to mind and shame engulfed her but she stiffened her shoulders against it.

'Miss Noble!' Doris Darlington waved frantically amidst the hustle and bustle of people, children, dogs and horses. The coach had just arrived and spilled out its human cargo, more souls all eager to try their hand at digging for gold.

'I'm sorry I'm late, Mrs Darlington.' Pippa dodged a small child and shook the older woman's hands. 'Are you all ready to go?'

'Aye, indeed we are, Miss Noble, and it's with thanks to you.' Doris nodded rapidly, sending her little black hat jiggling. She squeezed Pippa's hands again. 'You've given my family a new start and I never thought it would happen. Blasted gold, it's the ruination of every decent man.'

Pippa grinned at the woman's outrage, knowing that had the Darlingtons struck lucky, Doris would be singing a different tune. 'I'm sure you'll be happy in the valley. My family are wonderfully kind and will treat you well.'

'That's all I pray for now, Miss Noble, all I pray for now.' Doris sobered and tucked her arms under her large breasts. She was only a short woman but for all that, she ruled her husband and grown sons with an iron will.

Suddenly they were joined by the Darlington men, all laughing and joking, glad to be given another opportunity to live decently again. Once more they asked Pippa for descriptions of the valley, the people there and what work they'd be assigned.

As fresh horses were harnessed to the coach, Pippa gave introductory letters to Doris, looking at both Doris and her husband John. 'Now, give these to Robson, my overseer. He will meet the coach in Berrima. My family know all about you and will be expecting you.'

'Right you are, Miss Noble.' Doris tucked the letters into her bag.

John stepped forward and shook her hand. 'We appreciate this chance, Miss Noble. We'll work hard for you and your family.'

She nodded and smiled and, shortly after, the carriage driver blew the horn to hurry up the passengers. In a flurry of activity the coach was loaded and Pippa stepped back, waving to Doris who poked her head out of the window.

As the coach moved away to shouts and whistles, Pippa took a deep breath. The Darlingtons would see the valley soon. They would see her mother, standing on the verandah surveying her domain, and they would see Millie working in her vegetable garden with Davy helping.

She turned away, the coach gone from sight, leaving nothing but dust in its wake. Sadness weighed heavily on her heart, but it had been her decision to stay here, to earn more money in a few months than the stud could earn in a year. Summoning her courage, she lifted her chin and shook away the self-pity. Soon. Soon, she would go home.

'Miss Noble.'

Pippa stopped and stared at the working man who addressed her. His hat was pulled low, shadowing his face. 'Yes?'

'You don't remember me, do you?'

She frowned. 'Unless you hold your head up, I cannot even see you.'

Slowly he raised his face. Neil Chalker smirked, his eyes narrowing.

'Now you see me.'

For one terrifying second, Pippa couldn't move or comment. In the year since their last encounter she'd forgotten him and now she knew why. Chalker was nothing special, nothing memorable. Compared to Gil or Marshall, he was a nonentity. He looked older, rougher and by the state of his filthy clothes, obviously down on his luck. Abruptly, he didn't have the power to frighten her. 'I shouldn't be surprised to see you here. Gold attracts even the lowest of people.'

His cheeks whitened and the smirk faltered.

'Good day to you.' Pippa gathered her skirts and lifted them away, as if he contaminated her. 'I cannot say it was a pleasure, Mr Chalker.'

His hand shot out and gripped her elbow before she could walk away. 'Perhaps you have no idea of what pleasure is, Miss Noble?' The pitch of his voice threatened.

With one eyebrow raised, she stared down at his dirty hand. 'I suggest, Mr Chalker, that you release me before I scream so loud every man in the district will hear me.'

'Including Marshall, your current lapdog?'

She stilled, irritation racing through her body. 'Goodbye, Chalker.' She ripped her elbow out of his clasp and, head high, strode away.

When she knew she was out of his sight, she ducked into the nearest building, a dilapidated Chinese dwelling proclaiming to be a restaurant. The owner, standing behind a wooden counter at the back, quickly bowed to her. She blinked and impulsively bowed her head.

'Missy, need drink?' The small Chinese man stepped out from behind the counter but made no move towards her.

She nodded, berating herself for the sudden inability to act or think.

Light on his feet, his black pigtail swinging, he poured her a drink into a tiny blue cup, brought it to her and then quickly scuttled back behind his counter.

Pippa smiled and sipped the liquid, which tasted sweet. 'Thank you.'

He bowed again and grinned.

'My name is Phillippa Noble.'

'Phil No-bell.' He grinned and nodded, then pointed to his chest. 'Wong Ling.'

Smiling, Pippa took another sip and then stepped to the counter and gave him his cup back. 'Thank you, Wong Ling.'

His dark eyes lit his pleasant face. 'You come gain. I cook.'

'Yes. I will.' And she would. She didn't think of the new Chinese population as a plague to society like most others. As far as she was concerned there was room enough for everyone who spilled off the ships.

She looked around the fragile tables and stools, the timber walls with scraps of Chinese silk nailed to them. Yes, it was all primitive, but that was the way of the diggings, she'd become used to that now. She'd bring Marshall here, they'd have tea.

After a last wave goodbye, Pippa left Wong Ling and headed out into the sunshine. She was late retuning to the shop, Marshall would wonder where she'd got to.

With a force that lifted her off her feet, she was grabbed from behind, a hand over her mouth. Instinct made her scream against the rough fingers clamped over her lips, pressing them back into her teeth. She tasted blood and twisted violently to be free. The villain who held her swore as she struggled. His hat was knocked off and her boot kicked it to one side when he dragged her down the lane between two buildings and into a dim shed.

# CHAPTER SIXTEEN

Pippa woke to whispered arguing. Slowly, she raised her head, her neck creaked at the movement and a sharp pain made her wince. A throbbing alerted her to the tenderness of her left cheek. In the shadowy darkness, she made out two men having a heated disagreement in the far corner of the run-down shed. Dried blood caked her lips and she remembered the slap she'd received from the fellow who'd taken her. He'd not hesitated to administer punishment for her screaming and thrashing. His last smack had sent her world black.

The leather straps he'd tied her hands and ankles with cut into her skin, but she dare not move for the two men weren't aware she was awake yet. Her head throbbed, but she pushed it from her mind as she worked out a plan to escape.

Through the open doorway, the evening twilight descended. Being winter she knew that it must be around six o'clock. Hours. It seemed like hours since she had waved goodbye to the Darlingtons. Would Marshall be worried, possibly even looking for her?

She couldn't believe this had actually happened. Outrage filled her, squashing all fear. How dare someone abduct her! The very thought incensed her so much it made breathing difficult.

Sudden movement from the men forced her to be still. Quietly they approached and she closed her eyes, pretending to be still unconscious.

'You frigging fool, Reg. I told you not to hit her. She's still out cold.'

Pippa stifled a moan. Chalker. It was Chalker who kneeled close by, he who spoke. Reg was the man who'd accosted her on her first day in the diggings, and had since often jeered at her when they passed by each other in the street. Rage consumed her like a burning fever. She would kill them both!

'Now, listen Chalker,' Reg argued. 'You said to grab the wench and I did. The bitch screamed and fought like a madwoman. Did you want the whole town to hear her?'

'No, but now she has evidence to show people.'

'Then when we're finished with her, I'll slit her throat.'

Pippa's whimper silenced the men. She was roughly grabbed by the arm and jolted straight.

'Wake up now.' Chalker shook her shoulders, making her head wobble.

Pippa's eyes sprang open and she glared with every bit of hatred she could summon. 'You touch me once more and I'll see you hang.'

Reg laughed. 'See, told you we should have gagged her. The stuck-up cow has spirit that's for certain.' He rubbed his hands together and chuckled. 'I'll enjoy taming this one.'

Chalker sprang to his feet and gripped Reg by the shirt.'You touch her again and you'll deal with me.'

Reg held his hands up as if in surrender. 'Rightio mate. Settle.'

'I'll not tell you again, remember that.' Chalker threw Reg from him and turned to Pippa. 'You'll be all right.'

'Why have you done this? What do you hope to achieve by it?' she scoffed. 'Did you want to frighten me? Well, you've done your job. Congratulations. Now release me before I'm reported missing.'

Chalker glanced over to Reg and nodded. Silently, the man slunk outside. A horse snorted close by.

Pippa strained to hear other sounds. Nothing but the jingle of harness. 'Let me go, Chalker. I'll tell no one.'

He shook his head. 'No can do, Miss Noble. You see you're coming with me.'

'Not likely.'

'You have no choice in the matter.'

'Where do you plan to take me?'

'Now that would be telling, wouldn't it?' He kneeled, untied her ankles and helped her to stand. Being so close together, Chalker hesitated, he touched her hair that had come loose.'You know I won't harm you, don't you? I'll not let anyone hit you again,' he whispered.

Pippa swallowed. She read the desire in him and a tingle of fear as cold as mountain snow spread throughout her body. 'Please let me go.'

His fingers ran down her cheek, neck and across the top of her chest. She stood still, her chin raised in challenge and he smiled. 'You're the most delightful creature I've ever met, or will meet.'

'And I'll never be yours,' she taunted.

Chalker dropped his hand and stepped back.

Reg stuck his head around the door. 'Everything is set to go. Come on.'

Pippa's bravado left her. In panic she looked from one to the other. 'Where are you taking me?'

'We're going bush.' Chalker pushed her forward.

'Aye. A long way bush.' Reg grinned like the devil. 'We're off digging for gold far from this mangy town.'

Outside, Pippa halted at the sight of three saddled horses and two pack horses. It couldn't be real. She dug her heels in the dirt and refused to walk another step.

Reg sidled up to her. 'Just get on the horse, missy, and make no fuss.'

She wished her hands were free so she could slap his impertinent, ugly face.'You're stupider than you look, if you think I'll do as you say.'

His hand whipped out and struck her on the side of her head, knocking her to the ground. She landed with a thump and sat stunned.

'No, Reg!' Chalker's face twisted in disgust. 'I said not to hit her!'

Reg spat into the dirt. 'You might want to let her call the shots, but not me. She'll not speak to me as though I'm her lackey.'

Chalker came beside her and took her elbow. 'Come, mount up.'

Dazed, her head ringing, she allowed him to help her to her feet. 'You . . . You cannot do this. Let me go and I'll tell no one.'

He ignored her and guided her towards the horse.

Eyes wide, she stepped back, shaking her head. 'You're mad.'

'Very likely.'

'You cannot simply kidnap me.'

Reg swung up into the saddle, the leather creaking. 'We'll be long gone before anyone is aware you're not sleeping soundly in your bed, missy. They'll never find us.'

'No more talk.' Chalker lifted Pippa and thrust her on to the saddle. She sat like a limp doll and, swearing in frustration, he pushed her boots into the stirrups and placed the reins in her tied hands. Slapping the horse's rump, it walked obediently behind Reg's mount.

In a swift movement Chalker mounted, trotted up beside Pippa's horse and grabbed the reins from her stiff fingers and secured them on his own saddle. 'I know what a good rider you are. I'm not taking any chances.'

'Please, listen to me . . .' She stopped and stared as he whipped out a handkerchief, quickly reached across and gagged her. She squirmed in alarm, but in danger of falling from the horse, she stilled.

Satisfied, Chalker spurred the horses on and Pippa clung to the saddle as they rode past the outskirts of the town in near darkness. Looking over her shoulder, she watched the twinkling lights of the huts, tents and buildings fade. Tears ran down her cheeks and soaked into the gag.

When they entered thick bush on the fringes of the town, Pippa kept a constant record of the progress. Thankfully she was at the end of the line. Reg rode ahead, leading the packhorses and behind them, Chalker rode, leading her horse. Without him being aware of it, she could turn and look around her, to keep a mental record of their journey. They were heading direct north-west.

For a while they followed a meandering creek and when she believed them to be about ten miles from town, she used her fingertips to prise out her handkerchief from her pocket and drop it to the ground. She swivelled around to stare at it for a long time until they rounded a bend and she lost sight of it.

The moon rose high in the star-peppered sky as they rode for what seemed hours. She tried to keep focused. She thought of her family, the stud, recalled the times spent with Gil, remembered his laugh . . .

Despite her best efforts to stay alert, at times Pippa drifted into sleep only to jolt awake when she felt herself sliding from the saddle, and she'd struggle to sit upright again.

'We'll stop here, Reg.' Chalker called suddenly, bringing Pippa into full wakefulness.

She waited for the two men to dismount and Reg lead their horses to a creek. Chalker lifted her down without speaking and made her sit at the base of a large gum tree, its enormous branches hanging over the water. Her mouth and cheeks hurt from the gag and her throat convulsed with thirst.

'Secure her feet,' Reg spat, untying one of the packs.

Chalker shook his head and concentrated on making a fire. 'There's no point, we're miles from anywhere and if she escaped she'd be permanently lost.' He glanced at Pippa. 'She's no fool. She knows the bush can be a death trap.'

Reg laughed, the sound loud in the quiet of the bush. 'Aye, she's a woman. They're all dumb as shit.'

Pippa sat listening, watching everything they said and did. She leaned against the trunk, resting. Her stomach rumbled and she became desperate for a drink, but she remained quiet, uncomplaining. They thought her so stupid it made her want to laugh. Didn't Chalker understand that she'd learned a lot while living in her valley? She smiled inwardly. Gil and Robson had taught her many things. She knew how to safely climb a tree and use it as a look out, knew also that trees grew denser closer to water. When lost, always find water and follow its flow.

'Here.' Chalker thrust her a chunk of hard crusted bread and then squatted down to untie the gag. 'Eat. You need to keep up your strength.'

She took the bread in her fingertips and dropped it in her lap, all the while stretching her jaw and wincing at its stiffness. 'May I have a drink?'

He nodded and handed her his canteen.

'We lighting a fire?' Reg asked, chewing his own ration of bread.

Chalker turned away from her and as he and Reg discussed their options, Pippa drank deeply, awkwardly holding the canteen in her tied hands.

'I think we're far enough away to make camp for the night. It's dangerous to travel in the dark.' Reg walked back to his horse and took out a small bottle of rum. 'We've many days travel ahead and I don't want to lame the horses by pushing them too fast.'

'Right, we'll camp here for the night, but I want to be gone before sun up.' Chalker picked up a stick and snapped it over his knee. He looked towards Pippa. 'I'll make a fire. Are you cold?'

'No.'

He nodded and continued his task.

'Can you not untie my hands? I'll be able to help you.' She stared at him, issuing the dare to give her some freedom.

'I think not.' Chalker grinned.

Seething, she uttered vile curses in his direction. Being bound and a prisoner vulnerable to another's whims made her so angry and frustrated she wanted to scream and hit something hard!

In a swift movement, she pushed the bread into her pocket. It would be better saved, for she wasn't going to let the cowards truss her up like a chicken and transport her anywhere they wished to. She had to plan.

While Chalker worked on the fire, Reg unpacked the horses and hobbled them. She was given a blanket, which she draped over her lap and underneath the blanket she worked on getting her hands free. The constant wriggling and pulling of her wrists soon chafed the skin raw. Pain made her eyes water, but it also filled her with a desperate rage. With a sudden jerk, she snapped the leather strap and her hands were free.

'Are you hungry?' Chalker came closer, dusting his hands of flour. 'I've made damper.'

She stared at him in amazement. He was behaving as though they were on some summer picnic. Hatred blinded her reason.'I'd rather eat dirt.'

'Now listen—'

With a roar, Pippa pushed up from the ground and sprang at his throat, her motion toppled them both backwards. She landed on him, knocking the wind from his chest, before he had time to move, she scrambled over to the fire and grabbed a small branch poking from it.

'What the hell?' Reg emerged out of the darkness, adjusting his trousers as he did so.

Pippa spun, waving the blazing branch at him. 'Don't take another step!'

'Put that down,' Reg laughed. 'You'll take someone's eye out.

She backed away, keeping both men in her sight. 'I'll be taking my leave, thank you gentlemen,' she sneered.

Chalker, on his feet now, stepped closer. 'Don't be a fool. It's night and we're in the middle of nowhere. You'll be lost before you're twenty feet.'

'I'll take my chances.'

'No.' He took another step and she backed away another two steps. 'Pippa, I promise you, we'll not mistreat you.'

'Oh?' She chuckled, amazed at his stupidity. 'Kidnap is not mistreating?'

Reg, his face menacing in the firelight, walked around to the left of her. 'When I get my hands on you, you'll think kidnapping is a Sunday-school outing.'

Pippa turned to the right as Chalker came at her from one side and Reg on the other. She kept stepping backwards, but the stream was close behind. Her slight hesitation was enough for Reg to jump her. Pippa screamed as they fell to the ground. The burning stick flew from her hand and she twisted on to her stomach to grab it.

Reg clutched at her waist, climbing over her, impeding her reach. His fist smashed into her head, knocking her senseless for terrifying moments. He whipped her around on to her back, tearing at her bodice. He leaned down to spit into her face. 'I'll kill you, bitch, before I'm done.'

'No!' Chalker lunged for him, the force pushing Reg off her.

While the men fought, Pippa scrambled over and grasped the stick.

The red-hot heat had lessened on the tip but it still held enough to do harm. Without thinking she turned and as Chalker rolled Reg under him, Pippa thrust the stick into Reg's face.

His animal howl of pain barely registered in her brain. Chalker leaped from his injured partner and stared at Pippa as though he couldn't believe his eyes. He advanced on her and, beyond all reason, she brandished the stick wildly.

'Stay away.' She glared at him, dimly aware of Reg squirming in the dirt, crying for help. 'You come after me and I'll do the same to you, Chalker.'

She threw the stick towards him and, as he jumped out of the way, she dashed into the blackness of the bush. Instinctively, she lifted her skirts high and headed the way they'd come. Behind her she heard the crash of Chalker pursuing her, but she kept on going even when the air in her lungs burned like fire.

When suddenly she was grabbed and thrown on to the floor behind a tree, she had no time to react. A black ghost held her down, pushing her face into the ground. A pebble struck her cheek and grit crammed her mouth. Vaguely she was aware of running, thundering feet. For how long she was held, she didn't know, but breathing became difficult. Grass covered her nose and she squirmed, frantic for air.

The pressure on her back and head relaxed. Slowly, she raised her face from the ground and gulped.

'No talkie.' A phantom voice whispered in her ear.

Pippa trembled. Turning slightly, she stared, astonished at the Aboriginal man beside her. The whites of his eyes glowed eerily in the darkness. He held his finger to his lips and she nodded. No talkie.

Abruptly, he became rigid and cocked his head to one side, listening. He placed his palm flat on the ground. They heard Chalker calling her name making promises that she wouldn't be hurt. She shivered and stifled a moan.

After a second or two, the aborigine nodded and pointed behind her. She hesitated until he pushed her and then, stumbling, she scrambled up and into the darkness once more.

The Aborigine, clad in only cut off trousers, took the lead. Treading as lightly as a bird, he weaved through the trees, each foot placed carefully. Pippa watched his movements and copied. Within a short space of time they were near a shallow creek, but the native didn't stop until they had climbed a small cliff and walked on again for another few minutes.

As Pippa followed her silent companion, her mind went blank of all thought. Tiredness weighed her down, replacing the anger. She longed to simply curl up and go to sleep. Fleetingly, she wondered why she wasn't frightened, why wasn't she screaming in fear? Was the threat from an Aboriginal man any different to Chalker and Reg?

She tripped over a tree root and landed on her knees with a jolt. The fight went out of her and she stayed in that position, looking at the native.'Kill me if you must. I no longer care.'

He gazed at her without blinking for a moment and then turned and disappeared into the night.

His abandonment was final test to her endurance. She plopped on to her bottom and cried. Great heaving sobs broke from her, shaking her shoulders, drowning her in misery. She wanted her mother. She wanted Gil to rescue her.

'Phillippa.'

Caring little for what happened next, she raised her head, waiting for the next blow. Marshall stood a few feet away. She wiped her wet eyes to make certain she wasn't seeing an illusion. 'You found me.'

'Of course.'

'How?'

'Wong Ling.' He frowned. 'He watched you leave the shop and saw the men take you. He came to find me.'

She took a deep breath and hiccuped. The Chinaman had saved her from a fate worse than death.

Marshall held out his hand, showing her scrunched-up handkerchief. 'I had to employ an Aboriginal tracker, but you made his job easy.'

Swallowing back fresh tears, an overwhelming need to see her mother and Hilary swamped her. She needed to hear Millie's voice and feel Davy's soft arms cuddle her.

'Come sweetheart.' He bent and lifted her up into his arms.

Pippa nestled against his chest and closed her eyes. She was safe.

# CHAPTER SEVENTEEN

Pippa gazed up at the flock of white cockatoos screeching high above the treetops. The morning sunshine warmed her back as the cart jostled over the track through the scrub. Beside her, Marshall twitched the reins, whistling softly.

She glanced down at the letter in her hand, steeling herself to read her mother's words again. Why did she torment herself by reading it over and over?

> Of course I do not need to tell you that Hilary and Toby's visit was truly wonderful. We had a marvellous time, but we missed you. The house is quiet without you and I only have Millie to talk to most days.
>
> However Tabitha Ashford-Smith called just this morning with Augusta. They stayed only a short while, due to their leaving tomorrow for Sydney for a few weeks.
>
> Apparently, Gil has become quite taken with a young lady recently arrived from France, would you believe it? I imagine she would find it very different here after the delights of France. I guess we shall have to call on her, should she marry Gil. I imagine she'd be very fashionable and make us all feel rather uncivilized. It is such a shame he has turned his affections her way though, for I'd always believed you and he would make the perfect match. Sadly, it wasn't to be. Obviously your friendship means too much to him to ruin it with marriage . . .

Gil.

Pippa's heart seemed to shrivel and die as easily as a flower in the desert. She carefully folded the letter and put it in her pocket. She had nothing of Gil now. All thoughts of repairing their friendship on her return fled. What he'd offered her that night behind the inn was now given to another. Once more she tasted the bitter flavour of disappointment. It was all her own fault, of course. She had no one to blame but herself. Her silly ideas of independence and the urge to do everything her own way had cost her a good man, more than that it had cost her his special friendship that she treasured. How would she live without him in her life?

The wheels lurched into a hole and she gripped the small railing at the end of the seat to steady herself and at the same time she felt the letters in her skirt crinkle against her leg. They were her link to home. The two letters, one each from her mother and Millie had arrived late the previous evening and she'd read them repeatedly before exhaustion overruled and she fell into a fitful sleep dreaming of Gil.

'I really believe we could have sent someone else to do this run.' Marshall wiped the sweat from under his hat. 'This last week we've worked non-stop. We didn't need this trip and a break would've been more rewarding for us both.' He shifted his weight on the seat. 'Yes, I know you insist on showing how reliable we are. I guess the money makes up for it in the end. Actually, the last deposit I made into my bank gives me enough to buy another parcel of land. I thought I'd go to Melbourne and buy blocks near the city. Have you thought what you'll do with your money?'

She looked away, not wanting to answer. She'd already sent her money to her agent in Sydney and through him, she'd made an offer to purchase a new coal mine founded by Grant Lindfield. Yet, the whole process now left her empty, didn't give her the satisfaction it should. The kidnapping had changed her, woken her up to what was important in her life. Ruining Grant Lindfield, taking away his enterprises bit by bit, no longer appealed. The lump of hatred she'd fed on since that night in Sydney dissolved into nothingness.

She simply didn't care any more.

There would be no more buying of shares in his companies. No more dreams of owning his manor in Yorkshire. At long last she had eradicated Grant from her heart and mind. Life was too short to spend it on revenge – it was too short to waste on things that gave no comfort, no joy.

'Well, at least you could hold a conversation with me, since you dragged me out here again.' Marshall smiled and flicked the reins over the horses' rumps.

She managed a weak smile. 'Sorry.'

His grey eyes narrowed. 'You shouldn't have come. It was too soon.'

'I couldn't stay in town by myself, not after . . .'

'Definitely not.' He swore softly under his breath. 'Those two bastards will be caught and punished and if I happen to find them before the police then they'll hang from the nearest tree.'

Pippa shivered as his quiet words lingered in the cool air between them. She had no doubt he would carry out his threat. Chalker and Reg, to her knowledge, had escaped into the bush and not been seen since. The local constable and his small team who were severely overworked had soon given up looking for them, but they had posted notices for their arrest. It didn't matter to her that they hadn't been caught, not now. She wanted to forget them, forget that night and never have to think of it again.

In the last two weeks since her kidnap and rescue, she had pushed herself to work eighteen-hour days. The new shop, now completed, had her undivided attention as they stocked it ready for its reopening. Working so hard kept her in a constant state of tiredness, so that when she fell into bed at night she slept soundly and the nightmares that had plagued her for the first two nights after Marshall found her, were kept at bay.

Marshall had begged her to return home and she was solely tempted to, but something stopped her every time she went to pack. Sending men back to work in the valley had drawn her here, but it was the opportunity to make indecent amounts of money that kept her in the south – that and Marshall.

Guilt became a companion and it wasn't a very pleasant one either. She knew she wanted him, this quiet, larger-than-life man sitting beside her, she wanted him for a lover. The scandalous thing was this admission didn't even shock her. It seemed natural, right. To leave the diggings, to leave him behind without fulfilling the need they both felt for each other couldn't be considered. Her brush with death – and she fully believed Reg would have killed her – had cleared her mind of the social sensibilities that women were bound by. She would go home and live her life, but she would have Marshall first and damn the consequences. If it were not for him, she'd be dead by now and this second chance at life wasn't to be forfeited. After all, marriage would never be an option now Gil was lost to her, so why not have an experience to remember with Marshall?

*Penelope Johnstone.* Now why did she think of her, an old acquaintance? One who for a short time Pippa had mixed with in her circle.

The young woman had an enormously wealthy father, and it had been a good thing too, for he was able to buy silence every time Penelope disgraced herself, which was often, and always with a man. At eighteen Penelope had aborted a baby and nearly died, but it didn't stop her. She was insatiable with men, earning the scorn of all the women in their society, yet she was never ostracized because of her family name. Maneater they called her. Pippa frowned, was she turning into a Penelope Johnstone? Grant, Gil, Marshall and even Chalker at first, all had an effect on her in some form. Would she end up old and alone after wanting more than one man yet never actually having any?

'Have you had enough of me and the diggings now you've received letters from home?'

'No,' she sighed.

'Did the letters hold bad news?'

She gripped the seat tighter. 'Not exactly. Mother wants me home.'

He gave her a sideways look. 'Understandable. More so if she knew what had happened.'

'She never will. It stays between you and me.'

He nodded. 'Did she mention the Darlingtons?'

'Yes, they've settled in very well, as I knew they would.'

They trundled over a rise and down into a shallow, flat plain filled with white tents, and swarming with men working at diggings all along the length of a creek. To the right two men argued viciously, and Pippa glanced away, her emotions still raw since the kidnap. Violence of any kind made her feel ill.

'We'll set up under that tree over there.' Marshall nodded to a large gum tree on their left, at the edge of the plain.

It took them less than an hour to unharness the horses, set up the small table and weighing scales, open some of the crates, display the price list and ready themselves for trade.

As if understanding her need to be sheltered, Marshall did all the haggling with the men who wandered over to purchase supplies and gossip, leaving Pippa to stay behind him filling out the orders. Her sudden fragility irritated her, but there was no overcoming it at the moment. Chalker had not only taken her freedom that night, he'd taken her spirit.

She worked solidly all afternoon, measuring, weighing, counting and packing goods. Without meaning to, she shut out the humming noise around the cart, the men's chatter and laughter, the squabbles, the barking dogs, the hammering and swearing, the clattering of tins, the birdcalls and even Marshall to some extent. In a world devoid of noise, she continued to read the orders and stack the supplies until, blinking in surprise, she realized the crates were empty.

Pippa jumped when Marshall placed his hand on her shoulder. 'Sorry, I didn't mean to startle you.'

'No, it's my fault. I was . . . daydreaming.'

'We've done well. You look hot.'

Frowning, she put her hands to her cheeks and found them warm. She shook her head. This apathy wasn't her, she didn't like it and wanted to snap out of it, but she felt as though a veil had been placed over her, making everything distant, vague.

His expression hardened. 'You shouldn't have come. You're not yourself, which is no surprise considering what you've been through.' He took her elbow. 'Come, there's water under the seat. Drink while I harness the horses and we'll go home.'

Home.

The valley.

Yes, she wanted to go home urgently, not back to the hotel in Ballarat, but to the sweet valley, to her family. Today. Now. This very minute.

Spurred on by the abrupt and desperate longing to see her real home, she quickly packed away the crates and empty sacks into the cart. In frenzied haste, she cleared away their portable shop and then climbed aboard.

'What's the hurry?' Marshall laughed as he guided the horses around. 'Do you have a dinner engagement or something?'

Pippa took a deep breath, his smile melted her insides and she wished she could just ignore the world for a moment and beg him to hold her, but she needed to tell him her thoughts more. 'I want to go home.'

'Yes, sweetheart, I'll have you there in just over an hour.' He grinned.

'No, I mean I am going home.'

The laughter left his eyes and she bit her lip in torment. He concentrated on urging the horses, his face expressionless. 'I thought you might.'

'I'm sorry,' she whispered over the rumble of the wheels.

'Don't be sorry. I knew you would eventually.' He flashed her a wry smile. 'I'm glad you're going home, it's where you belong. I'm surprised you've stayed away so long.'

She plucked at her skirts. 'I do belong there and I'm eager to return, but I feel that I have unfinished business here still.'

'Meaning the shop?' Marshall rubbed his bad leg. 'Don't worry about that. We're partners and will continue to be long after you've left here. You trust me to take care of the business, don't you?'

'Absolutely.' She smiled sadly.

'Well then, we'll keep in contact and everything will go on as before. You've made an enormous amount of money. You're richer than any man who has found gold panning in those creeks.'

'I've come to realize that money is not everything.'

'No, it isn't, but it helps.'

Pippa looked out over the fields of waist-high dry grass. 'Once all I wanted was money. Money meant security.'

'There's nothing wrong with that.'

'No, but I let it rule my existence.' She frowned at her own folly. 'There were two reasons why I stayed here. One was to make enough wealth so I could ruin another man's life.'

Marshall balked, looking at her as though she was the devil incarnate. 'Ruin a man? Who? Me?'

'No, not you, never you. Sorry. I shouldn't have blurted it out like that.' She glanced away again, hating the person she'd become. 'He was a man I once loved, a man I would have easily died for. He . . . he rejected me and I thought nothing could be worse to suffer. Then, not so long ago, I found out he'd never respected my family. Our friendship was a lie. From that moment on, I swore to ruin him in any way I could. I thought that if I made enough money I could buy into his businesses until I was the major shareholder. I wanted to cut him off from all income. More than that, I wanted to buy his home in England, make him an offer he couldn't refuse. Make him feel what it was like to be displaced . . . I wished for him to suffer as I have done.'

'And have you? Have you ruined him?'

She blinked away sudden tears. 'No. Now, just when I possess enough money to make him a generous offer for his estate, I find I no longer want it. I don't care any more.' Tears trickled over her lashes and she wiped them away.

'Revenge is ugly, Phillippa. What does it matter if this man hurt you so long ago? Do you need him in your life now? Do you think ruining him will make you feel better?'

Her chin wobbled and another bout of tears gathered and spilled. 'I'm . . . I'm just so lost, Marshall. All that I thought I wanted, all that I thought I needed to do suddenly isn't there any more.'

'I told you once before you needed a man and children to fill that valley of yours.'

She fished for a handkerchief in her pocket. 'I lost my chance . . .' A sob broke from her, and swearing softly, Marshall, applied the brake and then turned to bring her into his arms to let her cry out her heartbreak. The haven of his arm gave her the release she needed. Sobs shook her body, memories plagued her, broken dreams and promises lost whirled through her mind.

When she hiccuped into silence, she felt better, easier of mind and heart. Again she had a desperate longing to hear her mother's voice, even if it was to simply scold a servant. She wanted to see Millie's smile, to watch Davy playing in the creek and to see Robson instructing the men. She shied from thinking of Gil, but yes she ached to see him again.

'Better?' He gave her a hand a gentle squeeze that sent her stomach tumbling.

Pippa looked down at their joined hands. Never had she been short of courage, but what she wanted to ask him next made her mouth go dry. 'I-I want to ask you a favour.'

'Oh?'

'My second reason for staying was . . .' She swallowed. Voicing it was more difficult than she thought it would be. 'Before I leave I want you to . . . I want us to be together properly, as men and women can be.'

'No.' He didn't even look at her, but kept his gaze fixed on the road ahead.

'Please, Marshall. You know how I feel about you. I want—'

'I said no.' He clicked his tongue spurring the horses into a faster trot.

'Why?'

'I'm not discussing it.'

Pippa turned in the seat to face him. 'Why won't you discuss it for heaven's sake? We're both adults. It is something we both want.'

'I don't.'

She blinked in surprise and stared at him. 'Liar.'

In a burst of temper, he called to the horses, jerked the reins and slammed his foot on the brake. As the cart came to a complete stop, he jumped down, stormed around to her side and dragged her off the seat.

Gathering her skirts up, she jogged alongside of him to keep up with his impatient strides. 'What are you doing?'

'You want to do it, then let's do it. Here, right now.'

Pippa's blood ran hot at the thought, but this wasn't what she had in mind, a quick tumble in the scrub wouldn't be the lasting memory of him she wanted to take away with her. He was angry with her for some reason, and this alone made her dig her heels into the ground and rip her elbow out of his grasp. 'Stop.'

Marshall raised one eyebrow, his mouth tight in a wry smile. 'Stop? I thought this is what you wanted?' He shrugged and folded his arms across his wide chest. 'A fumble in the grass with me taking your virginity, isn't it?'

'No, not like that.' His complexities frustrated her. 'I don't understand you. Why are you angry?'

He grabbed her upper arms and yanked her against him. 'I'm angry because you think of me as some stallion, here to do you a service.'

She gasped. 'That's not true! Not true at all.'

'Really?' He laughed and thrust her away. 'Well, I'm telling you sweetheart that afterwards that's exactly how you'd feel.'

'No, I wouldn't.' Pippa frowned, trying to make sense of it all. 'You know I think highly of you.'

'But you don't love me and the moment it's over, you'd regret it.'

'I'd never regret it, not with you.'

Shaking his head, Marshall moved away. 'I was mad to get involved with you. I should have listened to my gut instinct that first day.'

Although he hadn't hurt her, she rubbed her arms anyway, for comfort. 'What did your gut instinct tell you?'

'To ignore you, pretend you didn't exist, to get you out of my shop and never let you back in.'

His words tore at her heart. 'But you didn't know me that first day.'

'I wanted you though, badly.'

Pippa smiled and took a step closer. 'And I wanted you.'

Marshall ran his knuckles down her cheek. 'I know and I was all ready to seduce you, take you as my lover and then your friend Gil walked in.'

The mention of Gil made her stiffen. 'He means nothing to me.'

'Now who is the liar?'

'He doesn't.'

'Sweetheart, listen to your heart. What we share is a physical thing, that's all. Yet, with him, you can have marriage and babies, everything.'

'I don't want that.' She raised her chin, ignoring the inner voice that whispered she was fooling herself. 'Besides why couldn't I have those with you?'

He sucked in a deep breath and looked up into the tree canopys above. 'Because I'm already married. I have been for five years.'

If he'd slapped her she'd not have been more shocked. 'You . . .'

Marshall kicked at the tufts of grass. 'She is in America. We married in California while I was working there.'

'But . . .' Pippa bit her lip, she felt betrayed. There were so many things she didn't know about him.

He sighed and quirked his lips into some semblance of a smile. 'She's not here because I left her two years ago. I've been a drifter all my life. Living and working where I wanted to, content to move along as the need took me.'

He looked past her, over her head into the distance. 'She'd tricked me, you see. She, Lydia, had played loose before I met her. Yet, I believed her when she told me she was with child, my child. So, naturally, we got married. It wasn't until a few months later that I realized she'd lied. There was no child. Lydia and her brothers wanted out of the small town they lived in and I was the biggest fool to come along and, without knowing, I played into their plans. When we went to the new Californian gold fields, her brothers tagged along, three of them. Nasty pieces of work they were too. After a while I couldn't put up with them or her.

Pippa gazed at him, seeing his sadness. The humility of a proud man broke her tender heart anew.

'The day I left, Lydia was drunk, a common state for her to be in. She didn't want me to go, not because she loved me, but because I'd not be there to earn the money.' Marshall rubbed his bad leg. 'She shot at me.' He tapped his thigh. 'This is the legacy of my marriage.'

'Your wife is a fool not to know the worth of her husband.'

'I am no one special.'

Some part of her, some inner core wanted to banish his hurt, soothe away his pain and kiss him into oblivion, but she wouldn't. Her woman's mind, learning new things about him every day, told her not to torment him any more with offers of her body. He deserved more than that and so did she.

'I won't ask you to love me again, Marshall.' She smiled and reached to hold his hand. 'I won't make you suffer in making decisions you don't want to make.'

He groaned and then grinned at her. 'I am a man, Phillippa Noble, a man who wants to kiss you and lay you down on the grass and love you until you cannot remember your name, but I can't do it.' He stepped closer and tucked a strand of hair behind her ear. 'For if I did, I'd be lost for ever and I couldn't stand that as I know you're not mine. You never were. You, my sweetheart, belong in your green valley, not here in this dust bowl of humanity.'

She smiled and gently pressed her lips to his. 'I wish it were different.'

'So do I.' Marshall stroked her cheek with the back of his hand. 'We make a good team, you and I.'

'And we shall continue to do so. I might be miles away but I'll write often.'

'Send me a painting of your home, I want to imagine you there.'

Pippa nodded, blinking back tears. 'What you said earlier was wrong. I do love you. There is a special place in my heart just for you, Marshall.'

'Then I will be content.' He raised her hand to his lips. 'Now let us get you home, back to where you belong. I'm certain the people who love you are tired of waiting, especially that fellow you came down here with.'

She remained quiet as he helped her back into the wagon. It wouldn't do any good to tell him that Gil had cast his affections elsewhere, besides she couldn't really deal with thinking of that right now.

As they trundled away over the rough track away from one of the diggings and towards Ballarat, Pippa looked around, letting the scene, the sights enter her mind for all time. She didn't think she'd come back. Her time here was finished. She'd done all she needed and it was now time to go home and pick up her life again.

Smiling, she gazed at Marshall, her dear friend. He took her hand and squeezed it.

# CHAPTER EIGHTEEN

Pippa reined in Honey and, relaxing in the saddle, gazed over the valley spread below. The September spring breeze caressed the treetops and rippled through the long grasses. She'd been out riding since dawn, a habit that had sprung up since her return from the gold fields three weeks ago. A deep unhappy sigh escaped. She shifted in the saddle, restless.

Men were stirring around the homestead, getting ready for another day's work. A thin spiral of smoke wafted from the kitchen building, breakfast was being made. Millie and Robson emerged from their hut, Millie carried a washing basket under her arm and Robson headed for the stables. A smile played on Pippa's lips. Her dearest friends, the ones she trusted with her life seemed so happy. Gladness filled her that Millie had found love and Davy a father.

Noble Blaze whinnied, the sound drifted to her as if it were she he called. She should go down. A man was arriving today with his mares, but she knew Robson could handle the whole process like he'd done many times before. Even her mother didn't need her. Esther ran the household, organizing the servants with sharp efficiency.

It had been a shock to arrive home and find that the stud and the family had gone on without her, and done so wonderfully too. The Nobles were wealthier than they'd ever been. Her mother was happy, accepted, had many friends and acquaintances. Pippa knew she should be content, should be satisfied with her life, but she wasn't and she didn't know how to fix it.

On coming home, nothing had seemed out of place, yet subtly the changes appeared. The extra servants, like the Darlingtons had been integrated into the valley's small society, learning their place and what was required from them long before Pippa returned. Her mother kept good accounts of household expenditures and went visiting and shopping with the ease of someone born to such a country life.

Gil.

He constantly came to mind. She missed him, missed his laughter, his companionship, the way his green eyes sparkled when he looked at her. How could she live in the same district as him and not have his friendship? Worse than that, how could she live with him married to another? This was her punishment for rejecting such a good man, one that loved her. Why had she found out too late that she loved him in return?

She jerked the reins up, disturbing Honey's feed of grass and guided her back down the slope. Her heart thumped uncomfortably whenever she thought of Gil and what she'd lost. The Ashford-Smiths were in Sydney and she'd not seen them yet. Pippa worried that Augusta would distance herself too. They'd not communicated since she'd left her in the tent on the road to Ballarat.

Pippa shook her head at the thoughts playing on her mind. She should be grateful her family and the stud didn't need her constant attention. However, to be kept busy was the one thing she did want. It wasn't her nature to drift through her days idle and unoccupied. No one needed her. She wasn't indispensable. They'd learned to live without her while she was gone. Her rash decision to go to the gold fields had cut the ties binding her to the stud. More than that she had lost her friends in the process.

She'd come home to find her old life was redundant.

'Did I hear a transport, Phillippa?'

Pippa looked up from reading her letter as her mother entered the sitting-room. She smiled, for her mother looked well in a new copper-coloured silk gown. 'Yes, the cart has returned from town. Mrs Darlington just brought mail.' Pippa sorted out her mother's correspondence and handed it to her.

'Good, that means my bolts of material are here.' Esther took her mail and sat on the green and gold striped sofa placed under the front window. The afternoon sun streamed through the sitting-room's white lace curtains, giving good light to read by. 'Who is that letter from?'

'Douglas.' Pippa waved the letter and, at the same time, thrust a smaller note from Marshall under an envelope. Marshall had written that Chalker was dead; killed by a prospector, who claimed Chalker had been trying to steal his horse. She shivered, recalling Chalker's face, but he was gone now and thankfully she could close her mind to him and what he'd done.

'And how is dear Mr Meredith?'

'He's well.' Pippa tapped the pages, forcing a brightness to her tone. 'Though he says he'll remain in England. His son is happy and Douglas doesn't feel the need to return here. There are too many memories.'

Esther paused in opening a letter, her reading glasses perched on the end of her nose. 'What of his property?'

'He's given me first refusal.'

'Shall you buy it?'

Pippa nodded, instantly recalling the last time she visited the property when Gil and Augusta had been with her. After inspecting the cattle she pastured there, they'd shared a picnic. For hours they had laughed and talked, laying in the shade. She thrust the recollections from her mind and concentrated on business. 'Yes. I'll rebuild the original house and perhaps ask Robson to run the property for me.'

Her mother frowned. 'But if Millie and Robson move there how will we manage here without them?'

'Quite easily.' Pippa hesitated; an abrupt feeling of purpose filled her. 'I will fulfil Robson's role, as I have little else to do, and there is nothing I don't know about supervising the stud.' Satisfied she'd made the right decision, she turned back to her letter. However, Douglas's description of a recent trip to London couldn't hold her attention and her mind wandered. Work. Working was the best way to fill her life . . .

Gil.

Whenever she thought of him her stomach clenched and her heartbeat became erratic. She had to pull herself together and think of other things besides him or she would go mad. To throw herself into business was the only solution.

She stood and gathered up her mail. 'I'll have to make a trip to Sydney, Mother and meet with the bank. Did you wish to accompany me? We could visit Hilary and Toby.'

Mrs Darlington knocked on the opened door. 'Excuse me, Mrs Noble, there's a rider coming along the valley.

Esther, her letters forgotten went to the window. 'I'm not expecting anyone.'

Pippa joined her and with a sinking heart recognized Grant riding towards them. She glanced at her mother. 'It's Grant. You weren't expecting him?'

'Well no. Lord, I must see to things!' Flustered, Esther hurried Mrs

Darlington out with instructions to prepare a room and change the evening menu.

Alone, Pippa waited for Grant to dismount near the creek and walk the path up to the house. Within moments he was standing before her. His close presence did not affect her in any way and she was so glad for it. 'Welcome, Grant. Your arrival surprises us.'

His cold blue eyes stared at her as though he didn't recognize her. 'It's not a social visit.'

A knot of dread formed in her stomach. 'Oh?'

'Why?' His lips thinned into a tight line. 'Why did you do it?'

She nodded, knowing he meant her buying shares in his businesses. The time had come. 'How did you find out?'

'That's not important. Although I will say that I had some suspicions and once I learned of your agent's name it didn't take much gold to pass over his hand before he spilled his secrets. Now, just tell me why.'

Pippa took a deep breath. 'To ruin you, why else?'

A muscle along his jaw pulsed, his expression hardened with barely concealed anger. 'You failed.'

'I stopped trying.' Her hands shook and she hid them behind her back.

He took a step closer, his eyes narrowing. 'You'd never have succeeded.'

Tossing her head, she flicked her gaze over him, wondering what had driven her to feel such depths of love for him so long ago. Compared to Gil he was a pale shadow.'You think that, if it gives you comfort.'

Disgust flashed across his features. 'I don't know you. I doubt I even like you any more. You've changed beyond reason.'

Chuckling, Pippa folded her arms across her chest. 'You never knew me and I don't care a fig whether you like me or not. And yes, I have changed and gladly so. I see the gold from the dross now.'

'I want you out of my companies,' he sneered. 'I don't trust you and I don't want you involved in anything that belongs to me. Your revenge is ugly and I'll not let it ruin my life as it has ruined yours.'

She flinched, though remained defiant. 'If you want me out of your companies then you buy me out. I'd say that would then make us even.'

Grant jerked his head once in agreement, but his stiff manner showed his reluctance. 'Cynthia and I are going back to England. I'll arrange for all the paperwork to be drawn up before I go. I'll only pay the current market value and if you've lost money then that's your fault.'

'As you wish.' Relief seeped through her. She cared little about any monetary loss, she just wanted him gone.

'Our association as family is now at an end.'

'Absolutely.'

'I will answer no begging letters from you should all this collapse and you are left penniless. I am *not* my father.'

She raised her chin. 'And *I* am not *my* father.'

'Give my apologies to your mother.' He turned for the door only to pause and stare back at her. 'Find some happiness, Pippa, before you end up a mean-spirited old maid with no compassion in her soul.' With that parting remark he marched away.

Through the window, she watched him walk back down the path and mount his horse. In a heartbeat he was thundering across the valley and gone from her life for good. His words stung, but she mentally tossed them away. She would be happy, she'd make certain of it just to spite him. Besides, she had her family and her valley – they would save her from becoming a shrew.

Her mother, frowning in confusion, hesitated in the doorway. 'Where has he gone?'

'Home to England, Mother.'

'Well really!' Esther puffed. 'And I just changed the menus again!'

Smiling, feeling lighter of spirit, Pippa hugged her in a rare fit of emotional demonstration. 'Let us read our letters. You have one from Hilary.'

'Oh wonderful.' Esther clapped.

Grant was forgotten as they settled down to read and soon Pippa was engrossed in letters from her agent and other business matters. 'A Mr Baird from Sydney is enquiring again about Noble Blaze. He says he wrote last month and hasn't received a reply yet.' She looked up at her mother. 'What do you know of this?'

Esther slowly raised her gaze from her letter to Pippa. 'Oh sweet heaven!'

'What is it?' She frowned and looked at her letter again. 'Did you forget about it?'

'No, not that. Th-this letter is from Mrs Ashford-Smith, she says . . .' Esther glanced down at the page and back to Pippa. 'She says Gil is ill, dying. She is devastated . . .'

Pippa swayed. Her mother's mouth was moving but she couldn't hear the words. Gil? She felt numb all over. How could it be possible? Dying? Her Gil dying? It was a terrible lie.

'. . . they think it's scarlet fever . . .' her mother's words echoed around her brain.

'No!' She stared at her mother's shocked face. 'You're mistaken. Scarlet fever? It's a children's disease. Read it again, properly this time. How can you frighten me like this? He likely has no more than a cold.'

'Darling, I'm reading it correctly. Here,' Esther stood and gave her the piece of paper, 'read it yourself.'

Pippa took a hasty step back, staring at the page that held the accursed words. 'It's not true I tell you. A man of Gil's size having scarlet fever is laughable.'

'Anyone can succumb to it, Phillippa.' Esther hurried to the mahogany writing table. 'I shall write back immediately and offer any assistance, though what we can do I have no idea.'

Unable to move from the bit of carpet she stood on, Pippa watched her mother compose the letter. 'Is he . . . will he. . . ?' Her thoughts lay scattered around her mind like petals blown on the wind. Her Gil . . . Those two words repeated themselves like a chant. Her Gil . . .

Esther rang the small brass bell on the table. 'I'll send for a rider to deliver it.'

'To Sydney?'

'Sydney? Oh, no the Ashford-Smiths have all returned home to Sutton Forrest. They must be unhappy at that for there are better doctors in Sydney than here in the country. Of course a doctor can do nothing for scarlet fever—'

'When did they return?'

'Tabitha wrote they arrived three days ago and Gil has been ill ever since.' Esther picked up the short letter again and scanned it. 'Yes, they arrived . . .'

Pippa needed to hear no more. She dashed from the sitting-room, bumping into Mrs Darlington in the process, ran across the hall and into her bedroom, where she reached for her blue satin-lined cloak.

Esther came to stand in the doorway. 'What are you doing?'

Buttoning up her cloak, Pippa searched for her hat. 'I have to see him.'

'What!' Her mother gasped, her hand flying to her throat. 'You'll do no such thing, my girl. No such thing at all!'

'I must, Mother. Please don't make a scene.' Having found the hat that matched her linen dress, she rammed it on her head, uncaring.

'Make a scene?' Esther crowed. 'I'll not have to because you are not leaving this house!'

'I am.' Pippa stood, her mind whirling on what she should take with her.

Her mother marched into the room and grabbed her shoulders. 'I forbid it, do you hear me? I forbid you from going there.'

'Mother—'

'No Phillippa, I won't be persuaded on this. It's dangerous. The whole family could be infected for all we know. I'll not let you be at risk.'

Pippa stiffened and she took a deep breath. 'I need to see Gil.'

'Write a note, as I am doing.'

Gently, she kissed her mother's soft cheek and then swept out of the room. 'A note won't do.'

Esther followed her out on to the verandah and down the steps, arguing all the way, but Pippa ignored her and continued making for the stables.

'Pippa?' Millie called, as she hurried over from her cottage.'Is something wrong?'

'Yes, Gil is very sick and I must go to him.' Pippa kissed her cheek too, as though in farewell. She knew of the risk she was taking, she could catch the disease and never return to her valley, but she couldn't think of that now.

'Oh, Millie,' Esther puffed, seizing her arm. 'Stop her, oh please God stop her.'

Alarm filtered across Millie's face. 'Why?'

'Scarlet fever!' Esther cried. 'She's going to a house of scarlet fever!'

'Nothing will happen to me, Mother. Do not worry.' Pippa lifted her skirts and crossed the footbridge. 'Take care of her for me, Millie. I may be gone for the night.' Not wanting to hear their protests, she rushed across to the stable block and ducked inside. Unable to stand idle as John saddled Honey, Pippa tried to help, but in her eagerness to get to Sutton Forrest, she was all fingers and thumbs. With great patience John finished the task and led Honey outside.

As Pippa mounted, Millie came to her side. 'This is madness, Pippa. Your mother is awfully upset.'

'I cannot help that, not this time.'

'It is not your place to go, not now. He's to be married to another isn't he?'

Pippa braced against the pain that knifed her. 'He's my friend.'

'What good will it achieve to endanger yourself? What of the stud?'

Gripping the reins, she looked down on her dearest friend. 'Without Gil . . .' She couldn't finish the sentence for a lump the size of a rock seemed lodged in her throat.

Millie stepped forward and reached up to clutch at Pippa's hands. 'You are in love with him then?'

'Yes . . .' Pippa felt the urge to slump into the saddle and sob, but she couldn't weaken, not now. Gil needed her, just like she had needed him on so many occasions.

'For both your sakes' I hope he recovers, but you mustn't set yourself up for more hurt.'

'It's too late for that.'

'I want you to be happy. To find a good man to care for as I have found in Robson, but Gil is promised to another.'

'Tell that to my heart, Millie,' she snapped.

'I'm sorry.' Millie stepped back, breaking their contact. 'God speed.'

Pippa halted Honey at the entrance to the drive. Beyond the trees, she glimpsed carriages in front of the Ashford-Smith's grand house. A trickle of fear shivered over her skin. She didn't want to go any further and perhaps learn of soul-destroying news.

'Can I help ye, Miss Noble?'

Pippa jumped at the voice and twisted around to stare at the familiar old gardener who appeared from behind a tree.

He bowed and took off his hat, revealing a balding head. 'I didn't mean to startle ye, miss.'

Pippa licked her dry lips, summoning her courage. 'What is the news of Mr Gil?'

His expression softened, his eyes downcast. 'Nay, not good, miss, not good at all.'

'He lives?'

'By a slender thread I'm told.' He glanced at the house. 'They'd be happy to see a new face, miss, if you're going in. Miss Augusta is in a fearful torment as the Master and Mistress insist she goes away until the danger is over, but she won't. We could hear her yelling through the windows.'

Pippa nodded once and nudged Honey forward. What was she doing in the drive talking to the gardener when Gil and Augusta needed her? A groom standing near the carriage took Honey's bridle when Pippa dismounted by the steps. As she shook out her skirts, the could talk to him . . .'

'That's what I was saying!' Augusta darted back to her mother's side, her face aglow. 'Pippa just confessed to being in love with Gil. Isn't that splendid? Now he will get better again.'

Tabitha looked to Pippa. 'Is that true?'

'Yes, Mrs Ashford-Smith, it is.'

'Then let us pray it isn't too late.'

Above them a door opened and they turned to watch the doctor and Edgar descend the staircase. Pippa blinked at the elderly man Edgar had become. His smile for her was warm, yet tinged with sadness and Pippa's heart somersaulted against her ribs.

Tabitha swayed but Edgar steadied her. 'He's not gone, dear. He still clings to life.'

The doctor rubbed his forehead in weariness. 'There's a good chance he's over the worst of it. His vomiting has stopped in the last hour. I believe he's at day four or five of the disease as his tongue is coated in a thick white substance, but it should start to peel in the next day or two.'

'What can we do?' Augusta asked.

'Keep him cool, the fever is still on him. The rash will fade eventually. Try to get some water past his lips, but be careful as his tongue is swollen, so he'll have difficulty in swallowing. I'll call again later this evening.'

Weeping into a handkerchief, Tabitha allowed Augusta to guide her into the drawing-room while the doctor conversed with Edgar at the front door.

Pippa glanced at the staircase then back at the two men. Gathering up her skirts, she dashed upstairs. She didn't know which was Gil's bedroom and had to open three doors before finding the right one. On the threshold, she paused, uncertain.

The drawn curtains made the room dark, shadowy. Stale air tortured her nose. She jumped in surprise when a maid rose from a chair on the far side of the bed. On trembling legs, Pippa stepped closer, frightened by what she might see.

'He's resting for the moment, miss.' The maid bobbed her head.

Slowly, Pippa turned to gaze down at the man who'd come to mean so much to her. She frowned and blinked hard. There had to be some mistake, surely? The wasted man, whose flesh had been stripped from his bones couldn't be the handsome laughing Gil Ashford-Smith. For an instant she wanted to smile and call everyone in to tell them it was all right, they'd been wrong, that this wasn't Gil at all. Then suddenly reality crowded in on her, denying her the falsehood she so badly wanted to believe. It was very much her beloved Gil.

She crammed her knuckles into her mouth, smothering the groan of agony that erupted. Her knees gave out and she crumbled on to the floor beside his bed.

'Oh miss!' The maid rushed around to her, but Pippa waved her away.

'I-I wish to be left alone with him.'

The maid bobbed a curtsy. 'I'll be just outside the door if you need me.'

Pippa, on her knees, stared at Gil's flushed face. Where his strained skin wasn't red it was a dirty yellow colour. Sweat beaded his forehead and upper lip. On the small table next to the bed was a water bowl and towels. Pippa dampened a cloth and dabbed Gil's face. Heat radiated from him.

'See what happens to you when left to your own devices, Ashford-Smith?' She smiled, her tender love bruising her heart. 'Open your eyes, Gil. It's Pippa. I'm home again.'

He moved his head slightly and, taking courage from that, she slipped her fingers under his large hand and brought it up to her cheek. 'You have to get well again. Do you hear me?'

He remained perfectly still, only his chest rose in shallow breathing. Pippa stepped around the bed and sat in the chair the maid had used. Taking Gil's other hand, she kissed it and held it in both of hers. She settled into the chair, prepared to sit beside him for as long as it took.

The door opened and Tabitha entered, her gaze darting to her son's face and then to Pippa. 'He hasn't woken?'

'No.'

'Will you stay a while? I can send up a tray and have a room prepared for you should you wish it.'

'I'll stay, yes. Thank you.' Pippa glanced at Gil; she'd stay by him for the rest of her life if she could.

'Do whatever you can to keep him alive, Pippa, for I cannot lose my son.'

'I cannot lose him either.'

'I hope you mean it.' Tabitha straightened. 'He's been to hell and back because of what he feels for you. I'll not let you hurt him again.'

Gently stroking Gil's hot cheek, Pippa swallowed. 'As soon as he is well again, we'll be married. I promise you.'

'You will?' Tabitha's expression showed doubt. 'I'd always hoped so, but you didn't seem keen on the idea of marriage. He's been mad for you for so long. We've watched Gil suffer for the last couple of years, let me tell you.'

'I'm sorry for that. I didn't know what I wanted until I thought it was too late.'

'Yes, a common story for us all at one time or another.' Bending over, Gil's mother kissed his brow and then quietly left the room.

On the mantle above the small fireplace, a gold clock ticked softly as if to remind her of the hours and minutes she'd been away from Gil. Well, she'd make it up to him, if he'd let her.

Pippa woke and, as she moved her shoulders, darts of pain shot down her arms and she muttered a groan. She'd fallen asleep by the bed, her arms folded under her head. Flexing her neck and blinking to focus, she gazed at Gil before leaning forward to touch his flushed face. He tossed his head, frowning in his sleep. His legs twitched and his hand rose over the bedcovers only to fall down again with a thump.

Making soothing sounds, she settled him again and then dripped a few drops of water on to his dry lips. Gil's eyelids flickered and his throat convulsed before he became calm once more.

With a helpless sigh, she looked around the room, which had darkened while she'd slept. A gap in the curtains showed that dusk was making way for night. She lit the lamp by the bed, spilling a soft golden glow across the room. Restless, she walked to the tallboy standing against the far wall. On top of it lay Gil's hairbrush, razor and other personal items. Then she noticed the small drawing. Her sketch of Gil and Augusta as they sat around a picnic last spring. She couldn't remember giving it to Gil, but she must have done. Sketches and paintings littered her belongings and she was often giving them away to reduce her clutter.

'I . . . stole it.'

Pippa spun as Gil's weak words filtered through her daydreaming. She rushed to kneel by the bed, grasping his warm hand in hers. 'You have woken.'

He licked his parched, cracked lips. 'So . . . it seems. Wished . . . I hadn't.'

Anger at his negativity blotted at her happiness. 'Don't talk such foolishness. I won't have it.'

'Must always have your own way . . .' he croaked.

His words reminded her of their last meeting at the inn in Ballarat. Then, as now, he'd flung her selfishness in her face. He hadn't forgiven her and the thought chilled her to her marrow.

Frowning, clearly uncomfortable, Gil closed his eyes on a sigh. 'Drink?'

'Yes, of course.' After pouring a glass of water from the jug, she lifted his head to help him sip. The endeavour wasn't very successful, but Gil seemed satisfied despite his wet nightshirt. Pippa wiped away the spilled water and adjusted his pillows. 'Rest now. Sleep. I'll go down to tell your parents.'

'Too hot.'

'It's the fever.' She smoothed the damp hair on his forehead. 'Sleep, Gil.'

'Why . . . you here?' His green eyes narrowed. 'Deathbed farewell?'

Before she could think of a suitable answer, he closed his eyes as exhaustion overtook him.

Watching him sleep, she stemmed the tears his words caused. Ridiculously, she'd imagined their reunion would be affectionate, tender, romantic. Instead he was angry. No, not angry. He was uncaring. Whether he lived or died was of no concern to him and she had done that. She had made him feel he had nothing to live for. Shame and guilt filled her. While she'd been flirting with Marshall, looking for ways to earn more money, Gil had been sending himself to an early grave. And he'd nearly succeeded.

Resuming her seat, Pippa sighed with the weight of responsibility that sat on her chest, crushing her breath. Had she found her love for him too late? What if he no longer wanted her?

Hours passed with visits from the family and the doctor. The little gold timepiece struck midnight, then one o'clock. Pippa dozed in the chair, but never for more than twenty minutes. Her body decided to keep its own time and she'd jolt awake at intervals to check him, thinking she'd slept for hours instead of minutes.

When a rooster crowed, stirring her from another doze, Pippa stretched and smothered a yawn. Grey light seeped into the room. In shock, she realized that Gil was watching her. His green eyes lingered on her face. Reaching over, she felt his brow. It was warm but not unbearably hot as before. 'Good morning.'

'I-I thought I'd dreamt you.'

She smiled, love squeezing her heart.'You didn't. How do you feel?' She poured another glass of water for him and helped him up to sip it.

'Better.'

'Good.'

An awkward silence descended and Pippa wasn't certain what to say or do next. Her stomach twisted into knots. Suddenly, she couldn't meet his gaze. Instead, she stood and tugged the flat sheets straighter.

Gil lifted his hand and dropped it again. 'Looks like I couldn't . . . even die properly.'

'Perhaps the will to live is stronger than the one to die?' Tears gathered behind her lids, burning.

'You've been told of my . . . foolishness?'

She nodded. 'I'm sorry that I was the cause of it.'

'Don't be.' He winced as he swallowed. 'I've brains of my own.'

A scalding tear trickled down her cheek.

'Why do you cry? I'm not dead yet.'

Pippa threw back her head, blinking away the tears. 'That wasn't kind, Gil.'

His chest heaved with an inward sigh. 'Kindness has been stripped from me.'

She clenched her jaw with the effort not to retort and say something she'd later regret.

His hand moved again and touched her skirts. 'I'm sorry. I'm an ass.'

'I never meant to hurt you.'

'I know.' His gaze held hers.

The room lightened as the morning broke. Birds began their daylight chorus. In the attics above their heads they heard the servant girls awakening to a new day.

Squaring her shoulders, Pippa looked down on him and forced herself to be efficient because crying wouldn't help win him back. 'You must get better.'

'Must I?'

'Yes. I – we . . . that is . . .'

He turned his face away to stare blindly at the door. 'You should go. I'll sleep for a bit.'

Pippa closed her eyes, her courage withering away. 'Gil.'

'Don't Pip. I . . . cannot . . .'

Emotion closed her throat, but she had to speak, had to make him see and believe what she felt. 'Will you marry me?' she whispered.

Ever so slowly he turned to stare at her. His eyes were cold emerald gems in a red flushed face. His throat worked. 'Don't you ever pity me.'

Her chin trembled. 'I do not pity you.'

'Go away, Pip, please. I haven't the strength . . .' Tears spilled over his lashes and her heart shattered into razor-sharp pieces.

'I love you, Gil.' Her words rushed out, tumbling over themselves.'I think I've always loved you, but I didn't see it until I thought it was too late.' She grabbed his hot hand and held it tight. 'You must forgive me, Gil. I am nothing without you. My life is nothing without you in it.' Her tears splashed on to their joined hands.

'I am not enough for you. I know that.'

She jerked closer to him, eager to dispel his beliefs. 'You're wrong, very wrong.'

He sighed deeply. 'What of the man at the gold fields?'

'It was nothing, not important. You are everything to me. Everything.'

'Are you certain?' He tensed. 'For I couldn't—'

'Shh.' Cradling his hand against her wet cheek, she gazed at him. 'You once said to me that you wanted me as your friend, lover, wife, mother of your children. I wish it too.'

'But—'

'And now I ask you the same. Will you be my friend, lover, husband and father of my children?'

'My Pip . . .' The old wry smile that was his alone appeared. He touched her bottom lip with the tip of his finger, making her catch her breath. 'I'm unable to fulfil all those roles at the moment, but it'll be fun ticking them off my list.'

She grinned through her tears and kissed his hand, wishing he were well enough to be kissed properly. Still, they had time. They had the rest of their lives. 'I love you Gil Ashford-Smith.'

Gil relaxed against his pillows, exhausted. 'I'm rather pleased about that, since I adore *you*, Phillippa Noble.'